The Landmark Library
No. 26

THE CLOSED HARBOUR

The Landmark Library

THE CLOSED
HARBOUR

James Hanley

CHATTO & WINDUS

LONDON

Published by
Chatto & Windus Ltd
London

*

Clarke, Irwin & Co Ltd
Toronto

ISBN 0 7011 1655 2

First published in 1952
This edition first published in 1971

Printed in Great Britain by
Lewis Reprints Limited, Port Talbot,
Glamorgan

I

CERTAINLY HE was noticeable on the avenue, people stared at him as he passed by. The hard light of the sun was upon him, boring at his blackness, for he was black from head to foot, from his reefer jacket with its Captain's insignia to his shiny peaked cap pulled sharply down on the forehead. A stranger perhaps, but how oddly dressed, and on such a day. The avenue was long, the pavement seemed moving under the heat's pressure. It was half past four in the afternoon. He walked on, oblivious of those who passed by. He was unduly tall, very thin, he was certainly lost within the folds of his reefer, a threat to winter.

But making his way up, Marius saw nothing save the decrepit-looking building behind the Rue Lens. It was his vision up the desert, past the shops with their brightly coloured awnings, past the people in whom he was not interested, whom he scarcely saw as he moved forward, with a hesitant, wide-rolling gait. He never removed his hands from the depths of his pockets, and he stared defiantly at what his vision defined as the horizon line of the Avenue Croille. It was the ritual of determination, of defiance, of a certain hope in gullibility and forgetfulness, it was the day's stirring of the bones, setting in motion for the thousandth time the machinery of misery, the endless day. Reaching the end of the avenue, he paused, glanced about him, then moved swiftly between the dividing line of two shops, the bright jeweller's and the cheap toy shop, down a cool narrow alley, and so into the light again. And there he saw the building.

He stopped dead in his tracks, like a clockwork engine suddenly run down. The Company Heros and M. Philippe. Even the red bricks knew Marius, the windows stared at him like eyes, the stone steps, the brazen door that shut so often on the misery, the hugged misery inside the reefer, burdensome as his own flesh. The toot of a horn made him jump. He moved towards the Company Heros, Philippe bound. He mounted the steps, eased open the door with his body. He was in semi-darkness. Almost at once his nostrils were full of the strong smells, pitch, resin, manilla rope, oil. But the hall itself was cool. There were the stairs to climb. They knew Marius, too. The office of the Marine Superintendent. Forward.

He was there at last, and there was Monsieur Philippe, just as he was yesterday, very much himself, indifferent to visitors, always watching a clock, dreaming of home, his slippers, the roses in his garden. M. Philippe heard a movement, seemed to realise who it was. He glanced up at the clock, and so knew, and was linked with this, and the roses in his garden, his slippers, his favourite chair, the pleasure of his own person. Marius spoke.

Philippe barely noticed and he did not move. After all it was only yesterday's echo and the day before. Philippe had a coloured chart on the desk before him, and he continued to study it. He heard a match struck, and later drew in the aroma of Marius's cigarette. And he went on poring over the outspread chart, a hairy finger moving searchingly across it. It stopped, it had pin-pointed Oran. He had completely forgotten his visitor.

Marius for his part leaned heavily towards the desk, his body gave the impression that at any moment it might topple over M. Philippe and his attentive hairy finger. His elbows were pressed hard upon the glistening mahogany, through the surface of which he seemed to see a reflection that might be his own face. He was aware of the studied indifference of Monsieur Philippe, and the deep silence of the office, broken only by the fast tick of a clock that had the high prattling sound of a child. It seemed to accentuate the presence of the two men, the sheer physical weight of their bodies.

Again Marius spoke. The finger on the chart suddenly departed from Oran.

6

What did Marius want?

To see Monsieur Follet.

That would be quite impossible.

Marius stiffened. One day Monsieur Philippe would get a great surprise, a terrible shock; he would open his mouth to speak and only sawdust would fall out. Why, it was not yet five o'clock and the offices never closed till the moment of five, after all the Heros people were far too miserable ever to think of closing it a moment before.

Please, Marius said. He had come so many many times. There was a ship lying in the harbour, the *Clarte*, he had seen her, he knew Manos personally, she was loading for Salonika and other Greek ports, and then on through the Black Sea. Would not Monsieur Follet see him? He was a patient man, he would wait, he had been here yesterday and the day before and the day before that, and last week and last month. Didn't he, Philippe realise what this meant, the endeavour, the hope, this land was only hell. He, Philippe had only to lift a finger, wink an eye, press a button, and Follet would see him, the magic door would open.

Monsieur Philippe stirred slightly.

Nevertheless the office was closed.

Marius drew himself up to full height, he dominated Philippe by nearly six inches. He willed the other to move, to look at him, and suddenly he moved, he looked up at Marius.

He first saw the shiny peaked cap, a three day growth of beard on the long sallow face, the bloodshot eyes. He noticed some wisps of straw adhering to the magnificent jacket. Its buttons were tarnished. He noticed the long thin hands, the powerful wrists protruding from the sleeves like pistons. Monsieur Marius must lengthen those sleeves. He met his eye. Marius met his. But think, for one moment, Marius seemed to say.

He, Monsieur Philippe, was a powerful man, and he, Marius, admitted it, cringed before him. A move could be a

7

miracle, a lift of the finger all the difference between being upright and horribly stooping, turning a wonderful key. Why, if only Monsieur Philippe out of the goodness of his heart, turned this key, he, Marius, would hear it inside his brain like some great golden bell, he Marius, would be resurrected. He was drowned and his ship was drowned, they were like Lazarus, trying to rise, their eyes were clogged with death. Perhaps Monsieur Philippe would realise. The walk on this hot day had been a mile, going back it would be a desert-ridden thousand.

Nevertheless, M. Philippe said, the office was closed and Monsieur Follet was not available. He presumed Captain Marius—he paused to allow the mockery to sink in—he *presumed* he was of a certain intelligence. No doubt he had known, in the early days that M. Follet, too, was of a certain intelligence. But also there was moral integrity. Did he suppose Follet would forget himself? Did he not think it unwise to keep calling, pestering? The fact was there were no berths and that was the answer. There was nothing doing. Who knew better than he, Philippe? In life there was always a certain point to be reached, for good or bad, and he Marius had reached it. Did he not appreciate the position. He had no ticket, he had lost his ticket. Dethroned captains did not rise again. It was a law of the sea that they should not, there was also a point where trust stopped.

He leaned away from the desk, his eyes moved towards the door.

" Captain Marius, I believe that the sea would refuse to drown you."

" And he will not see me ? "

" He will not see you."

" Then I must go ? "

" If you must" Philippe said, and he looked away, and downwards, and the finger was active again, and he had Oran, the red dot and the blue circle round it.

" Then Heros can congratulate itself" Marius said.

He stood there, glaring at the man behind the counter, and

he watched the finger and he watched the dot. There was a moment when the dot could shine as fierce as flame. Looking at the chart, Marius, for a fleeting moment saw the sea and the ship live, and breathe and draw him to her. His being longed, as suddenly froze.

" Am I to thank you ? "

" It is customary, but not necessary" Monsieur Philippe said.

" Damn you."

Marius turned and went out, the swing door shut swiftly, smooth as a knife. Marius was in the dark again, lost again. He thought of the *Clarte* loading at the quay, he hoped it would sink from a mighty wave, burn, smash upon rocks. Damn him. Damn them.

The world was no longer wide. The sea was rolling up, the great expanse of it, the miles of it, narrowing, shutting out, they had turned the key again, those God-forsaken agents of the sea. Damn and blast them.

" I would have cringed, kissed his rotten feet."

He went slowly down, dropped from stair to stair, heavily, aimlessly, there were no precise directions. And at the outer door he paused, looked through the glass. There they were, still at it, these people hurrying and scurrying, and that tram rocking as in a frenzy, the hard white light still there, and the walk home. The long walk home.

True, there were others, and he had tried others. If he could get out of here, out of this infernal port, he would never return, never, and he swore as he pushed again at the outer swing doors.

" I am as low as low—and it is not hard for them. They have their knives into me."

He stood there, hesitant, watching, and he hated it. They were all a part of it, these indifferent people, what the hell did Philippe care anyhow? How he loathed the place, if *only* he could get away.

" As what? Nothing."

He moved back into the avenue.

"Instead, I must walk back again, I must think again," and it was no longer simple.

"Everything is simple until you are alone," Marius exclaimed, as though he were addressing the red bricks that sheltered the hides of Philippe and Follet.

"Damn them" he cried.

"She will be sitting there when I get back, they both will, like stones. They know things before I know them. They will draw me tomorrow's map, describe my day by a look."

"Where the hell are you going to?"

"What was that?" asked Marius, but the man had gone on, cursing him.

"If there were a road, a direction, a course set, I could drive myself to it, by my own will, and by the horror of this place. I'd give my heart to get out of it."

He hardly realised he was in the Bistro until he was up against the counter, feeling the cold wet brass of counter top under his hot hands.

"Cognac." And louder, more demanding, "coffee."

Where had that thing come from on such a fine afternoon as this? And the barman raised his eyebrows.

At a table in the corner Marius talked to himself. He had talked to himself for a long time now, and, after all, it was better than no company. He could hear the heavy breathing of the occupant of a nearby table. He was a fat man, and Marius's endless sotto-voce upset his nerves. He banged down his glass and went out.

"The Heros—I spit at it. Closed, he said. Yet it was not yet five o'clock. Perhaps it is a dream after all. Yet they have seventeen ships and they are manned, and they have seventeen captains and they are as proud as peacocks. But I *will* find a ship, there is a certain place, if I can get to it—if—— I'm not a bird and cannot fly, and unlike the Saviour I can't walk it. But somehow I can see that ship, I can smell it, wondrous, aching as I ache, to be out of it, out of it."

It was not far now. Already he could hear through the

open window the loud rattle of winches. It made him think of Manos.

"Manos is old, very old, he might drop dead. Follet might send for me. I will then say, 'go to hell'."

"Cognac" he shouted, and when it was brought, "more coffee."

"There they go, I can hear them pounding away, she's her head to the sea," and again he thought of Manos, and the *Clarte* and the sea beyond.

When cognac and coffee came, he drank both quickly, got up and went out.

He leaned against the wall, his captain's cap askew on his well shaped head, covered with thick bluish-black hair. His hands disappeared again into the reefer pockets, the street seemed swarming with people, he watched Marseilles go by.

"I have been at many places, let me see—there was—— ah, but it is always the same. There are many captains, France is full of Captains, the world stinks with them. But there is yet me" he thought.

You saw it in the office boy's smile, the closing doors, you heard a ship blowing in your brain.

He drew the collar of the jacket higher about his neck, the lower part of his face was almost invisible.

"Blast them."

The hovering policeman watched, and then came up.

"You are not ill?"

"*I am not ill*," brusquely.

"And you are not civil either."

"Shall I go?"

"Go."

"I will remain." Marius tried to laugh.

"You will get along" the policeman said, pushing him.

Marius, not resisting, went staggering forward.

"And you need a wash perhaps" the policeman called after him.

" Of course " thought Marius, " I might have shaved, perhaps I forgot. No matter, I must get away, I will perhaps draw a crowd."

He dragged himself off, turned a street corner sharply, this road was not so crowded, and the noise of winches came louder to his ears. Somewhere there was an end, somewhere there must be a stop.

" They will be sitting there like stones " he thought as he moved on.

He saw before him the forests of masts, the funnels, the cranes, and the winches were roaring, eating up cargo like lions. He saw all this and it was his country, the edge of the sea.

" Tonight I will go to Madame Lustigne's and I will forget myself. And then I will go home and the house will be silent, as graves are, and they sleeping or waiting or watching, the latter most likely, they are always watching me."

Suddenly he stopped dead, staring round. Then he crossed the road, sat down, his back against the wall of an old shed, shaded from the sun, he watched the *Clarte* load.

" Lucky Manos " he said, " lucky man."

The *Clarte* clouded over, the winches stopped, there was dead silence, he could see nothing but a high building, a towering wall. He was at Nantes. He was mounting stairs, he was at the desk.

" My name is Marius. Captain Eugene Marius. . . ."

And the man said, " you're not the only one who knows that," and laughed, and Marius went out, and the laughter followed him down the stairs, he could feel it driving into his back like knives.

He was in Bordeaux, the Rue du Soleil, no eye could escape the brass model of the ship, high and shining in the summer sun. The Bilter Line.

" My name is Marius, Captain Eugene Marius. . . ."

" Sorry. . . ."

" And here I am " he thought, stiffening where he sat.

A ship's siren had blown, it struck him like a cry, he sat up sharply, a boat was coming in, he could see her, the sun streaming her decks, the smoke triumphant from her funnel, a voyage ended, she was coming home.

Marius got up and walked nearer to the quay. Already he could see the short stocky figure leaning against her poop rail, and knew it was lucky Manos.

"Never lost a ship, never lost anything in his life, not even a button off his coat, the lucky swine." He cried within himself, "you self-pitying bastard."

Twenty yards from where the *Clarte* lay he stopped, sat down on a bollard.

"If I could sail in her, as I was, as I used to be, at my full height, if they were not silent, all the days silent, if it had never happened."

He could see the cargo pouring down into her after hold, saw the others battened down and secure, she would soon be gone.

"In the end I will swim out of it."

He fell asleep. Later he woke, a hand on his arm, he felt chill, the sun was going, a voice said, "you ought to get home," and he got up and he went away, never once looked back, and the policeman following with his eye thought, "this place is full of bums," and watched the tall thin figure vanish round the corner.

Marius took the back streets, and here, unlike the avenue, people were not so important, the tempo was different, the very climate breathed an air of acceptance, of resignation. People passed him by and hardly gave him a glance. There was a moment in the long day when Marius's spirit lightened, he thought of his room, the climb upstairs, past the silent women, the door closing, the door locked behind him. Alone. Everything in it had become intensely personal to him. He saw everything clearly. The black bed in the corner, the plain scrubbed wooden chair alongside, some flowers in a vase, always fresh, he could never understand who put them there, but he was touched by this. The bundle of charts lying on the mantelpiece, wrapped like mysteries in their brown paper, the sextant on the table under the window, the telescope, a collection of brass buttons, a pipe, a hard plug of tobacco. Always he would look at the picture of the *Mercury*, his first ship, the proud moment. The picture of his father, resplendent in uniform, his boyhood hero. He had loved his father.

He stopped by a bistro, he searched in his pocket, counted two hundred francs, he went inside, but was out again in two minutes, his throat fiery from the brandy.

"Tomorrow will be tomorrow" he thought, "and they will still be there", thinking of them, his mother, his sister, sitting so silently in the window, looking out, always looking out, at what, the sea? At everything, and perhaps nothing.

"If I could get away. And the sooner the better. That Philippe, blast him, he could have given me a berth on the *Clarte* as easy as winking, but no, he is so bloody upright and moral and horribly good, and Follet's no better. When you are down you are down, and there's the end of it."

He removed his cap which he crushed into his pocket, he ruffled his hair, wiped his forehead, suddenly dived into an alley. Cooler here, but the smells rose as high as heaven. He was not far from home.

"They hate it, and yet she will follow me, as though I had not anchors enough around my neck. I'll stow away. Now if I could get to Greece. Ah, that's the place. Ships there are owned by the devil, and he mans them too. Well. . . ."

There was the house. He stood for a moment by the door, looked right and left, then went inside.

The whispers sounded to him like prayers, but the moment he had pushed open the door they ceased, they had seen him come, and there was silence again, and they were so still they might have been seated thus for a hundred years. Neither of the women looked at him when he came in.

14

They were sat side by side in the window as they always were. Often the evening hours were spent in this way, it was an elected silence. They would look out to the broad sea, and the restless breakers. Their very pose, locked in this silence, gave them the appearance of conspirators, eternal watchers, an alertness against the world.

For a moment Marius looked at them, then removed his coat which he hung upon a hook inside the door. He went into the kitchen and brought back bread, wine, and an onion. He sat down and began to eat. They could hear the grind of the onion in his teeth. A hungry man. A miserable man.

The young woman rose from her chair and went out. Marius heard her climbing the stairs, and later her slow, almost ponderous movements to and fro in the bedroom. A person uncertain of something, a person tired of waiting, a person always listening.

The old woman, seated in her high-backed wooden chair, had turned round, but not to speak, only to stare. And he did not speak to her, and he did not look her way, but calmly went on eating, making coarse noises as he did so.

She was aged, pinned to the chair by weight of years, by the horrible silence. He could feel her eye upon him, as a pressure; it upset him.

The fierce light of the sun was all about them, the glass of wine caught in it seemed shimmering, forever moving, and as though Marius had sensed this he put his hand, flat upon the glass top and pressed. Watching her, he saw the day's end, her repose. The labours of it slept peacefully under her bones.

As he looked at her he saw how quickly she averted her glance, as if only now she had realised she had been staring at her son.

This house is of four rooms only, its walls a shattering white in the evening sun. As Marius ate he looked about him, it broke the stare, lightened the silence. Around them the simple furniture, but here and there an object that sharpened his memory. He looked at everything, sipped at his wine. The bones of home, of their life, of what it had been. For a few moments it served to screen off a certain blackness in Marius's mind. He heard the slow, tumbril-like tick of the old clock. Above it on the mantelpiece yet another picture of a naval man. A handsome man, his own father, whose first fruit came out of the sea.

" I, too, was born in the sea " he thought.

Looking at the picture he was conscious of a certain secret pride, then suddenly his mother, too, was there, she had climbed into the frame beside her husband, and she was young then, and innocent and charming, nothing in the severe black of her dress could hide it, she beside his father, the bright Captain.

Now he was looking at his mother again, thinking of her long life, her honourable life, it was impossible not to look at the statue-like figure.

Though she now returned his gaze there was nothing in it save a vast, stony indifference.

Marius leaned back in his chair and lit a cigarette, sent smoke clouds madly climbing. He could still hear the restless to and fro movement from the bedroom above, a human pendulum, ticking out a kind of time that was not his time and never could be.

" I shall go out," thought Marius.

And he went out, leaving the old woman staring at the remains of his meal. He climbed stairs to his room, and met his sister coming down. As he passed her he was aware of her quick movement away from him, she cringed against the wall.

" I am what I am " he thought.

When she heard his door close, she steadied herself, then went down.

She cleared away the things from the table, then laid upon it a large dark-green cloth. She resumed her seat by the window with her mother.

16

" He is back again."

" So I see."

The old woman's mouth was as drawn and tight as a shut purse, she said quickly, " and I'll bet he has been cringing to the Heros again. Imagine it! A gang of ruffians calling themselves shipowners."

" But nothing happened ? "

The old woman laughed. " He may yet drown in the sea," she said.

" Listen to him," Madeleine said.

" Aren't I always listening ? He's back again in his cage. He'll be happy when he finds somebody as miserable as himself. I wish he would go. That is a hard thing to say of a son, but I say it, and every time I see him I think of how he saved himself. Your father could not have done that."

" Please, mother."

" All right, I will say no more."

" I am glad of that," said Madeleine, she took her mother's large, fleshy hand and placed it on her knee, and stroked it, and smiled warmly to her.

" Is Father Nollet coming this evening ? "

" Father Nollet is coming, you seem to doubt," Madame Marius said.

" I am not."

" And I am glad you are not. Do you know I begin to feel the gutter climbing into my bones, think of it. Your father, God have mercy on him, would have cried from shame. Your brother slinking about, crawling for a ship, hands and knees to the job, no dignity, no pride, nothing. Think of that. A Marius. In and out of shipping offices. It is not so much that he lost a ship, many ships have been lost, no, it is something else about him, like a whine in the Marius flesh, I don't understand it. He belongs to the gutter. It is very strange."

She put her hands on her daughter's shoulders, looked earnestly at her.

" Mighty Jesus! That it should have happened to us."

"But it has happened" Madeleine said, "it has happened, it has——"

Madame Marius could already feel the tension rising in her daughter, she pressed downwards with her terrible strength, pressed hard on the shoulders.

"Enough" she said, "enough."

"This is not our home" Madeleine said.

"I am well aware of that. He is yet the son of his mother."

"If I were not here, I wonder if you would embrace him."

The old woman raised her hand and struck her daughter across the mouth.

"The last time I struck at Marius flesh was that time your brother uttered a filthy remark about his uncle, and I did it because it saved your father's hand. Your father at least was French, and lies in an ocean that will never drag down his son's bones."

"I'm sorry, mother."

"And you have the right to be sorry." She looked at the clock. "I will go up" she said.

"The house where no one speaks is hateful" Madame Marius said, she rose heavily from her chair, and suddenly her daughter's hand was behind her.

"Come."

Madame Marius pushed away the hand. They slowly left the room.

At the stairfoot Madeleine paused, listening. But there was not a sound from her brother's room. She often thought about him, hours behind the closed door, what did he do. Did he perhaps just sit there and think? And of what?

She allowed the old woman to precede her, and as she watched the slow, tortuous climb she seemed to feel age crying aloud to her. She put her hand behind her mother's back.

"Don't do that," her mother said. "Ah, it will be nice to be cooler."

" Yes."

" Perhaps Father Nollet will not come after all, it is gone seven."

" But if he does ? "

" Well, naturally he will come up to my room," the old woman had turned and was looking at her daughter, " or is it perhaps that you are glad he is not ? "

She turned and went on, the daughter following.

" How long have we been here ? "

" Four months."

" It seems four years. Often I think of my lovely house at Nantes and I weep for it."

" You did not have to follow him here," Madeleine said. " Don't speak to me, I'm too tired to listen" . . . and after a momentary silence, " I shall go on myself, I am not that helpless, leave me."

Madeleine stood still. The aged bones dragged upwards.

" But I had better follow " she thought.

She helped to undress her mother, put her to bed, crossed to the window, shut out the sun, then went away and left her. As she stood on the landing she heard her brother moving in his room.

" He is going out as usual " she thought, " it is always the same, out all day, out all night, it's a wearing out, that's what it is, a wearing out."

Behind the door Marius's hand was upon the latch. He had heard the voices, the tread upon the stairs, they had gone up.

" Now if I were to hear a sudden knock, then I would go down, and at the front door I would find one from the Heros office.

" Manos fell down the hatch this evening and was killed. They are looking for a skipper.

" Perhaps " thought Marius, " I am truly finished."

He lifted the latch, then dropped it, he had heard the feet moving downstairs.

" Soon she, too, will go to bed."

Madeleine returned to the small sitting-room, took her chair by the window and sat down. Looking out she realised that everything tired her, the sight of the sea, the yet merciless sun, the hard light, the restless tormenting breakers, the ships, that, from this window looked so much like toys. She sat stiff, tense, and remained so for some time. Later she heard Marius go out. She saw his tall figure pass the window.

" Poor Eugene, I am yet sorry for him, and yet I hate him."

She laid her hands flat upon the table and looked at them.

" I am not like the others " she told herself, " I never was. But I know what I am."

Rising from the chair she crossed to the mirror on the wall and stared into it. She pointed a finger at the reflection and said slowly, " this is you. I wonder which one of us will wear out the other."

She walked about the room, undecided, aimless, she looked at the clock again and again. No, it was too late for the priest now, something must have kept him back.

" And when he comes I will say yes, because it is best for both of us," her mind leaping back days, to a simpler time, a happier time, " there was never any other place but Nantes.

" I am tired too, I am even tired of being tired, perhaps I will go to bed also. Yet it is so early. Still. . . ."

She shut the door silently behind her.

" I am closest to her, we are closest to each other. It will be like that until the end. He will always look another way, he is not of us."

She found her mother lying awake, staring at the low ceiling. She crossed to the bed, knelt, she said her prayers aloud. Then she undressed and climbed in beside her. She put an arm round the old woman.

Madame Marius felt the head heavy upon her breast, felt the body heave, listened to the sobs. She neither spoke nor moved. This was not new, this lying together, clutched and

clutching, this silence and this weeping, it was a year of age.
After a while she spoke.

" He has gone ? "

The daughter's head moved a little, this meant yes.

Later, as the light began to fall, they fell asleep, bound to
each other, easily, casually, as children do.

II

"THERE IS something I have to do today, yet I cannot for the life of me think what it is" and Monsieur Follet went round and round in his swivel chair, head high, thinking hard. It was a certain method of reviving the memory. Suddenly he stopped, "Ah, of course. That rise for Labiche."

"Labiche" called Follet. "Labiche."

He might have been calling his dog. Nevertheless it was a man who came, four foot six in height, large-headed, extraordinarily broad in the shoulder. A dwarf-like creature in the fifties. Aristide Labiche was of curious shape. At the Heros he was referred to as the "pregnant man," and sometimes "the little bull." His bulbous nose was a standing joke amongst the staff. He had a heavy, sensual chin. Monsieur Follet had some regard for him. He worked hard, he was loyal, it was rare to discover that Labiche was *not* at his high desk, his head lost in a mass of documents. He liked Labiche's eyes, which were large and of a soft brown; he thought they looked exactly like those of his retriever, and sometimes that they should have lain in a woman's head.

"Ah Labiche! Please sit down."

"Yes sir."

"What are you working on at present?"

"The *Orlando's* time-sheets, sir."

He glanced up questioningly at the other, it was not often that he was asked to come into the director's office.

"Of course, that overhauling job, yes. Healthy, Labiche, or unhealthy?"

Labiche only smiled, giving Follet a wonderful view of his single gold tooth. There were the inevitable jokes, Labiche expected them, they came.

" Still working hard for the salvation of France ? " he asked, his fingers tapping on the blotting pad.

Follet's slow, somewhat greasy smile was not returned.

" Have I any important appointments today, Labiche, you have such an excellent memory."

" Manos at three o'clock, sir " replied the other.

" That brings me to the point " said Follet, " it links up at once with an efficiency, a loyalty that I wish to reward. As from Friday, Labiche, your salary goes up by one hundred francs a month."

Labiche got out of his chair, stood erect, looked at the director.

" I am grateful, sir " he said.

Follet was struck by the dignified, though somewhat ridiculous pose.

" That's all right " he said. " But do not give it all away, Labiche, you are a far too generous man——"

" No sir."

" There was an altercation outside my office, Labiche," said Follet, "you are in the next office to Philippe, you can see everything that happens."

" It was that Captain again, they say he's a Captain, look-ing for a berth. He is always asking .for you, Monsieur Follet."

" So I gather."

Follet stuck his thumbs into his vest and sighed, his voice sounded tired.

" Sometimes, Labiche, I'm sick of the very sight of sailors, that's why I've delegated Philippe to do all the interviewing, given him the requisite authority. This city, it stinks with them. But you, living where you do, there's no need for me to enlarge on it," and he saw the little clerk smile. " Yes, far too many, and not enough ships, Labiche. Come to think of it, it's cruel. What we owners lost in tonnage in two wars, is nobody's business, I suppose. Consider Heros. We've seventeen ships and once we had something like seventy, think of it, and every berth occupied, packed tight, securely locked, not another berth, not a single one, and a waiting list today of over two hundred.

"An odd thing, Labiche. I'm struck by the number of men seeking to get to the Orient, something starting there perhaps, but my broker is silent," he gave the clerk a quick pat on the back, it made the dust fly.

He got up, "this rise, Labiche, it is purely between ourselves."

Labiche stared. It gave the episode a conspiratorial air, yet to him nothing seemed more simple, one more clerk getting a rise in salary.

He was moving towards the door, Follet following, who now picked up his hat and gave Labiche a final instruction.

"Tell Marcelle that Manos will be at my office at three o'clock prompt, and that he's to make the usual arrangements."

"Very good, sir" and Labiche went out.

Follet called after him, "tell Philippe I'm ready, it's a quarter to one."

"Yes sir."

"If Labiche ever dies" he thought, "the Saint Vincent de Paul Society will collapse, little Labiche is the rock that holds it up."

Philippe came in.

"Ready?"

"Ready" Philippe replied.

They both went out.

Labiche, after this unexpected call to Follet's office, and his more unexpected rise in the estimation of the Heros concern, had returned to his own cubicle, sat down at his desk. He was soon buried deeply in the *Orlando's* affairs. He was a very careful man, conscientious, scrupulous. He not only dotted down the last minute and the last sou for the ultimate benefit of the Heros Company, but would often, in imagination, go

24

aboard the ship upon whose time-sheets he happened to be working. He was generally escorted to the best cabin, then sailed away in her, the Captain's special guest for the remainder of the voyage.

In the twelve years in which he had worked in the red-brick building behind the Rue Lens, he had sailed many voyages, travelled to many countries. He had, indeed, been round the world six times. This apart, he had never at any time travelled further than the Place de Lenche or the Canna-biere except on a single occasion when he had gone to Lyons with a party of the Saint Vincent de Paul Society, of which he was the local secretary.

And every evening, promptly at five o'clock, he ran down the iron stairs and out of the building, to mount his bright green and redoubtable bicycle, on which he pedalled furiously until he reached the bottom of the hill. Thenceforth he climbed, laboriously, up and up, what Monsieur Follet had once described as climbing into hell. And it was somewhere on its second floor that Aristide Labiche lived with his wife and two children.

Heros liked Labiche, he was so faithful, punctual, he gave a good day's work for what might not be a good day's pay. Monsieur Follet had not forgotten that this year he had promised him a rise. Now, Labiche toiled away with the time-sheets, all the time enjoying a feeling of happiness, like a long, secret, un-ending smile, that shone inwards like the sun.

That their best clerk was able to split himself into two persons was a matter upon which the Heros concern was entirely indifferent. So long as the clerical side functioned well, all was well. What Labiche did after five o'clock was his own business. The Heros would never interfere. All knew how his spare time was spent; they admired him in a distant, cynical sort of way, but they never commented upon it.

Philippe, a home-loving person if ever there was one, could never understand why Labiche's wife put up with it all, for the man was hardly home from his work and enjoying his supper, than his mind was made up to be out again. Madame Labiche was totally resigned to his mission, and the green hat and the umbrella, the parting smile as he reached the door was only a signal to her that another creature had fallen.

Labiche loved creatures. A man of serious purpose, with a mission in life, a clerk who sat in the dingiest of the Heros offices, but who in the evening wandered off into the dark places. One was not a member of the Saint Vincent de Paul for nothing.

There were creatures who spent more than forty days and forty nights in the desert, and Labiche was after them. There was always somebody on the rack. His brain contained a large, outspread map of hell, full of wandering creatures who could be saved. His was a continuous descending movement. He was familiar with abysses, dark corners, lost holes, concealed turnings, labyrinths. He visited the sick, prisons, hospitals, hostels for the dying, whore houses; he climbed the gangways of ships, found his way into malodorous foc'sles, then came down again, going on, scattering good intentions, scattering seed as he went. His country lay behind the locked door, the closed window, he travelled in the night as though on wings. He watched out for the bent, the stooping, the blunderers, the night leaners against walls, the lost, flat on their backs in the knocking shops. He arrived after the last word had been said, after the clock had stopped, he was the extension on Hope. Dereliction drew him as powerfully as light, he believed in redemption, the resurrection of souls.

There were depths lower than abyss, and he knew them, miseries as solid as walls, sin as affrighting and fierce as flame. Labiche never paused, but went forward, hope had the solidity of rock. Mercy was not just some blind leap of the heart.

But after the nightmare hours there was the morning, the quieter day, the ordinary, the normal hours, yet Labiche often drew after him a kind of hallucinatory thread, and sometimes the very ordinary objects in his office took on an unreality. . . .

" There ! " he said, having finished the last of the *Orlando's* sheets, " there ", and he made them into a neat pile and put them away in the top drawer of his desk, which he locked. He pushed in his chair, went and looked through the window, to see the sky and a desert of roofings. He put on his hat, picked up the umbrella, and went out into the corridor. He tore down the iron stairway, he always took it at a run, as though never a minute must be wasted. He met the cleaner coming up, armed with his cloths, his brush and pail.

" Good-day."

" Good-day " the cleaner said turning to watch him go. Nothing seemed funnier to the cleaner than the sight of Labiche's odd shape careering madly down the stairs.

" Poor sod. Quite mad, I'm sure."

Labiche went off to Fred's. Meanwhile Follet and Philippe had reached Madame Gaston's establishment. They never lunched anywhere else.

Monsieur Follet was a fat man, he never sat comfortably anywhere. To-day he draped one of Madame Gaston's chairs, enjoying his lunch with M. Philippe. He toyed with a cutlet, and at the same time kept his eye on Madame, seated at her high desk, whose present function was one of dispensing smiles, as one after another of her favourite customers came in. Follet was always attracted to Madame Gaston by her wonderful red hair, he sometimes expected it to burst into flame. A glance from her to M. Philippe made him realise what a reedy instrument his assistant really was.

" You were saying ? " said Follet.

Philippe sat back in his chair. " I said that Nantes bum was in again yesterday, sir."

" Indeed! I was unaware of it " replied Follet; he looked quickly round the room as though an eavesdropper lay in every corner.

" By the way, that Toulon agent says that the stuff is on the way, and a long way, too, I think. If I did not think it paved the way for future business I would never dream of accepting it, but agents are mighty people as you well know, Philippe, and one must not offend them. But the *Clarte* is held up, and her hatch yawning open for the stuff. And Manos is irritable, I cannot offend my best skipper, although he is at the nodding age. He desires to be under way by seven o'clock. I am seeing him at three o'clock. You might get on to Marcelle as soon as you get back, we *must* know when this bloody consignment is arriving."

" Yes sir."

" What did you say to this Nantes bum ? "

" Nothing, sir. What does one say ? If one's a parrot perhaps the same as one said yesterday. There are no vacancies, and indeed we of the Heros like to keep the concern a family affair, we do not like strangers——"

Follet smiled. " Quite so. What sort of job, Philippe."

" Commander."

" Nothing less than that ? " Follet roared. " Indeed, with his record."

" With his record, sir " Philippe replied, wiping his hands carefully on his napkin.

" I've never seen him. What's he like. I've heard of him, of course, and indeed I may say that I've the strongest feelings I've met people of that name, years ago of course."

" I never looked, sir " Philippe said.

" And he standing in front of you ? "

" What could happen if I'd looked at him ? A miracle ? There are no berths, our ships are manned. Isn't that correct, sir ? "

" Why yes, of course, of course. And there are other Lines " said Follet.

" Then let him try them " said Philippe.

" Quite so."

Follet began wiping his mouth, he looked towards the high desk, smiled, received one back, the cheese was coming.

" He asked for you, sir " Philippe said, " but he always does."

"Naturally. Everybody asks for me, Philippe. But one is far too busy. It's a long way to come looking for a ship, anyhow, a long way——"

"If one comes to Marseilles looking for a ship the circumstances may be exceptional, sir," said Philippe.

"That is very true. I gather his people are here, too. Am I correct?"

"They say his mother and sister followed him here."

"Intriguing, but far too hot to-day to pursue anything."

"The family is quite respectable, I understand that the father was a Commander in the Navy, went down with the *Croilus* in the First World War——"

"That's it. I remember now, I met a Madame Marius and her husband years ago, at a launching, so long ago I've almost forgotten it."

"I wonder he did not follow in the father's footsteps, sir" Philippe said.

"Well, as to that, I could tell you that his own father had the Admiralty turn the son down, the father didn't think he was good enough for the Navy, not French enough if I may say so, a stuffy, thick-headed provincial but a thorough good fellow, and loyal, that counts; there's little loyalty about to-day, Philippe," and Philippe nodded an immediate approval.

"He'd a suspension some years ago, too."

"Yes. A heavy loss for her owners, a very young Captain, twenty five or six, no more, at the time."

"A heavy loss to her owners?"

"It was indeed. Marius did well in the Marine, but somehow he always steered clear of decent owners, the riff-raff attracted, I've heard tales about him, seeing sailors every day of one's life——"

"Yes yes, of course. His stock fell."

"Then you have this other affair, the *Corsican*. There was supposed to have been an enquiry about it——"

"It didn't happen, hardly the time, people were too busy killing each other . . . the war."

"That's true."

" But it hasn't been forgotten, sir " said Philippe.

" By whom ? "

" Sailors."

" Is he a heavy drinker ? "

" They say he likes his drop, but he's no exception. He's a splendid sailor. Yet they say there's a contradiction in him, a sort of flaw. A good commander but not always able to carry the authority of one. He is a proud man, too, and a jealous one."

" You seem to know a hell of a lot about this man, and you seem to be making an exception of him."

" You asked me about him, sir and I'm telling you. I'm seeing sailors in the office every day of my life, stories get about, it's natural, some say they wouldn't ship with a man like Marius, call him a Jonah. That's what is hurting him to-day. Nobody questions him, nobody enquires, companies just ignore him, it's worse than a direct kick."

" I should say so. Poor swine. How long's he been calling on us?"

" Almost daily, well at least three times a week for the past four months. . . ."

" It almost makes me feel ashamed " replied Follet.

" The rule of iron is the one hold on a powerful element, and men are dependent on it " said Philippe.

This made Follet burst out laughing, " now you're talking like an actor, Philippe, please keep to business."

" Quite so, sir. Take the *Corsican* then. If Marius was wrong on that night then he's not the one to admit it. Such men are liabilities to any company."

" But you are an asset to mine " cried Follet, and he slapped heartily at Philippe's knee. " I'm enjoying my lunch, Philippe, and I hope you are, too."

" I am indeed, sir."

" I'm trying to recall that matter," Follet's brow was furrowing, " there were two survivors, they say."

" It was this man Royat who first spread the story of Marius having had a row with his mate and with the helmsman,

Madeau, on a matter of the correct course, a difference of nearly four degrees. It is interesting to note that he broke with all tradition by surviving."

" There are no longer traditions " Follet said, " one does not stand at the mast-head like a fool, saluting as his ship goes down. Rumour is like fire " he added, " who believes in gossip, anyhow ? " He sat back, waited for his coffee.

" Black and a brandy, Philippe ? "

" If you please, Monsieur Follet. Thank you."

" Thank you, Jean," when the coffee came.

" Ah," exclaimed Follet, after the first sip, he looked at Philippe.

" It all comes to this," he said, " this man is looking for a berth, and we have no berths, and we are glad there are no berths. Is not that so ? "

Philippe smiled assent.

And then he returned to his bone.

" D'you know what I think sir ? "

" What do you think ? "

" I think there's something fishy about the whole thing."

" Why ? "

" Because Madeau did not survive. And it's plain, too, that it was the end for Marius, he had already suffered a suspension, he'd be bound to lose his ticket, nothing else for it, inescapable, I can see him facing the issue, see any Captain of that ripe age facing it. One does not require much imagina-tion——" continued Philippe, but he was interrupted by Follet, who waved a hand violently in the air.

" My God, Philippe, how you love sensation," he leaned closer, lowered his voice, " and how the love for it seems to feed on quiet, respectable lives, such as yours Philippe, grow-ing out of your rose garden, even out of your house slippers. Rubbish. I never listen to stories, anyway."

" A man came to me for a job some three months ago, sir " said Philippe ; " he'd been sent along to me by a quarter-master under Manos, he said he'd got it from a stoker that there *was* a violent row between Gasse the first officer and

Marius, and that Madeau who was at the wheel at the time sided with Gasse and angered the other. Consider. If this was so, Marius's end as a skipper was inevitable. He might consider the humiliation, the downfall, he might do anything——"

" Your imagination does you credit " said Follet.

Philippe, the bone firmly between his teeth, replied quietly, " I'm serious, sir."

" No. No. That is Fate giving too hard a knock to a creature " said Follet, his voice full of protest. " Spare me, Philippe. Besides, look at the clock. It is time to get back to business. So you think that Marius, to save his pride might have killed his own nephew. Well well. I would advise you, Philippe, to keep a careful control over the tongue in your head. If this were so, well, there are such things as justice, somebody would do something——"

" France was in pieces, Monsieur Follet. France was fleeing. The matter of a single ship is a tossed fragment, besides there is a kind of honour——"

Follet was up, calling loudly for his bill.

" Enough, Philippe, I've a conference at three o'clock, but perhaps you forget."

" Labiche says that France has not fallen far enough, she has yet to sink further——"

Smiling, Follet paid his bill, spoke low into Philippe's ear.

" And this morning I gave him a rise in salary."

" The Marius affair is a ripple in the ocean, sir," remarked Philippe as they moved towards the door.

" Good. That will close the matter. Let it be a ripple in the ocean, and let the ocean alone, Philippe, and let your imagination alone, too. I'm off. I cannot afford to be late with Manos, I haven't seen him for some time now, and he is our best man."

They had reached the steps.

" It's been interesting " Follet said, " but shall we now let Marius rot ? "

" Very well, sir we'll let him rot " Philippe replied, and together they went out into the bright sunshine.

" Manos is waiting for you in your office, sir " Marcelle said, as soon as Follet came in.

" Thank you."

" Ah Manos. A pleasure. I so rarely see my Captains. How are you, my dear fellow ? "

Grunting a little Manos replied, " you rarely see your ships, either. I am quite well, thank you."

" But I dream about them," Follet said, " do sit down."

Manos was as Spanish as Jerez. Follet often thought he had in him the blood of an old pirate, he often stared at the Captain's ears, they used at one time to carry ear-rings. He sprawled in the chair.

" Have a cigar ? "

" Thank you, sir. Some stuff is not yet through, Monsieur Follet, and my hatch is waiting. Beyond number five we are battened down and derricks home, we are indeed ready. Again, I want to be off."

He sent smoke flying round the office.

" Is that all you called about ? "

" Of course, and you yourself are only waiting for me to be under way."

Follet growled. " Time has never stopped being money."

Manos tossed back his head. " Indeed ! I was unaware of it."

Noticing a mass of papers, Manos remarked that Monsieur Follet was somewhat busy.

" I was checking up on a certain matter."

" I see."

" I've often wondered what you thought about it ? "

" About it, about what ? "

" Nothing, really."

Manos shrugged his shoulders. " One thing upon

which you may congratulate yourself Monsieur Follet, is that we have such a splendid lot of men."

" Including Captains ? "

" I thank you."

Follet sat up in his chair. " Well now ? Have you had a man by the name of Marius looking for a job aboard the *Clarte* ? "

" I'm not interested. It's the Nantes man, no, not at all. Many skippers have lost their tickets and will do again."

He turned round, swept the office at a glance.

" How comfortable you are here" he said. " To return to important matters, I hope I'll see this consignment on the quay before five o'clock. It's important, you know it is."

" It will be there."

" Good. Then I am satisfied."

" Tell me, Manos, would you ship this Marius ? "

" If he were a good sailor and I was a hand short."

" Isn't he a good sailor ? "

" I'm not as close to him as that " replied Manos.

He was staring down at the red carpet, he liked this, he wished he had one as good for his cabin in the *Clarte*.

" But you are tight-minded as well as tight-fisted."

" I have to respect my crew."

" So there is something in it ? "

Manos shook his head.

" Nothing in it. If this bum's dragging through the gutter, then it's his own fault. When a man with his record refuses to ship below his rank—well, I ask you——" and Manos threw out his hands in a despairing gesture, " the man's crazy. There are ways of climbing. No one can find them for you, you find them yourself. Marius will."

" At fifty ? "

" I must be off, Monsieur Follet. Thanks for the cigar."

" Suppose he came to you for a job ? "

" With great respect to you, I refuse to discuss the matter."

" Your ears are closed to the stories then ? "

" The common mouth is a very large one " replied Manos,

" anything may come out of it," he tossed his cigar into the grate. " I *must* go. I've things to do," and he picked up his hat.

He paused at the door. " You'll find out about the lorries ? "
" I'll ring at once."
" Shall I wait while you ring ? "
" There's no need," and Follet's voice sounded somewhat stiff. He stretched out a hand.
" Well Manos—sailor's affairs are sailor's affairs, eh ? "
" Sailor's affairs are most often sailor's affairs. Good-bye."
" Good-bye. Pleasant voyage."
" Thanks " and Manos went out through the door.
Follet threw away his cigar, sat down and rang up Marcelle.

Manos waddled his way out. He had a beautiful roll, it often made passers-by think he was drunk. In a considerate way they would steer their way past him. He reached the *Clarte* in a leisurely, comfortable walk, having had a drink or two on the way just to assure himself that he could still take it.

" I'm not getting younger."

He leaned now upon her foc'sle head rail. There was some-thing, peaceful, satisfying about the late afternoon, now drawing to evening. The noise of winches rattled in his ears, but it did not disturb a sudden feeling of content that he felt within himself. It was good to have a job, to be safe, to be understood. He looked seawards with some longing, away past the loud chattering little motor boats carrying their excursionists to the Chateau d'If. Like Marius, he had been too long hard bound.

Had he heard ? Of course he'd heard. Who hadn't. Poor devil. It's what he doesn't know that'll scare the guts out of him. They'll find Royat in the end, people aren't fools. Now if he'd only come down off his Captain's throne, why, I'd try to find him something myself. At the best I could stick him in the hold, but would he go ? Trotting about the place with his record.

He turned lazily, put a hand to his eyes. " Ah! This country's far too civilized, everybody has *feelings*, consciences— the happy state is complete anonymity."

He pulled out and lit his seventh cigar, he liked cigars.

His eye met the sun as one thin line of fire, he took in the whole harbour, the far off line where the water danced, beyond the breakers he seemed to see continuously moving ribbons of light.

" He may have made a mistake, who knows, and saw his sacred ticket crumbling to ash before his eyes, he might have done what they say—all the same he has served ships well, that's remembered."

He left the foc'sle head, walked aft.

" This is the place to come, anyhow, the meanest dog can find a way out, and if he wants to be forgotten forever he need not travel any further than beyond the Cannabiere."

" By God " thought Manos, " that snake Follet might well be trying to find an excuse for getting rid of me. Yes, he might even be quixotically generous and give that bum my job, he'd take him for less salary of course, that's his way——"

He had a momentary vision of Marius, Marius shadowing the Heros building, Marius wearing them down.

" So many years my junior, just fifty, no no, what's this crazy imagination of mine doing to me—yes, it might happen, I'm getting old, and that's a worse terror than losing a ship, even killing a man, when one begins to feel the assaults of age —no no. Rubbish. Pull yourself together, you're crazy, man, crazy. Isn't it Manos, isn't it ? You're an honourable man, and you've served Heros well, and Follet knows it, and after all it's he who's got most of the shares."

A hand on his shoulder made him jump and he swung round.

" Why Laurent. Good. Good. Let's go to my cabin," and they went off together, the mate following behind the waddling Manos.

" Just come away from seeing, Follet " Manos said as he sat down. " So rarely do I meet that fellow, and it's my instinct that keeps me away, that this time I hardly realized it was him, barely recognized him. I was annoyed with him, even a little disgusted. Such a well fed animal, so certain of himself, such a greedy swine, so indifferent to people unless they're putting money in his pocket. He asked me if I'd ship that Nantes bum."

"Ah " he cried, " listen to that. Something is happening, let's go out."

The crew were coming up the gangway, and there on the quay something that shed his terrors at a blow, made him smile, the two great lorries had arrived.

He watched the loading. " Good, good" thought Manos, " no man is free until he's away, and that's the living truth of it."

" Get for'ard and check up on the men, Laurent."

" Yes sir " and Laurent went for'ard.

At half past six the final sling had swung downwards, the limp fall came up. The hatches crashed down. There were shouts on the quay, the lorries were drawing away. Somebody was calling to Manos.

The sound of the *Clarte's* syren split the air.

Manos hurried to the bridge. He saw the first hawser go, heard the sullen crash.

" All clear aft." Manos listened. " Away for'ard."

He pulled his watch from his pocket, cried to himself, " beautiful, beautiful."

The *Clarte* was under way at a quarter after seven. She blew again.

" What about Marius now " he thought, standing triumphantly on his bridge, " to hell with Marius."

He gave a sigh of relief. The threshold of voyages always yielded up a kind of warmth, he was under way, he was free.

III

EVERY evening Labiche sat with his children on his knee and rocked them and sang to them, whilst in the kitchen his wife prepared the supper. In between snatches of song they exchanged conversation.

" I'm going out at nine o'clock, Marie " Labiche said. " D'you remember Madame Gilliat's girl, you know, the one they dote on, Jeanette, well she's somehow found her way into that Madame Lustigne's house."

" Mother of God."

" Yes, Father Prideau was telling me yesterday, her mother's in a terrible state. I'm seeing Madame Lustigne this evening. But I won't be late," and then Labiche forgot every thing as he lowered his head between those of his children and he hugged them and was happy.

But only when he got inside the house, and he was glad to do that, the journey up the hill always saddened him, the faces of children, he would sometimes stand and stare at them, leaning on his bicycle, looking at the dirt, the rags, the big eyes of innocence full of a dreadful melancholy.

He had once brought Philippe to tea, it was Yvonne's fifth birthday, and Philippe had found it difficult to refuse, but not so difficult to resolve that never again would he climb the hill of Accoules. The long dark street in which Labiche lived he called " the whore's left leg ".

" How the hell you live and like it " said Philippe.

" Many people live here" replied Labiche.

When Madame Labiche appeared, Aristide picked up his children and carried them off to bed.

To celebrate his rise in fortune there was a special bottle, a special salad.

" Perhaps " remarked Marie, " we could now move further away, one ought to get on," to which Labiche replied in an absent-minded way, " why, get on, where ? "

" I don't know " she said, and didn't, it left her bewildered.

She was a foot and a half taller than her husband, large, fat and comfortable looking, she was a simple girl from the farm.

" You could try, for the children's sake, for Yvonne's anyhow."

" Many are worse than us " he said, he leaned forward and kissed her lightly on the cheek, and then, re-assuringly, " I shan't be late."

" Diderot called this afternoon for the Mission money. I gave it him."

" I hope it's a bigger collection than last time."

" And the man from the hospital called, they want a shirt for Lanier."

" Poor Lanier " said Labiche, he wiped his mouth, " a beautiful meal " he said and pushed in his chair.

He took out his pipe, sat himself in the armchair and puffed contentedly. Marie cleared the table. Most evenings she sat and sewed. Watching her now as she bent over the table he thought she looked a little sad.

" Anything the matter, dear ? "

" Nothing " she said.

" I'm not *always* out."

" You're not always in," she was on the point of saying, " you don't see things, though you think you do."

She was always glad to draw the curtains, even on a hot night.

" Sometimes I wish you'd give up the St Vincent de Paul, you're never in."

He noted her hands sudden gripping of the table, he sensed a tensity rising, it was most unusual. He got up.

" What's the matter, darling ? "

" Nothing."

" Well then——"

39

" Everybody *uses* you " she said.

She went to the bureau, came back and showed him a letter from her parents. Was she never coming for a holiday, were they never to see Jacque, two years old now and they had never seen him.

" But I do not harm, I only help people, Marie, don't you understand me ? "

" Sometimes " she said, " sometimes."

He stood by her, an arm round her shoulder, his huge, ugly head reached upwards, " don't you understand ? "

She cried a little.

" There there." He held her tightly. " Then shall I not go out ? " he asked.

When she looked at him she saw his eyes were on the clock.

" I don't know, please yourself, Ariste," and she walked away and left him and went upstairs.

" Am I wrong ? he asked himself. " Am I right ? What is *really* just ? "

He went to the window and looked out. " The noise, yes, the tramp tramp up and down these streets, perhaps Philippe is right, we are living on a whore's back. Nothing stops," and he was watching some children playing, one of whom lay flat on its back in the gutter. He looked down the hill, and thought, " swarms with people, like lice, and yet it's miraculous."

He went to the foot of the stairs. " Marie. Shall I come up ? " and when he heard no reply, he went up. He found her sitting on the stool between the children's beds. They were both asleep.

" I tell you this, Marie, I do tell you this, we'll take that holiday, yes, I'll ask Monsieur Follet if I can go next month, instead of November, somehow I always seem to be the last for my holidays."

He knelt down by her, placed his hands on her knees, looked gently at her. " Marie."

" I want to live myself " she said.

" Yes yes, I know, dear, of course, why not, and we shall, with the help of God we shall, but when I go out, when I go down this street, and I turn this corner, and that, and down that other street and I see what I see——"

" People should help themselves."

" They do, Marie, think of Madame Sorel ? "

She gave him a wan smile and said, " Ariste, you'd better go then."

He held her in a fierce embrace. It was not often that she sobbed, but she did so now.

" All day, all this day, it's strange, I could think of nothing, I just dreamed, I dreamed of our getting out of it, of our going, we *will* go, we will go ? "

And he said, " ssh ! ssh ! We will go, Marie, my own love. Now may I go. Think of this child, with *that* woman ? "

" Go."

He turned and left her sitting in the darkened room and seemed to hear more deeply the short, quick breathing of his sleeping children.

She heard the door close, but still sat on between her children. Labiche had hardly travelled ten yards before he heard his name called from a high window, and looking up saw Madame Sorel frantically waving to him from behind a curtain.

Her door was open, it was rarely closed, and Labiche went straight in and up the stairs. He found the old woman in some difficulties, she was on her knees by the door.

" Oh Madame, what is this ? " he asked, " what is this ? Has not Marie given you your supper ? "

The face, crawling with lupus, was turned upwards, the old woman nodded her head.

" I can't get back into bed " she said, " please Monsieur Labiche," and he helped her back to bed and covered her.

" Good-night Madame Sorel " he said, and closed the door, went downstairs and into the street and continued his journey downwards.

" Poor creature " he said, it came to his lips so often that it had a robot-like sound to it.

He looked at the long row of houses, how they hugged each other, embracing the ugliness of all, and this continued to the very end, and lower, to the next street, and lower to the next, and over it all the sun shone, hard and bright, and Labiche took a handkerchief from his pocket and wiped his neck.

" There are some holes here " he said to himself " where the sun never shines, it is much cooler in those places."

Labiche always paused when he came to the Rue Danielle. If there had been any other way of dodging it he would have taken it, for here in this street were the people who laughed loudest, youths who called after him, " the little black pudding", and once two drunken sailors had stopped him, tried to get him to dance, the memory of it had never left him, he would sweat when he thought of it. But when he turned into it, the place was almost empty, as though all in this street had died. And then he heard the noises through the open windows.

" If I'm not mistaken her house lies somewhere between the Quai de Belge and the Cannabiere. This is the second time she's stolen somebody, says they come to her, rubbish."

" Philippe should come late at night," he thought, " it glows with horror," it made him think of Marie, quiet, sad, between those innocent beds.

" Am I right? Or wrong? And yet it's the first time she has wavered, ever."

Doubt flung itself up as powerful as a wave, fell quickly as he thought of Follet.

" There is a man who believes in nothing but himself, yet in some queer way, when I tell about my work, for he often asks me, then he says, ' I wish I were you, you are good, Labiche.' "

Where is the truth of it?

There was a tiny shop at the end of the Rue Thomí, and always by its door an old, old man, who would wait for Labiche to pass. He would say good-evening, Monsieur Labiche, are you after the devil again? and he would smile, and thinking of him as he approached the shop, Labiche hoped he would yet be there, there was something in the old man's smile that pleased him.

To-night the shop was closed, and no Monsieur Noste was to be seen. Labiche turned the corner.

Children everywhere, old people seated on doorsteps, women in shifts, a mass of rubbish to kick under one's feet, he always called this, " the street of floating trash", and sometimes he asked himself if this were the children, or merely the rubbish of that day flung rudely out of doors. The grey of the stone, the blood shine of the brick, it struck at the eyes. The air stank.

"Not far to go now " he thought, and almost without realizing it he had reached the bottom of the hill.

"Now for that woman."

You could tell Madame Lustigne's house anywhere, because it looked the most respectable, and its high walls, pock-marked, smeared, with its one solitary climbing rose. It seemed to grin in the sun. It was situated at the end of the road. One high wall directly facing the hill was completely blank, windowless, and held only a large hideous Michelin placard, which now hung mournfully downwards, having been torn from the wall by a high wind, and needing only a single gust to send it flying into the road. And there was the door which was of brightest green, and in front of it the wrecked street lamp, headless, and above this the tall narrow windows, glittering in the sun.

Labiche had been here once before. He had used the front entrance. To-night he would use the back, and so passed through a court-yard littered with household utensils, pails, brushes, a heap of old clothes, an empty barrel, a bundle of soiled newspapers, and above this a long clothes line, but Labiche did not look that far. He found the door and knocked.

It opened. The interior was so dark that Labiche could not at first discern who the opener was. And he got the smell of scent and stale smoke and new wine to his nostrils.

"Madame Lustigne" he said.

"Who're you?"

"Aristide Labiche."

"Doesn't mean a bloody thing to me, names never do, what d'you want?

"I've already said, Madame Lustigne?"

"Are you from the police? The girls were examined on Tuesday. I say are you from the police?"

"*Me?*" said Labiche, and laughed, then wondered why he had laughed.

"I'm not the police Inspector."

"In which case you'd better come in."

"Thank you."

He saw him then, and recognized him. Henri. Her husband.

A man in the early sixties, his mouse-coloured, tousled grey hair upset Labiche at sight, and he noted that the man wore only a vest and black trousers, heel-less slippers. The face was grey and ashen, the eyes dull.

"This way" Henri said, and went off down the corridor, closely followed by Labiche, he talked as he walked.

"If you're a customer, the price's up five francs, how anybody lives to-day astounds me. This way" he said again.

"Who's that, Henri?"

"A Monsieur Labiche."

"Bring him in."

Labiche blinked a little as he passed from darkness to light.

"Oh" she said, "it's you. You're a menace, Labiche, a menace."

Labiche smiled. "You know why I've come?"

Madame Lustigne was seated on a sort of throne, it always reminded him of a throne, and she was looking at him, and

44

smiling, but this was to his disadvantage, she goaded and tormented Labiche about his figure.

" You may sit down ? You are always saving somebody, why can't you let people alone ? You're wrong anyhow, she came of her own accord."

The door was open, Madame Lustigne was looking, not at Labiche, but out through this open door. There was a voice outside. Labiche looked, too.

It was at this moment that he saw Marius who had just come in by the front door. His startled look made the woman ask, " anything the matter ?"

" That man " said Labiche, " I know him, at least I've seen him before."

" So have I, Monsieur " said Madame Lustigne, " a generous gentleman."

Marius passed the door.

" Where is she ? " asked Labiche.

" Where d'you suppose a girl would be at this hour ? "

" You have the advantage of me."

" Then go and see. Room fourteen, and mind she doesn't take advantage of you, these girls who look like nuns——."

" I'll find it " Labiche said, and went to the door, just as Marius was coming in.

" Ah Captain. There you are. Is it Lucy again ? "

She rose, and went to him, put out her hands, held his own, " I'm always glad to see you, Captain."

Marius drew away his hands, went and closed the door. He did not like Madame's smile when he came towards her.

" That man " said Marius, " who's that man. That's twice I've seen him."

" How excited you are, my Captain. Please to sit down, I'll call Henri for a drink. Brandy ? "

He did not answer, but heard her go to the door, open it and call Henri.

" This bloody man, where've I seen him before, I believe he's following me."

" Your drink, my Captain."

45

He looked up. She was standing there, smiling down at him.

" You do not wear very well to-day " she said, she lifted his cap off his head and laid it on her dressing-table.

She brought a chair and sat beside him, put an arm round him.

" Tell me your sins, Captain. What have you done to-day."

She put her hand under his chin, " you should shave more often."

She stroked the rough beard, " is it Lucy again ? " she asked, " perhaps you're in love with my Lucy, Captain, a beautiful girl, but so's champagne when the bottle's full. She's no brains, poor child, but who on earth wants brains."

Her scent was clouding over him, he could feel her breath. He sat there, not speaking, not responding, she thought, " to-night, he looks utterly stupid."

Marius had waked up shivering, somewhat surprised to find himself still on the timbers. He had dragged himself away, he could still hear the laughter of the pair who were sitting at the other end of the pile.

" Young lovers" he said, and had hurried away.

He had not been " back there." The very thought of it chilled him, the silence like a knife, the meal spread out, the two staring, wooden faces.

" They know, of course they know. I'll tell her to-night, I can't stand it any longer. Poor Madeleine——"

" Do wake up, you're falling asleep " Madame Lustigne said, " you can't possibly see Lucy like that."

" Leave me alone."

" I can't. You're in my room, I want you to get out. Lucy is waiting."

" Who's that man ? "

" Him. A miserable little clerk " she said, " why. You're becoming afraid of your own shadow. Are the police after you ? "

He looked so dejected that she flung her arms about him, " come, come, don't be sad, Captain, life's far too short.

Enjoy yourself. I'm just going to have my supper. Would you like to join me?"

He sat up. "I *am* hungry" Marius said.

"You've been out all day?"

He nodded.

"No luck?"

"No luck."

"Oh dear, how sad. Perhaps to-morrow. You've not been home all this day?"

"No."

"Of course, you're hungry, that's what it is."

He kept looking towards the door.

"Nobody will disturb us" she said.

"What's his name?"

"Labiche, he's a sort of saint, but an ugly one" replied Madame Lustigne. "He's actually here to steal one of my girls. And I'm letting him. Think of that?"

Marius couldn't think. He had fallen fast asleep.

He ate greedily enough when he woke.

"Perhaps the Captain came here to hide?"

"I came here to look for a man."

"And have you found him?"

"He won't see me."

"A friend of yours?"

"Of my father's."

"You have a father then?"

"He's dead."

"But if it was to hide, well then—this is the place, the world knows that."

"Why d'you say I'm hiding" he protested stubbornly, "I'm looking for a ship."

"Plenty of them."

He was as stubborn with his silences.

"I could see a certain person."

"I'm a Captain" Marius said, "I have my merits."

"Oh God. You've Captain on the brain. Here, more bread."

" I wish I knew why that man is following me."

" Him. He's not following anybody except his own inclinations, he's a damned nuisance. St Vincent de Paul indeed. And the Apostleship of Seamen. There, Captain, I've got it. He will help you."

" Him ? "

" Why not. You want a ship, he works in a shipping office."

" Where ? "

" The Heros."

Marius slapped his knee. " There. I knew I'd seen him before. The Heros. All the same he's following me, I feel he is, it scares me——"

" You'd think a murder had been committed. Now get out, Captain, will you, I have other friends, and one is waiting outside. Please get out."

She pushed him out through the door.

" Perhaps I'm getting a little tired of him, all the same " she thought.

" Sometimes he's such a nuisance, in spite of his money, and one can't afford nuisances. Perhaps he *is* hiding. Perhaps he's made away with somebody. In which case——."

She sat down at her dressing-table, began powdering her face.

" One does not want trouble with the police, who does? Come in " she called, hearing the knock, and Labiche walked in.

" Madame Lustigne."

" Well ? " She saw his reflection in her mirror.

" I am taking Jeanette now " he said. " She wept bitterly, her mother was broken-hearted about it. You understand ? "

He had a feeling she was smiling.

She swung round on him. " Are you following that Captain ? "

" Captain ? "

" You know who I mean. He's here now, you've scared the very guts out of him. He's a good patron here. I don't like my patrons followed around. Are you following him ? "

" I came for Jeanette. True, I've seen this man, he is continually at the Heros, but Monsieur Follet refuses to see him, says he's beyond the pale."

" Indeed ? "

She turned her back on Labiche and continued her toilet.

" Can't nobody make a living without you barging in ? "

" I've the girl outside, I'm quite satisfied, Madame Lustigne. As to the Captain, you judge me wrong. I'm sorry for him. I've seen him every day for weeks, sometimes I feel sad at the way Philippe treats him, it must be humiliating. If only Captain Marius would let me talk to him, I'm sure something could be done. It's sad for his womenfolk. They are here, too."

" I didn't know that. Has he done a crime ? "

" A ship of his was lost under mysterious circumstances———"

" That's nothing, I thought he'd murdered somebody, that's all."

She looked at the little watch on her wrist.

" Get out, Labiche, I've a friend coming in."

She could hear heavy steps in the stone corridor.

" He walks like an elephant " she thought.

She got up, walked across to the door, opened it wide, said, " get out."

She saw Jeanette against the wall, she supposed it must be Labiche's outsize handkerchief she was holding to her eyes. She looked straight at the girl, and seemed to pin her to the wall by her fierce, penetrating look.

" Miserable little bitch " she said, and banged the door the moment Labiche reached the corridor. She stood behind it listening to them go.

" This Captain. I must talk to him. There is something about him———" she smiled, and it spread all over the mirror ———" I wish he did not always choose Lucy."

" Come in, Lucien " she called, and the elephant came in, tall, blonde, grey suited, his hat in his hand.

" Come " she said, and as he sat down on a corner of the bed she stroked his balding head.

49

" The people I've had in today " she exclaimed angrily,
" first that Inspector saying I hadn't done this and I hadn't
done that, then a miserable Captain and on top of that something—oh well," and she tittered and showed her teeth and
leaned against Lucien.

" D'you think I'm a very wicked person, Lucien ? "

" You're lovely " he said.

" Call Henri " she said.

It was turned seven o'clock. Marius had not come in.
Madame Marius and her daughter were seated in the kitchen.
The old woman stared with some disgust at the table, the
laid out meal.

" One evening he will not come back at all " she thought.
She looked at her daughter. " Madeleine ? "

" Yes mother ? "

" I think I'll go to the Benediction to-night." They so
rarely went out in the evenings that it came as a surprise to
Madeleine when she said this. She did not wish to go, but
felt she must.

" Very well " she said.

So they had got ready and left the house. Madame Marius
walked beside her daughter, very erect. Sometimes she would
glance down at the woman beside her. And sometimes she
hated her:

" She has the calmness—oh, she's like a cow."

Such docility, such resignation, such terrible calm. It
seemed too much to bear.

It was only a few hundred yards to St Sulpice's, but Madame
Marius walked to it as with closed eyes, she seemed neither
to see nor sense the things about her, there was only this
daughter at her side, following meekly, silently, devotedly.

" Perhaps I am indeed lucky with such a daughter " she
thought. She looked at her, gripping her arm.

" If it wasn't for where one had to walk, the things through which one had to pass, I would dearly love to go to the High Mass to-morrow for the celebration—but no, it doesn't matter," and Madeleine detected a sudden sad note in her mother's voice.

"Let's think about it" she said, and smiled up to her mother.

There were some people just ahead of them, making for the evening service, already they had turned into the gravel path leading up to the church. And then they themselves had reached its door, pausing only for a moment to bless themselves at the font, then as they usually did, to seek the darkest corner of St Sulpice's, the last bench but one. They knelt for a moment or two, then sat down.

Madame Marius had already fixed her rosary upon her wrist, the small silver crucifix gripped tight between finger and thumb. She did not pray. The mouth was shut tight, she stared steadily ahead, she seemed to be watching God.

Each morning they came for the Mass, for the Sacrament, and they sat in the same place. Now they were like mice, drawn into the deep silence of the church.

In contrast to her mother's tenseness, this folding in on herself as it were, Madeleine appeared always relaxed, at ease, prayed as was her heart's wont, never took her eyes from the altar. Her mother sat stiffly, knelt stiffly, as though she were on some kind of sentry duty.

"Oh God! I have forgiven him. I am now content. Please make mother charitable, pardon the cruelty of her years, through Christ our Lord."

She was kneeling, but the mother had not noticed her movement. She still sat still, as stone is, she felt the beads cool within her hand, she looked towards the Tabernacle.

The soft organ strains stole into the air almost like that of water, and Madame Marius listened to the music.

Everywhere there were flowers, tall proud lilies, piled velvety roses, and at the feet of the Virgin the green herbage whose scent rose high, climbing beyond the tall pillars, it seemed to be locked about the Virgin's feet. Saint Francis held the child, whose pink cheek brushed the bright nosegay reaching upwards. St John, tall and lean seemed shadowed by nothing but his own bone. Madeleine had noticed the absence of flowers here, but she remembered his life, and she understood.

People came in, walked slowly and quietly up the aisles, she watched them genuflect, and they seemed to carry about their persons the last remaining warmth of the sun, and the dying light. The organ strains grew louder, she knew it would soon be time. The music leaped like fountains, the air vibrated under the mass of sound. Madeleine remained kneeling and did not once turn to look at her mother, but if she had done so she would have found the eyes closed at last, and nothing coming from her save her laboured breathing.

" Oh God ! Help Eugene. Forgive him, through Christ our Lord."

As her lips trembled under the words she was suddenly conscious of eyes staring at her, and knew that her mother was watching her. She sensed the powerful body leaning towards her.

She spoke in a low voice, and Madeleine slightly turned to her, straining her ears to listen.

" What mother ? "

" You have made up your mind, Madeleine ? " she asked, and the slack of the beads swung to and fro as she spoke.

" You are sure of this, certain ? "

" Yes mother, I know it is right. I will always be with you, mother."

" I'm old " her mother said, " I knew long ago."

" Yes " Madeleine said, " I know you are old. I have made up my mind."

" I only wished to be certain, Madeleine."

" I am certain. Isn't that enough ? "

Madeleine watched the candles spluttering in their holders, the rock-still blooms in their vases.

" The priest was unable to come last evening, he was called out to the dying."

" Of course " her mother said, " one understands that, one is not stupid."

The church had become strangely silent. Madame Marius knew that at any moment now, the altar boys would come out through the little dark door, preceding Father Nollet. She took her daughter's hand and pressed it.

" Don't imagine I do not understand" she said, pressing more tightly, " I do. I *am* old. And you will not re-marry. Some things are always too late."

" Ssh ! " Madeleine said.

The little procession came through the door and they both knelt down.

" Did you hear what I said ? " whispered the old woman.

Madeleine fixed her eyes on the statue of St Joseph. She had heard, but would not answer. Some things were not discussed in the house of God. Later, Father Nollet was in the pulpit, speaking, but they did not hear him.

" What is that ? " asked Madeleine, she glanced shyly about her.

" I said we've been here too long. That is all. I'll be glad to be out of it."

Madeleine was suddenly very close to her mother.

" You had a letter this morning. I saw it, I mean the post-mark. From home ? "

She never mentioned Nantes by name, simply referred to it as ' home '.

" From Father Gerard."

" What does he say ? "

" I haven't read it."

They were suddenly silent for the blessing. Father Nollet followed the boys out, people were rising to their feet.

" Let us go."

" I'll just speak to the priest before I go " Madeleine said, and suddenly was gone.

Madame Marius knelt down again. " Help us now, Mighty God."

As she prayed she stared about the church, and behind her

heard the steady, deep tick of the clock below the choir stall.

" I follow him because there is something he must tell us."

" And he can't hold it in much longer, it is too dreadful for that, he knows—and when he speaks I shall be satisfied. But what of her ? "

She did not kneel long, her knees hurt, she rose and sat back in the seat.

" At the end one is always asking for help."

The rosary came alive in her hands, the beads moved through her fingers, she kneaded them, bead on bead, and stared at the Tabernacle.

" I shall be glad to get home, my back is aching a little, I hope she won't be too long."

She suddenly saw her daughter, she was at the breast, she saw her for the first time.

" Nature plays tricks, how plain she really is. Unlike the Marius lot, how handsome they were," and she felt again the full rigour of that initial shock.

" To-day she is as plain as a pancake."

She struggled to her feet, her sharp ear had already heard approaching footsteps. She put an arm through that of her daughter and they left the church.

" You have everything ? "

" Everything."

" Then we will go back to that house" Madame Marius said.

There was something hesitant, uncertain in their very steps, as though this were a task, a duty to be done, the heart pulled another way.

On occasions the old woman would cry " stop " and the daughter stopped.

Madame Marius regained her breath, and as she stood she held on tightly to her daughter's arm.

" It's a terrible place, so huge, like a big melting pot, if one falls into it, well, you never know how you come out. Ah, I shall be glad to go."

" Are you ready ? "

" I'm ready."

They walked on, Madame Marius erect, her head slightly forward, on her shoulders, Madeleine held tight to her arm.

" I wonder if he'll be out ? "

" Is he ever in ? "

A silence fell between them and they did not speak again until they were safe inside the house. Madame Marius freed herself from the clutching arm. She stared about the kitchen.

" Well at least he has taken his peasant's suit" she said. " You know there is something terribly stupid in his stubbornness, I'll bet he is cringing around the Heros again. My God, if *I* could get in to see that Follet gentleman—— You had better bring in the coffee. I am going into the other room," and she left her daughter standing in the centre of the kitchen. When she brought in the bread and coffee her mother had already resumed her seat in the window.

" This morning I had half a mind to go into his room " Madame Marius said, as she took the mug from her daughter. " Sometimes I think one may know what that person has been thinking."

" What are you staring at ? " she asked suddenly, and Madeleine replied quickly, " nothing," but she was.

To-day, this very evening she seemed to be looking at her mother as for the first time. How big she was, how strong, how determined, and yet withal, how suddenly calm. In the night something had risen in her, a resolve, a decision.

" Then what she said in the church is true " thought Madeleine.

" Why don't you sit down ? "

" I am," sitting down.

Her mother made coarse noises as she ate, she dropped lumps of bread into her coffee and sucked at the sodden mass.

" I expect he was thinking what you were thinking " Madeleine said.

" What was that ? " Madame Marius spoke sharply, " give me more coffee."

" Your pride " she said.

" Since you had none, it cannot affect you very much."

" Where is the letter of Father Gerard ? "

" I have it here. Read it to me."

" Give it here."

Holding it in her hand, Madeleine felt for a moment as though all Nantes were there, all her life, the grace of her days, she heard laughter, saw her heart-happy man.

" Then read it " Madame Marius said.

" Yes " Madeleine said, faltering, the break in her voice.

" Spare me, please, I thought we had done with that. Read the letter."

She opened out the sheet of paper and began to read.

" Dear Madame Marius,

I am glad that you have written me. This morning I was on my way to see our old friend, Jules Cordon, you will remember him. And as you know my way lies past your house, and coming by it I chanced to see bursting over the wall the white lilac, heavily in flower. And I thought then that perhaps, as I passed, I would hear you call to me from behind it, as in the old days. But there was only the strong light and the whiteness and silence, and I knew you had gone. But at the same time I wondered too, if you would not come back——"

" Will you go on, or must I read it myself ? "

" I am reading it " Madeleine said.

" It has always seemed to me a foolish decision to have made, to have turned your back on your home, there was so much spirit there, so much bone and heart. It is your place. It is yet empty because there is a feeling abroad that you will still come back, to where you belong, to where your place is, since there is no other. Nobody thinks any the less of you because your son has erred, and as for the rumour, the disgrace, surely you place far too high a price upon this. A man may sink a hundred ships, and yet not be disgraced, your son has erred and you think it is the end of France. My dear Madame Marius, if I may say so, I fear your pride is strangling you——"

" I said go on reading didn't I ? "

" I am reading " Madeleine said, and was in that house, hard by the river, in a room opening on the garden, and this was cool. There was a man stood there, and he was looking at her, she at him, and she said, " where is Jean ? "

" Gone," and she heard the word again, and felt it and saw it, dropping as stone into the sea, and into that room where the sea was, flowed there, carrying this man.

" Where is my son ? "

" I said he is gone. Poor, poor lad."

With her clenched fists she hammered at his breast, and this was iron.

" Where is he, where is Jean ? Christ Jesus " she cried at him, " you saved yourself," and struck, and went on striking, and he was as rock, immovable, taller than she by a foot, and as she looked up at him, taller, as high as heaven in his silence. Something like steel held her, she was caught, tight in his arms.

" Madeleine."

And she remembered it was he who cried, and not she.

" Don't touch me " she screamed, and ran, and left him, in the sea and silence.

" Will you give me that letter ? " Madame Marius said, " what has come over you, cannot you read ? Or is it that awful weakness in you, come again, after last night, after this morning, what we said, the resolution was made——"

" How far you have travelled since that morning. I often think of you, and your good daughter, God help her in her wretchedness. I have had the mind to come to you, to see you, and to talk to you. How is your son ? Has he yet been lucky, and maybe gone, or is he still hoping as we all must hope. Every day people are asking about you, and let me tell you consternation is still with us, as real and rising as a tree. You seem to have decided when end was without perhaps realizing what end means. I do beg of you, my dear Madame Marius, for the sake of your family, and of your name, to return to us and live again. On the other hand I tell myself how devoted you are to that son, to have broken up your home and followed him, and no less with her, who has suffered so much. Nothing will ever erase from my mind the dignity of this simple woman in her worst hours. Poor child. . . ."

"I should never have let him go" Madeleine said, the letter was limp in her hand, her hand fell to her side, she stared stupidly at her mother.

"And I could have said that of your father, God have mercy on his soul, I could have said, ' why did I let you go?' Perhaps because the sea is blue. Give me that letter at once."

Madeleine reached out and handed her the letter.

"Here, I will not read any more of it," said Madeleine, and went out, and upstairs to her room.

"Poor creature. It was a blow, and it will never cease to be one."

Slowly, with great deliberation she began to tear up the letter, the muscles of her face contracted—" we could never have stayed, never, my man was gone. And then she goes and marries this Madeau, so that we are forced to ask ourselves ' who in the name of God is this?' ", tearing and tearing, into the tiniest fragments, " and then the son, a fine name he made for himself, drunk, they said, when he lost that first ship, as to the other——" and suddenly she had flung a hundred tiny fragments into the air, " that cannot be answered " she said, " I would never go back. Never. I should never have let her read it, it was silly of me, I could see her falling to pieces before my eyes. Her poor son. We may have heart, but sometimes I think there must be iron. Anyway our minds are made up. It is only for Father Nollet to speak his own. Poor child. She thinks she may be happy again. Rubbish. That is something you have only the once."

She turned away from the window, she called loudly, " Madeleine, Madeleine." There was no reply. She waited, listening.

"I thought all that was finished, these secret weepings, these regrets, these—— Madeleine, cannot you hear me calling you?"

She went out and stood at the foot of the stairs. In her right hand she carried a stick, and with it she now struck sharply on the floor.

"I did not ask you to come" she shouted.

And louder, "I say I did not ask you to follow me here. Go back then if that is what you wish."

She began to climb the stairs.

IV

" WHEN I feel disgusted with myself " he said, " I always come to you."

" We can take anything " she said, " even disgust."

With a quick shake of her shoulder her hair fell loose.

" You haven't bought me a drink yet " Lucy said, making a face at him.

" I'll get one " Marius said and jumped up, but she pulled him back.

" Call Henri " she said, " that's what he's here for."

" Henri ? "

" Madame's husband, he understands everything."

" He must be very clever indeed——"

" You're actually laughing, Captain, it's the first time. Call him in. He won't fail to come, he's a mongrel man and everybody's his master."

Marius went to the door, opened it and called loudly, " Henri."

They had not long to wait. There was a knock on the door.

" Come in " cried Lucy.

Henri had mousy grey hair and a cast in one eye. He stood there in vest and black trousers, carpet slippers, looking at them indifferently.

" What is it, Lucy ? "

" I'd like a long, long Cinzano."

" Two long long Cinzano's " Marius said.

He seemed no sooner departed than he was back again, he did not knock this time, but walked right in and placed the drinks on the wicker table near the bed. His single good eye was focused on the couch.

" Two Cinzano's for Room 10," he stared at Marius, then at Lucy.

There was something in his eye that Marius did not like, and he shouted, " clear to hell out ", and Henri, grinning, turned and went out.

" And when we've had this drink, Captain, the lights go out, they hurt my eyes."

" You're very beautiful, Lucy, did you know that ? "

Lucy only laughed, she laughed at anything.

" How old are you, really ? "

" Me. I'm twenty," she said.

" Ought I to envy you, I'm forty eight," and Lucy laughed again, because she always did, she couldn't help it.

" At least " he said, " you're happy—yes ? "

" Of course I'm happy," she pulled his hair.

" And never sad ? "

She noticed the Captain's quick change of expression, " and *never* sad ? " he repeated.

" Why should I be sad ? " she asked, she made a loud gurgling noise when she drank.

" Well consider " Marius said, he had noticed a sudden boldness in her voice.

" Well—consider," his mouth touched her ear, " consider," and then her hand was flat against his mouth.

" Please, no sermons—now you're being fatherly—are you married?"

He shook his head, " Never."

" Had she been married ? "

" Twice " Lucy said, " it was no good, I'm not like that, Captain," her mouth widened to a smile and he looked admiringly at the firm white teeth.

" You're sloppy " she said.

" All the same you are beautiful " Marius said, his look was so intense that Lucy suddenly shut her eyes against it.

" Why d'you think I'm unhappy ? "

She pressed her hands on his chest, obliterating the barque that sailed so triumphantly across it.

" Well——" he found himself stuttering, " you're so beautiful—so young—this life—this *sort* of life——"

Lucy positively shook with laughter.

" Good Lord ! That's what makes me happy " Lucy said, " this *is* my life, silly old fool, it's what I am," she went on laughing.

She sensed a sudden stiffening of his body, Marius felt as though he had been struck.

" I'm a hard creature " he thought, " and unshockable, too, but that——" and when he looked at her he knew there was no answer to that.

" You mustn't drink any more, if you do, I'll kick you out " Lucy said, leaning heavily against him, " look " she cried, " look."

" What ? "

" There," and she pointed to the tattooed snake on Marius's long, hairy right arm. " It's moving."

They both laughed.

The hand heavy on her shoulder, had moved to her hair, lost itself in the black mass, he played with it, spreading the tresses either side of her head.

" Poor Lucy " he said, " who parted her legs before she parted her lips."

She pulled at his ear again.

" And you, Captain, what about you."

" Oh, I'm still waiting for the tide, so to speak."

" For that ship ? "

" For that ship."

" Is it that difficult ? "

" It depends on what you can pull from your pocket on the right occasion," he said.

" Sometimes sailors come here, and they haven't any papers, but Madame gets them away, she knows people."

" Does she. Imagine that" he said.

" Sometimes, when I look at you, quickly, when you're not noticing, I think, ' there's a frightened man, frightened of his own shadow.' Are you frightened, Captain ? "

" Sometimes I try to remember, try hard " Marius said.

She felt her shoulders gripped, his breath on her face,

" I've talked to you before, you're not even listening, Lucy."

" What the hell are you talking about " Lucy said.

She went off into another peal of laughter, then switched out the light, " the things I get told when I'm flat on my back," and her un-controllable laughter made Marius really frightened for the first time.

He shook her roughly, "what the hell are you laughing at ? "

" You " she said, and clung hard to him.

" I've never been closer to a creature than I have to you " said Marius, and she felt his finger moving over her face, as though he were tracing its structure in the darkness.

" They all say that " she said. " Rubbish."

Feeling the warmth of her cheek he clung more tightly, as though never until this moment had he really been warm.

" And then again " she continued, " I think he's so full of something he wants to get rid of, like a person trying hard to be sick. You want to be sick, Captain, isn't that it, get something off your chest. You could tell me anything, I wouldn't say a word."

He did not answer.

" To be sick in public is not very nice " Lucy said, " you can tell me anything here, I wouldn't snitch, not me, are you being watched, Captain, you are always looking over your shoulder, we girls notice things."

Suddenly she realized he was not there, he had left her, moved away to the bed's edge, had thrown out his arms, one of which hung heavily over the side, one knee was raised, she saw his open eyes staring up at the ceiling.

" I'm not wanted by *anybody* " Marius said, " that's my trouble."

He felt her arm on his neck, heard her say, " be sick here, Captain, with me, it's safer."

" Open the bloody window " he cried, " I'm stifling," and she got up and threw back the curtains.

" There."

Moonlight seeped into the room, the tiny box-like room with its high, narrow cell-like window.

" I should never have arrived " he said.

The silence of the room was suddenly heightened, it seemed an eternity before he heard her say, " that's nothing. Lots of people never arrive. Don't talk any more, Captain " she said.

" To hell with talk " Marius said, and turned towards her.

He did not stir again, and in the sudden silence she could hear the heavy breathing.

" Miserable man " she thought, her hand moving up, feeling his mouth, and higher, the muscle, the bone, the flesh that gave to the touch.

The air smelt strongly of scent and sweat, and she was conscious too of a strength in the room. Marius lay quite still. He had fallen asleep. Lucy held to him and shut her eyes.

The house was curiously silent, and only in the yard below did the mongrel dog proclaim a wakefulness that struck flat against the walls, it barked and went on barking. Above their heads an alarm-clock ticked away merrily, and in the red glass bowl under the altar, rocking gently upon the holy oil, the flickering night-light, swaying to and fro like some minute, drunken ship, under the lightest of breezes that came through the window. Each time it flickered the face of the plaster Virgin was illuminated, it seemed to move through continuing patches of light and darkness.

She could feel the relaxed muscles of his forearms, the slackness of the powerful back, the long arm upon her grow heavier still. She wanted to move, but did not. Something had gone out of him, something withdrawn, she had felt it go. She opened her eyes, then quickly closed them, she drew back her head. The eye had opened hard up against an unfamiliar darkness, something strange. She had been staring into the interior of Marius's wide nostrils, at the hair and bone.

In the distance she heard the sound of a lorry moving towards the basin, and almost at the same time the hoot of a tug. Her head lay comfortable in the crook of his arm.

" He says he loves me, he'd marry me. They all say that sort of thing."

She felt the light fluttering upon her eye-lids, and she woke gently to a sun-filling room. Marius was still talking, but in his sleep.

Lucy lay back, drew up her knees, she felt a pleasurable exhaustion, her hands were clasped and lay uppermost upon the greyish-coloured sheet. Below she heard Henri shout, the mongrel starting his day.

She planted a strong foot in the middle of Marius's back.

" It's turned five o'clock " she cried.

In his sleep he turned towards her.

Gradually the eyes opened, to the light, the new landfall. He was so close to Lucy that he could see those fluttering eyelids, the gentlest movements of the long lashes, that seemed to be fanning the bright eyes below them. His strong thumb lay at the corner of her mouth. He felt her hand run the length of his arm.

" You'd better get out " Lucy said, she gave him another push.

Marius sat up, then reached out for his coat, hanging over the nearby chair. From this he took his wallet. He extracted some notes from it and handed them to her.

" For you. Madame need not know."

She took them from him with a smile, but did not speak.

She got up and started to dress.

" When are you coming again ? "

" Soon " Marius said, he was dressing, too. " Does that include a cup of coffee, Lucy, I've a throat like the bottom of your bird-cage."

She broke the day with her first laugh.

" Henri's down. I'll go and get you some."

She flung on a heavily flowered blue dressing-gown and went out.

Marius finished dressing. He washed in the basin, used Lucy's comb and brush.

" Only another bloody day " he said.

" Here's your coffee. Drink it and get out."

" And you ? "

He sat down by her, and she watched him drinking the thick, hot brown liquid.

" Go out by the rear door " she said.

" Why the rear door ?

" Go out by the rear door " Lucy said again.

He finished his coffee, laid the cup on the floor at his feet, turned to her.

" Lucy."

" Hell ! Not again " she said, avoiding threatening arms.

" Shall I come again ? "

" If you like. Now get out."

He picked up his cap and made for the door, and in a moment she was after him, a hand on his own. " I'll help you if you wish it " she said.

" With what ? "

" You talked your head off " she said, " and when I woke up you were still talking. . . ."

" Then it must be true " he said.

" What must be true ?

" Nothing," he said, gave her a quick pat, a kiss, and then went out.

" I believe he's still drunk," thought Lucy.

She stood by the open door, listening to his heavy steps down the corridor, then a quick, clumsy run down the iron stairway, a banged door, and he was gone.

" He was a little nervous, and I like that " she said, " and clumsy, too, but I liked that also. He's not a common sailor, I do know that. And he comes here and he never asks for anybody but me."

She stood arranging her hair in front of the small mirror— hanging over the table. Through this she noticed that the night-light had gone out, and immediately she went and put in a new one. She could hear opening and closing of doors, one after another, footsteps, she recognised Madame Lustigne's high, tremulous voice, Henri's, high and flute-y, an emasculated voice, then Simone singing through her teeth, continued descendings on the iron stairs. It was time to go.

She picked up her bag, put the money in, burst into song, a popular tune, then ran off lightly down the corridor to the stairway.

Marius was long forgotten. Marius might well have been on the furthermost sea.

V

"SOMETIMES I ask myself why I am here" Madame Marius said, and at once she raised her hand to silence the other. "Let me speak.

"Sometimes I think he was lucky. Coming back like that, the place in flames, yes, it would be like that for him, he has the devil's luck, and poor old Berthelot and his precious offices a heap of dust. These days you need only have one ship to call yourself a shipowner. I once saw that *Corsican*, and if that ship had anything it had the right to sink. And what was she carrying for Algiers? I ask you? And you may well ask till the last day. I doubt if anybody knew she had really sailed. In the morning there was nothing but dunnage where she had been. That was the ship your brother sailed, but then I don't think he ever in his life had the Captaincy of a decent ship. Even the *Mercury* stank. And nobody asked whether she returned or not, perhaps they didn't care, except the poor souls who had lost men in her. And think on that. Millions dying. Who has the right to fuss about two score of men?"

After a momentary silence, she added, "I haven't heard him come in. Out all night again."

Madeleine's lips seemed never to have parted, and yet she had spoken.

"Are we staying here forever?"

"I hope not" replied Madame Marius.

"I know I talk like a parrot" Madeleine said, "but I ask again, what are we waiting for?"

"I want the truth out of him, and I want justice. It would be terrible to have lived a long life and never to have seen it. And we are here because we cannot go back. We are finished *there*. Everything is finished. Never can I look some people in the face. Never."

" The priest thinks you're the fool, throwing everything up for your pride."

" Would you have stayed ? " asked her mother, but Madeleine turned her head abruptly and did not answer. "Would you ? "

Madeleine got up and went out of the room. Madame Marius heard her climbing the stairs.

" She will have her little weep," she thought.

In this low chair, hard by the window Madame Marius looked mountainous. There was something implacable, the sleeping strength of some powerful animal. She sat erect, the heavy, fleshy hands clasped gently together in her lap. Only the eyes moved. And by her side lay the black bag with its powerful lock. This bag never left her side day or night, she dragged it with her everywhere, she lay with it under her pillow. Her life was locked inside it, her memories, her pride, the family history, the days that were gone and the days to come. Sometimes, unconsciously, her hand would stray towards it and grip it, and if she were talking she would lift it up and plant it firmly on her knee, then continue with her conversation, staring at the other in a defiant way, as though to say, "well, try and take it from me".

She had once been handsome. Height only redeemed this shapeless body. The fine nose still remained, but one could see where other blows had struck, one after another, the swollen ankles, the outsize arms, the chin as powerful as a man's, and ready to pull down and destroy the remaining structure of the face. The eyes were almost black, but completely without lashes, the lips had dwindled, tightened, giving the mouth the appearance of a half shut purse. Everywhere the skin was coarsened, excepting the fine forehead from which the hair had been rudely drawn back. It was smooth yet carried an unhealthy shine about it.

Moving, she was conscious only of height, of weight, and yet she bore this mass with some dignity.

Before a mirror in the morning she would suddenly tilt back her head, stretching the fullness of the flesh, and shut tight her eyes, and this action was like a duty in the sad, brutal moments of revelation.

She wore long plain dresses that draped, and sat carefully in every chair. Her teeth were her glory and she was forever cleaning them.

She suddenly heard Madeleine moving in the bedroom, and thought, " well that's over, she'd had her little weep."

She thought the regularity of this weeping had removed from it the last trace of any sadness, the whole thing was undignified. Sometimes she would exclaim, " horrible, listening to it, why can't she brace herself why does she go on and on. No miracle can happen. Nothing could bring him back now. I'll be glad when we've gone. Thank God when the day comes. I wish Father Nollet would come. Perhaps he will, this very day."

Sometimes she saw her son, but always to his disadvantage. She would see him eating, it made her think of peasants, she would note the grip of a fist on a wine-glass, as though he were holding a bunch of carrots.

" I shall never understand why he was different. To-day I am glad I burned his rags. I feel sure that he will at least look distinguished," and the smile was fleeting.

Madeleine was down again, she could hear her in the kitchen.

" Such a blow " thought the old woman, " if I'd been an elephant it would have felled me. But her—she's got the docility of a cow."

She called then, and Madeleine came in.

" What time d'you suppose he'll come ? "

" I can't say, mother, some time to-day, I'm sure."

" I'm going to lie down " Madame Marius said, and without another word she went out.

Madeleine followed her to the stairs.

" I do not want your help " her mother said, and she started to climb, leaning well forward, hands pressed upon her knees.

She called over her shoulder, " and every time you go to your room you do not have to lock yourself in. I heard the key turn. Perhaps you think somebody will come in and kill you."

And from the top of the stairs, staring down at her daughter who leaned against the banister.

" Somebody called for him to-day, too. Looked like something out of a circus. Gave no name. Probably hasn't got one."

She went in and banged the door.

Sometimes she would pause, stand as in the act of listening by the door of the remaining room, but she heard nothing, it was always empty.

" Perhaps he never sleeps at all," she would tell herself, " and I'm not surprised."

She had hardly lain down and settled herself when she heard the knock.

" There is somebody knocking."

" I heard it."

" Then answer the door. If it's the priest, we cannot keep him standing in the street."

" Yes mother."

" If it's him, I'm in my room."

" Shall he come up, mother ? "

" I'll come down."

She heard the door opened, the sound of a man's voice.

" Why, Father Nollet " she heard Madeleine exclaim, " how good of you to call. Please come in, Father. I'll tell my mother."

She threw wide the door, saying, " excuse our untidiness, Father Nollet."

She led him through the kitchen into the sitting-room.

" Is that the priest ? " her mother called.

" Excuse me a moment, Father, my mother is calling me."

" Yes mother."

" Come up."

" Coming."

Madame Marius was lying full length on the bed.

" A moment ago I felt so exhausted, I had to lie down at once——"

" Mother ! "

But Madeleine's concern was waved away.

" I'm all right, only ask the good priest to excuse me for
ten minutes. I shall be down."

" You're really tired, mother, he'll come up here, I'll ask
him."

" I said I'll come down."

" As you will."

She returned to the sitting-room to find Father Nollet
seated in her mother's chair in the window. He was studying
his hands, closely inspecting his finger-nails, he was so
absorbed he hardly noticed she had returned.

" You have a beautiful view from this window " he said,
and turned to look at her, he had the close, searching look of a
short-sighted man.

" And yet we hate it " he heard her reply, and then she sat
down.

" You're Madame Madeau ? " he asked.

" Yes Father."

He sat somewhat gingerly on the chair edge, and in the
moments when she was not looking he stared about him, and
gave the impression that at any moment he might jump up and
run out. Certainly he might not stay very long, like somebody
who has got into the wrong house by mistake.

Madeleine was looking at him. They smiled at each other,
it was the signal for calmness.

She saw a small and wiry man, with a wind-beaten, sun
drenched skin, eyes barely discernable, they seemed only half-
open, it made her think of an aged farmer, and certainly the
hands were hardly those of a priest. They were hard, leathery,
the veins stood out, and here and there the skin was flecked
by brownish spots.

" He is a man of the deep country certainly " she thought.

A man of rude health, nut-shining cheeks, a very blue chin.

" Well, as you see, I have called. Where is your mother ? "

" She will be down directly, Father," and watched him
dangling his hat in his hand.

" I'm sorry, Father " and she took it hastily from him and
hung it behind the door.

72

" You are strangers here " he said.

" That is true, Father."

" How long have you been here ? " he asked.

He seemed a little more at ease, he had made himself more comfortable, sitting right back in the chair. She noticed that his feet were unduly large and clad in rough black boots with laces of heavy leather.

" Some weeks now."

" I had noticed you first at the altar rails " he said, " you are daily communicants."

" Yes Father.

" At first " she went on, " it was very lonely and we did not go out."

" Naturally, a big city like this. From where have you come, Madame ? "

She told him, yet spoke so low that he had to crane forward, a quick hand to his ear to grasp what she said. She told him that they had moved to various places on their journey, and he said, laughingly, " you get about."

A woman of middle age was sitting before him, run to fullness of figure, a woman, who, though she may have had some pretensions to prettiness when she was young, was certainly at this moment very plain, very matronly. Looking more closely at her features he told himself that they might be those of a man *or* a woman, it was a curiously sexless face, only its human-ness looked out at him. Even her hands were plain, thick, short-fingered, they might have been the hands of a small man.

" Forty four or five " he thought, noticing her eyes.

They seemed devoid of any colour ; he might have been looking into clear water.

" Of course I don't know what your mother wishes to see me about. She has never on any occasion spoken to me beyond saying a good-morning. You have both been somewhat reserved I feel. I am the priest of this parish. I am quite in the air," and he gave Madeleine a searching look.

" I promise I'll make all endeavours to help you in any way

73

I can, my child " he said, and suddenly threw one knee across the other.

She thought he looked somewhat grave as he said this.

" You are unhappy " he said.

" Perhaps I am."

" And your mother ? Does she like Marseilles ? Are you settled here ? Are you alone ? "

" We are not settling, Father and we are not alone. My brother is here, too."

" I see. He works here ? "

" No Father. He's a sailor. He has come to look for a ship."

" Times are not very good. One time ships cried out for men. Now its the other way round. You think your brother will find a ship ? "

" I don't know. We hope so, Father."

" I hope so, too " Father Nollet replied. " What is your mother's name ? "

" Marius. Genevieve Marius, Father."

" You have come far " he said. " A pretty little place that is, though I have never seen it."

" It was our home."

" And you are not returning ? "

" No Father."

" May I ask you why you have left. I can see that you are not happy, my child."

She was unable to speak, and he said gently, " I will not press you, Madame Madeau."

Madeleine sat up in her chair and blurted out, " I'll tell you everything, Father, everything——"

" Perhaps its something your mother can better explain. It was she who sent for me."

" Whichever speaks, it's the same " she said.

He left his chair, crossed the room. Bending down he put a hand on her own.

" I will do what I can, my child."

" We both of us wish to enter a religious house " she said,

74

and avoided his glance, as though for an instant she had regretted her words.

" Perhaps I'll wait for your mother " he said, and returned to his chair.

" Tell me about your brother. What kind of person is he ? Perhaps I've seen him at the Mass."

" He does not attend the church, Father, though we Marius's are all of us good Catholics."

" Where is your father ?

" Dead in the first war——"

" I see," and added quickly, " just the three of you."

" Yes Father."

She kept looking anxiously towards the door, wishing her mother would come.

" I'm sorry she's keeping you waiting, Father, I'm sure she'll be down any minute now."

His smile was re-assuring.

" I'm in no great hurry " he said.

" A furnished place " he thought, remembering the kitchen, " the language of squalor, it could frighten such people."

" How do you pass your time here, Madame Madeau ? "

" Very quietly. We hardly ever go out. In the morning certainly, then perhaps a little shopping and back home again. If the evenings are cool we may go to Benediction."

" And your brother ? What is his name ? "

" Eugene."

" Has he friends ? "

" I don't think he has any friends " she said.

" You all of you seem pretty isolated " said Father Nollet, " I don't think that is very good for you. You do not know this city at all?"

Madeleine hearing steps on the stairs, had risen, as she replied, " no, Father, we do not."

" An enormous place, my child, it's like no other city on earth. I cannot think how you came to this part, it might be said that you are amongst the animals——"

75

He stood up, waiting, the door opened, and Madame Marius came in.

She crossed at once to the priest and offered her hand, and a slow smile, she was measuring him up, as a man, she had only seen him remotely upon the altar.

" My mother, Father Nollet," said Madeleine.

" How are you, Madame Marius ? We have met before of course, but at a distance, never so intimately as now. I'm always glad to meet my parishioners," and he hurried forward to get a chair, but she disdained this and made for her usual place in the window.

" This is my place, Father. I always sit here. It is good of you to call."

" I have an hour to spare, the rest of my day is heavily tied up."

He resumed his seat. He felt quite insignificant sitting there, he had never seen so big a woman.

" So tall, so fat " he thought, trying to define her age, sixty—seventy ?

" Well Madame Marius " he said.

" You're not very comfortable there, Father " she said.

" I am quite comfortable, thank you," he waved away all help, " you wished to speak with me on some matter or other. If there is any help or advice I can give you—I shall be glad to do so."

" Madeleine, you will go out now, and later perhaps you will bring the coffee, and a cup for the Father " she said.

" Yes mother."

When the door closed behind her, they found themselves looking steadily at each other.

" Well now " he said.

" There's a time in life " said Madame Marius, " when there is a sudden stop, as though we had ceased to grow. One has had some happiness, has done the things one wished to do, and sometimes those things which one has not, still one hopes, as God meant them. One has seen enough, has had what one's wanted, some dreams have come true and some have broken. But there is nothing more. It is time to be off, it is like that. I am old, my only daughter will not re-marry, some things are too late and one knows it."

Father Nollet leaned forward in his chair, clapped hands on his knees.

" It's like an ultimatum, Madame Marius " he replied.

She appeared not to have heard, as though she had not been listening, not waiting, had for the moment forgotten him.

Her attention had been drawn by the high prattle of some children who were playing outside the window. Beyond their cluttered heads she saw a great ship moving seawards.

" There were some happy times with my husband, my father. I like to remember them. Even my children. There was even a grandson. A little plain, but my daughter is plain as you will have noticed. It seemed strange to me."

" You were somewhat disappointed in her marriage I take it " said Father Nollet.

" It does not matter now."

Father Nollet looked at his watch.

" And about this advice, Madame Marius."

The old woman picked up her black bag and laid it at her feet.

" My daughter and I wish to enter a religious house. That is our great desire, Father. We have thought this over, and over again and again and again. It would make us happy——"

" One would have to think carefully about that. Such things are major decisions " he said.

" I'm a hard one to satisfy, Father " said Madame Marius. " I do not like this " she lifted a great arm and waved it towards the window. " We have had enough of it. Enough. It is too much. In these months I have felt gutter slime on my skin, and I'm not used to that. I never thought I would reach so low, I may in all honesty acquaint you with my feelings, Father."

" You seem to be pitying yourself " said the priest, " and we are no further on, anywhere. Am I to say whether you should retire from the world, Madame ? In matters like this one does not think of oneself alone, but of others, and there are others. You have not yet spoken to your son ? "

" He knows best," she replied, flinging the words down hard, like stones.

" You mean he may look after himself ? "

Already the priest could feel a pressure here, a dominant force. In this room the mother was everywhere. Madame Marius might be a ventriloquist, the daughter seemed like a puppet.

" I shall come to the son " she said.

When she laughed it shocked him, yet at the same time it released the sense of pressure, of power. But the body was yet obedient to the will, it was yet motionless.

" At fifty, or nearly so " she went on, " well—he is a man. At least he says he is."

She saw him turn away his head, he had indeed fixed his eye on the lamp-post outside.

" You appear to have a grievance against your son " he said, and thought, " if one squeezed her words long enough acid would drip out."

" I could well say that. At one time in my life I had my name. That was something. It always is. Something growing up around one, and it's like a light. I mean one's name, if that is good."

Ignoring this he asked, " what have you against him ? "

" Madeleine " she called, " please to bring the coffee in. We are waiting. You will honour us, Father Nollet. Thank you," and then she forgot him again, waiting for her daughter.

" You had best speak with my daughter, after all " she said.

" And now " she said to herself, " I shall split myself clean in halves, I shall be opened up at last."

Madeleine handed out the coffee. Madame Marius got up and drew down the blinds.

" It's like this most days, no shade anywhere, one goes to bed to keep cool. The light can be bitter on the eyes," she had noticed the priest's sudden discomfort.

Madeleine's hand touched his own as he took the cup from her, and he was struck by its coolness.

" Thank-you."

" You despise your son ? " he asked.

There seemed hardly any need for her to answer, her expression was enough.

" For one so despised you seem to have followed him a long way " he went on, as he slowly sipped his coffee.

" I shall come to that " she said.

" Then I can only ask you Madame Marius, to come to it soon, for I must be off, I have much work to do, and mine is a large parish as you may know."

" I know nothing whatever about your parish, Father " she replied.

He was aware of a continuous grudging note in the old woman's voice.

" Well ! " he asked.

" He came here " said Madame Marius, " and we followed him, that is but natural. In any case we could not remain where we were."

" Why not ?

" The disgrace of it."

" Of what ? "

The old woman had shifted her glance from Father Nollet to Madeleine, and she said slowly, and with some effort.

" Madeleine, that letter for Father Gerard, I did want it to catch the early post."

At once her daughter got up and left them, and later they heard the door close, a latch fall, and then there was silence again.

Madeleine had understood, it was only another way of saying, " you are not wanted here."

" He had taken a ship out to sea and he had returned without it, but worse than that he had returned alone. I shall not soon forget that terrible night, for believe well that the whole place was in flames, even now I often feel myself turning slowly in the hall of my home, it was filled with a most unnatural light, and my daughter hearing voices walked into it. One might have felled an ox. He stood there silent—and when he spoke—the crudity—the sheer clumsiness of his explanation—it made me want to shriek. He had taken with him on his third trip a certain person and he had not brought him back. Worse still, *he* had survived, imagine it, a Captain saving himself, I thank God this day my husband was not there to see it, he at least was honourable and went down with his ship———"

" Your husband was a sailor, too, Madame Marius ? " Father Nollet put back the cup on the tray.

She was silent for a moment or two.

" He was a naval Commander Father Nollet, and he was *French*, he went down with his ship in the First war. He was a good man. To-day that sort of thing does not exist. There is no more pride anywhere———"

" Pride is not all, Madame Marius."

" The world might be a better place for a little more of it, Father."

" You were saying " Father Nollet leaned forward in his chair, Madame Marius had got off the track, " you were saying —about the night he returned———"

With a sudden weariness she exclaimed, " oh I don't know, Father, I really don't know—there is something on his mind, something he can tell us, that's why we're here, something he can tell that poor child who has just gone out to the post."

" Perhaps I should come again, Madame Marius " said Father Nollet, " you are somewhat distressed," and he half rose from the chair, and quickly she flung out a detaining arm, and he remembered it as her first violent movement.

" He is not like us, Father, he is different, he believes in nothing but himself, it was a shock to my husband, who often said that his real place was the gutter, I do not know—still—a reckless man, a wandering man, and yet I suppose there was something there, a sort of affection for his nephew—for his sister—an intelligent man, but he could not help being that, we have that at least——"

The priest looked at his watch again.

" They were landed some miles down the coast, he and another man——"

" What other man ? "

There was a slight note of irritation in Father Nollet's voice, he felt the old woman was unequal to it, she kept moving away from the facts he was waiting for.

" I presume your son reported to the required authority ? "

" Authority ? There was no authority, it had ceased to exist. And consider he was the only one arriving, it was the time of great departures, everybody was flying. I remember a train flying through the station, the roar it made sounded like the end of the world. They say there was a driver but no guard, a single passenger in the end compartment, a frightened child, it never stopped they say, but went tearing through station after station. The whole of France might have been packed inside it, that's how it was."

" Who was the other man, Madame Marius ? "

" I've reason to believe it was a man named Royat, a deck hand under my son. He has never been seen since, they say he's in America——"

" A long way from here."

" A long long way, away " she said.

" But who's cares about that " she went on, " I have my daughter to think about. You have seen her. I believe something dreadful happened aboard that ship, and I have the feeling, and it is strong, Father Nollet, that he has lost the right to exist——"

" Be plain, Madame Marius, *who* ? "

" My own son " she said.

" He committed some crime ? "

She did not answer.

" Please go on, Madame Marius " said the priest.

She suddenly realized that he was lying far back in his chair, and his eyes were closed.

" I'm listening " he said quietly.

Yes, she said, they had spent their lifetime there, their hearts were in that place, and as she said this she gave him the impression of a person lost under a wave, who if he will but use some giant endeavour of will and bone may yet rise above it. For a moment he seemed to sense a sudden leap of the heart, out of this squalid room, back to where she belonged, where the roots were deep, the genius of being embedded in the solid rock.

No, she said, after her son had joined the Marine, he was not fit to join his father's service, after he had joined the Marine they had seen little of him in the following years. He roamed a lot, the vagabond in him was something new to the Marius family, and somehow he had the knack of finding the dross of the shipping world, questionable ships, questionable owners, hard dealings in dark corners and some dirty ones, that kind of person. Yes, mostly tramp ships.

He had sailed much in the Mediterranean waters, in many kinds of ships, but never a decent one, never a proud or stately one. No, he had never married, but she added, tartly, he did not lack experience.

Sightless, he seemed to see this woman more clearly, the great body anchored in the chair, motionless, only the eyes alive there, watching, watching. He noted a change in the voice, as though the inner fount of her strength was beginning to dry up, the mountain beginning to wilt, something was breaking.

Yes, she had sold up. That was the sensible thing to do. And when he had cleared out, they had cleared out, too.

But always at her side, like a wound, a cry in her ear, her defeated daughter,

"God's simpleton" she said.

But to return like that, on such a night, as though he had fallen out of the sky. If things had been normal, one might have paused, tried to understand, but the world was quite mad and France was taking blows, everywhere flames, and everywhere running people.

"I dared not ask him how he arrived, what had truly happened, where that child was. Even that doorway through which he came, even that very door had heightened, become huge because there was not behind him the one he had taken away. Where was he? Gone, he said. And the others: Gone, too, everything gone, ship and all. As easily as that, like dropping your scissors, closing your bedroom door."

In the momentary silence both heard the hurried, rasping tick of the little clock. He heard her sigh. His own hands were raised, the fingers spread out to meet each other, tip to tip, the elbows hard down upon the chair's wooden arms.

"Sometimes I am lying flat on my back beside her. For hours together nothing passes between us except a great understanding. Then we may fall asleep, but I am never deaf to her weeping, silent though it is. Many blows can be struck, but I can only think of the one she received. Poor creature. Every day I'm close to it, every night. Sometimes she goes quietly away and shuts herself in the bedroom."

Her voice had dropped, it came over to the priest as a whisper, as a tremble of words, like leaves under wind.

"She has her pitiful little dreams, I know, and son and brother are often in them. It is not for myself that I wish to go, Father Nollet, but for her also. She is not like me, she has no resources. A simple heart and that is all. Home to such creatures is all."

"Yet in your own pride you drove her from her own" he said, sitting up abruptly.

83

" Some people may have happiness but the once, and they know this, and she is one of them and she knows it, too. Her husband was as herself, a simple man, who was lost years ago with the fishing fleet. His name was Madeau. There was one Madeau only, there will never be two, she knows that too, she has told me so, not in tears, but in a great calmness. She is all I have got now."

At that very moment the door opened and Madeleine came in. She gave a quick, shy smile to the priest, then seated herself.

Father Nollet declined another coffee, gave himself a rude shake, adjusted his vest, then glanced towards the door.

He rose and walked across at the room.

" If I may say so, Madame Marius, yours is a big decision to take, but it's hardly right that you should decide for your daughter also. She is not a child. At the same time she's not old, either. She may yet re-marry."

The old woman lowered her head, it seemed like a direct rebuff to the priest, for she did not answer him.

" I must go," he said and was on his feet instantly. He stood by the old woman, a hand on her shoulder.

" As to your intentions, Madame Marius, I must have more time to consider it. I would like to speak to your daughter— alone. Could she come and see me at the presbytery this evening, after supper, say about eight o'clock. I'm not at all satisfied with the motives, Madame Marius. To-morrow I may be the better able to tell you what I think——"

Madame Marius rose, towering over the priest, " you do not approve of our action. Father Nollet ? "

It was impossible for him to avoid her eyes.

" You do not approve of our action ? "

" Our action ? Is it truly like that ? " he asked, his little finger began to play with his watch-chain.

" As to that, you are free to talk to my daughter " she replied.

" Your son " he enquired, " where is your son ? Could I see him ? "

84

" We hardly see him ourselves, Father Nollet, but if you asked me what he is doing I would say that most of his days are spent going from one shipping office to another, begging for a job, on his knees to them all—behind his back they must surely smile. Poor man. He can never forget that he was once a Captain, he's got it on the brain, I think. Perhaps he thinks life a fairy-tale——"

The priest retreated as she moved, he felt she was slowly pushing him towards the door.

" He's gone about the place in his filthy old uniform until one got sick of the sight of it, and at last I found my opportunity and I took it away from him. He lies about in the wrong places, that Madame Lustigne's for instance, everybody knows what that harpy is—and when he's not there you may find him in his room, soaking in his misery. It's sad for me, but for *her*——"

" Sometimes we may see dereliction for ourselves, Madame Marius," and he put out his hand, " good-bye, remember, I will see your daughter this evening," and then he felt the hand being slowly withdrawn from his own.

" Good-bye, Father Nollet " she said. " I will only say that you've not heard the half of it."

He smiled and turned away, and Madeleine preceded him through the kitchen that he would not forget, the clutter of things, the high smell, the dreadful hard light on everything, the picture on the wall, the resplendent figure looking down on the squalor.

He glanced at Madeleine.

" Why did you choose to come here ? " he asked, and she said softly, looking behind her, as though she expected her mother was following them, " because he was here. Mother calls it being on his track, but I do not like it."

He grasped her hand, held it firmly.

" And I really believe you, Madame Madeau. This evening then. Good-bye."

" Good-bye, Father " Madeleine said, and saw him through the door.

She stood watching his quick, nervous walk until he had vanished round the corner.

" A man of the deep country " she thought, " like a jolly little apple man." She closed the door and returned to her mother.

VI

Marius talked to Marius.

" You are a fool."

" You are a fool, and at fifty that is unpardonable."

" You are on the ice cap."

" You are on the ice cap and may stay there."

" I am scared."

"That is because last night you had a curious feeling that somebody was on your track."

" Last night I was at Madame Lustigne's and I talked too much."

" Lucy said I even cried, but I don't believe it. Never in my whole life have I cried. I can remember the first time my father struck me, and it was a hard blow, but I never even flinched. I think he always disliked me after that."

" That was one blow. This is another. But all the same you cried about it, you were drunk."

" Yes, I am weak there. I lay with Lucy and I positively stank, but she did not seem to mind."

" She said you said, ' I only came here because I am disgusted with myself. Even my own body disgusts me.' "

" I remember her laughing, she kicked off her dress, I can see the flash of her heel as she kicked shut the door. ' We can take anything,' she said, ' even disgust.' "

" Poor Lucy."

" But you must keep away from Lustigne's. There is that man Labiche, a horror, so respectable, so correct, reminded me of a certain kind of fish. I heard Madame enquiring after the health of his wife and daughters. Respectability held together with string."

" I must get away."

" You are wondering what they will do ? "

" I suppose I am. The way they cling to me, at least she does, motherly love I suppose. It is not so simple. I had better think it over."

" Nothing is simple."

" You have not shaved or washed for four days and you will go about with that horrible coat and cap, it has become your second skin, Marius."

" I must really straighten myself up, some terrible lethargy has got hold of me, I seem to have no will, except to hide away when I am not cringing before somebody."

" You are perhaps a little crazy. For instance you think because you have sunk two ships somebody will just come along and give you complete liberty to sink another one. You may be proud, you may at times have taken leave of your senses, but you are not stupid, surely you are not stupid ? "

" God ! The terrible position I am in. I am afraid to tell myself what."

" The hell of it is they don't even know."

" The hell of it is they may have to."

Marius rolled over on his back. Through a slit in the curtain he caught a pencil line of sky, a swift vision of blue, the sea, it was always there. He saw it with a lazy, indifferent eye.

" Consider certain things. They are broken. They have sold up and left their home, which was once your home, you have broken the roots of something you never really understood. They are here, below there. They have followed where you went. Blood is blood anywhere on earth."

" I have been here nearly four months, each day like a ladder, climbing, somewhere there is a rung missing, there always is. I cannot even find a berth here. And now I will ship away as anything, I have made up my mind. There is one thing of which I can never be sure. Who saw? Who is dead and who is alive ? The timbers are rotting but there is always more timber. There are yet ships upon the sea."

" You know perfectly well that if you could once see Follet things might look different. He is only formidable because not seen. He is an intelligent man, a man of character, but one has to get past his little henchman. If one knew where Follet lived. You would go. You would beg for a berth. You would begin at the very bottom. Work upwards."

" I am perhaps telling myself a fairy-tale."

" You are talking for the sake of talking, Marius has been talking to Marius for some weeks now, like a parrot."

" I cannot remain here any longer."

" I should think not. Get this into your thick head at once, that if once you were a commander, you are not so now, and never will be again. The only ship whose bridge you will stride is a fairy ship and she sails in a fairy sea. Though you hug your misery you also hug your infernal illusion."

" Christ ! I must get up and go out."

He sat up, stretching his legs, he swung round and out of the bed.

He sat on its edge, his head between his hands.

There came to his ears a shout, a single word. " Nine."

It seemed to strike on the door like a hammer, it made Marius jump.

Then the front door banged. The house was silent again.

" Nine."

Which meant " it is nine o'clock and there is food on the table."

He stood up, shivered a little, then crossed to the door in his shirt. He opened it, and from the top of the stairs called, " all right."

But there was only the silence. He came into the room again, shut the door violently, went to the chair to get his clothes. There were no clothes.

" Am I still drunk, where the hell are my clothes ? "

He searched frantically around the room, he tossed the bed-clothes this way and that, finally flung them in a great heap on the floor, he rushed to the only cupboard, this was empty.

"I must be drunk. I undressed here. Somebody has stolen my clothes."

He stood by the window, bewildered, what on earth had happened? Then he sat down on the disordered bed and stared round the room.

No mistake at all. This was his own room. It certainly was not Lucy's. He went out, stood listening on the landing. Then he crept down the stairs. He quietly opened the kitchen door, peered round, there was nobody there. He saw the table, the coffee, the roll. He entered. Then on the chair he saw the bundle.

"I burnt your rags."

He picked up the piece of paper, read again.

"Burnt them. My God, she's burnt my uniform."

He picked up the bundle, opened it, let the garments fall slowly, one after the other. He watched them fall. A black suit and vest, a white muffler, a loud patterned check cap.

"She thinks I'm a peasant" he shouted, "she thinks I'm a peasant."

He sat down.

"They are both out. At the mass. Of course. Would I be happy if I went to mass? Would I be happy in my peasant's clothes?"

He shook with laughter.

"It means something else. 'Get out.' I shall.'

He picked up the clothes and returned to his be om. He dressed, washed, he shaved, stared at himself in e mirror for some time. Then he went down and had his breakfast.

"Another day. Only the clock talking, sometimes I hate that clock so much I would like to dash it to pieces. They will come back, wearing their sackcloth. Words are so precious with them that I suppose if they pressed one out, it would bleed. They will soon be back from the mass, I had better get out."

He crossed to the hanging mirror and stared at it, the reflection in the glass attracted him.

"To-day I do not even know who I am," he played about with the peaked cap, "Marius you hardly know yourself."

He pulled down hard on the peak, gave a shrug of the shoulders, then quickly left the house by the rear door. It was turned ten o'clock. Two women were gossiping over a fence, a boy played in the gutter. He hurried away, but from time to time glanced behind him.

" I am getting into a bad habit " he thought.

He stood on the pavement edge, he looked West. Over there lay Heros, a big firm, if he went this morning it was possible that Philippe would scarcely recognise him. They had many ships. One might say one had tried for the last time, then try again. But suddenly he had turned on his heel and was hurrying off in another direction. He walked faster, then, hardly realizing it he began to run. And he did not stop until he had reached the tall ugly house on the corner.

There was the loose Michelin poster swinging away from the wall, and there in front of the door the battered-looking lamp that was never lighted. Its door was closed. He did not knock but pushed against it, and it did not give. He turned the handle, the door gave to him, he pushed and went inside. He stood still in the half darkened lobby, then he felt for the bolt and shot this back. The sound echoed through the house.

" Who is there ? "

He recognised Madame's voice, but did not answer. He knew where he wanted to go. Mounting the three stairs he went off down a long narrow corridor. When he came to the door he wanted he heard voices, girls chattering. He gripped the handle and pushed, there was some resistance. Seized with a sudden fury he threw himself against it.

Behind it stood two naked women.

" Shift your great arse " Marius said, he still knew where to go, what he wanted, he had already seen her lying in the bed. She was still asleep.

" Lucy."

" Christ ! She looks even more naked when she's asleep,"

staring down at her, the mouth was partly open, " I could not see her more clearly if she was split wide open."

" Lucy ! Wake up."

He began shaking her. Behind him the two girls were still so astonished by the intrusion that they remained speechless.

" Here, you bitch, wake up " Marius shouted, " come on," his hands gripped her shoulders, " damn you for a bitch, wake up, was I talking in my sleep last night ? Was I drunk, very drunk ? "

Lucy slowly opened her eyes, then instinctively raised her hands and covered her bosom.

" Who the hell are you ? "

" You know who I am. You knew last night, and the night before, tell me what did I say last night ? "

" What do you want ? "

The expression on her face angered him, " injured innocence, by God."

" Not you. Was I talking in my sleep last night. What did I say ? Lucy, please tell me what I said."

His manner changed, she at length sat up in the bed. Her mouth was still open, and she continued to stare at him.

" For God's sake " he said, " can't you wake up, at least you would not look so ugly. Lucy, please tell me, tell me now, what did I say ? "

" Tell you what ? " She yawned, stretched up her arms. " What bloody right have you in here, you haven't even paid."

He caught her arms and pulled them down, he leaned over her.

" I beg you to tell me this one thing, Lucy, what did I say, you must have heard me, we weren't both snoring like pigs, I'm sure, I know I parroted in my sleep, but what was it I said. Please, Lucy."

He added, without meaning too, " that Labiche was here, too, that fish——."

" How do I know what you said, let go of my arms, I don't know *who* you are. Anyhow I hate your suit, get off my bed."

She pushed vigorously and he did not resist. He turned, saw the two girls.

" Please " Marius, said.

They went out without a word, he was alone with Lucy.

" Madame will be here any moment, I have to go shopping with her. It is my morning."

She went and sat down at the dressing-table, and he sat watching her.

" This flesh-house stinks of the cheapest perfume " Marius said, " what kind do you use, Lucy, I could find you better smelling stuff than that."

She washed in the basin, combed her hair, smiled at herself in the glass, she could see him sitting there.

" You do not even take off your horrible cap," she said.

He removed this and flung it to the floor.

" Is that snake still crawling about your upper arm ? " she asked.

" What did I say last night. Christ blast you, can't you answer ? "

" You certainly do not look like a captain, Mr. Marius. There ! Now that is Madame, you had better scoot," but the door opened and Madame Lustigne was standing there.

" What are you doing here ? " she asked, she had not recognised him. " We have our hours of business like everybody else."

" It is that nice man in a peasant's suit " Lucy said, she turned and added, " I am quite ready, Madame Lustigne."

" Go and get your breakfast " Madame Lustigne said, and was so determined that she should not miss it that she took the girl by the arm and pushed her out through the door. She came back and faced Marius.

" This sort of thing does not help anybody, I heard you come in, you might try not to be so clumsy another time. What do you require now that you may not have at the proper time, Captain Marius ? It is half-past ten o'clock. Are the gangways everywhere pulled up and the ships gone ? "

She was standing very close to him, and he watched her high bosoms, they seemed to prance at him.

" I came to talk to Lucy " Marius said.

" You are yet miserable, you are now here four months and a day. And yet no ship."

She watched him swinging his cap as he sat there.

" Not yet " he said.

" Shame. Shame. So unfair. My poor captain, tell me, did you in fact kill the creature ? "

When he did not answer she went on, " you are unhappy, yes, well of course I can see that. Many people are, my Captain, very many. Outside in the world everything is well—you, will come with me, Mr. Marius, we will have breakfast together, in some way I like you, yet I do not know why. Come along."

She caught him by the arm, he followed her out.

" I see that you have washed yourself and even changed " she said.

" Poor creature " she thought, " he has lost what he calls his ticket, how he talks when he has had a drop. A captain, a sailor, a bum."

In the narrow corridor she paused and smiled up at him.

" At half past ten in the morning, sailor, I should not do this for anybody else, but then you *are* a sailor, and they are our best customers and I am honest enough to value their patronage."

The small poorly lighted room gave Marius a feeling of claustrophobia.

" Sit down, Captain. Now I will bring in the breakfast," and she left him.

There was a uniformity about these rooms, all small and of the same size, they might have been tailored, the same curtain on the windows, the same floor covering. Only Madame Lustigne's bed was different, and this was of wood, the best oak.

Marius admired a sheer cleanliness here, absent from the other rooms, it lacked their scruff and stuffiness, and also the

94

window was open. The bedsheets were of the purest linen, and clean, the blankets thick and a warm green in colour. The whole covered with a heavily decorated counterpane.

" A sailor's payment," he thought.

The window was small and barred. The sight of it un-nerved him yet he did not know why. He stood by it, looking down into a courtyard, where he saw a mass of litter and debris, and a great clothes-line of shifts, in varying colours, from orange to the brightest blue, bellying in the breeze like sails. He walked slowly round the room. At the altar he stopped.

" Always the Virgin, when it isn't Magdalene " he muttered.

The dressing-table fascinated him. He sat down on the small stool, looked at everything at once, and then piece by piece, particularly the array of bottles, of all shapes. One after another, he lifted the objects up and examined them. He un-screwed each fancy bottle and smelt it. A number of brightly-coloured tubes contained paint, perfume, lipstick, miraculous mud, Eau-de-Cologne, mascara. A single silver-backed hair-brush, some loose hairs, shampoos in bottles and packets, powder clotted on the corner of the mirror like a small white cloud. He picked up two tiny handkerchiefs.

" This is what smells " he said, holding them to his nose, " this is the perfume that stinks out the house."

A photograph of Madame, ten years younger, he thought, and looking her very best, did not attract him. He was sitting there, idly eavesdropping, when the door opened and Madame returned with a tray.

" You like my room, Captain ? "

She put down the tray.

" This is most unusual, and I do not mind, do you ? "

" I am not hungry " Marius said.

" But you are thirsty, I'm sure " replied Madame, she began pouring out coffee.

" I have just had coffee, indeed, my breakfast."

" Tut! tut! Have more " she said.

" You may talk to Lucy this evening if you wish to, and everything will be the same as usual, Captain, three hundred francs. Perhaps I can save you some time and indeed expense. I miss nothing of what goes on here, Captain. If you have talked in your sleep last evening, then be sure I already know what you have said. There is an hour in the morning when my girls and I get together, and most often the night's customers are discussed. It is most interesting, though we have our dull evenings like everybody else, beds are subject to a rise and fall, to economic laws, at least I find it so——"

He had her hand in his own, he pressed hard.

She smiled at him and said, " well, Captain ? "

" Did I talk in my sleep last night, I know you would have heard me, I am loud-mouthed when I am drunk, it is just my nature, I have been called a fog-horn in my time, Madame."

He released her hand, and he realized at once that it was an attitude in her that had made him so quickly let go. He leaned on the back of the chair.

" Possibly. If one is drunk, there are sometimes drunks, do try to understand Captain that you are only like some others. But if you did, well—I am the soul of discretion. Also I am quite unshockable, and I may assure you that you are quite safe here. Consider. I am myself always glad to return, if only after a single hour. I like to be in. Outside——" she waved a hand towards the window, " well—you have seen it, what do *you* think ? "

Smiling she showed him all her pretty teeth.

She began scratching vigorously under an arm, " I believe I have a flea, and I believe that Labiche creature brought it in the other evening. Well, Captain ? "

Marius seemed as though dumb, he sat there trying to understand, trying to measure up this woman. After a while he said, " I am a lawless man myself."

" I am not as bad as that, thank heaven. Sometimes, out there, in the world, one is imperilled, there is always somebody who will not leave you alone, somebody watching, following perhaps, people—they can be terrible——"

She said, a little sternly, " you are not drinking your coffee," and stared at the hairy hand that completely enclosed the cup.

" A strong creature," she thought.

" You know now that I begin to think " she continued, " now that I begin to think, I ask myself if I really have seen you before ? "

He sipped coffee through dry lips.

" You have, nevertheless," he said.

" You have not your uniform to-day, perhaps that is it."

" I burnt it."

" Indeed ? An accident ? "

" What time will Lucy be back, Madame ? "

" My name is Flo, you may call me that " she smiled across at him.

" When I was here last night " Marius said, " a man came in, do you remember, a middle-aged, rather stout dwarf, with heavy moustaches, he was wearing a stiff black suit and a black hat, he had also an umbrella."

" Well ?

" A man named Labiche, I think that was the name."

" Correct. He is a friend of mine. A charming man, very respectable, he has a wife and two children. What of him ? "

" Did he question you about me ? " asked Marius.

" He asked who you were. After all, though we have many sailors here, it is not so often that we have Captains in their uniforms. I said you were a stranger here——"

" What did he say ? "

" He just said, ' does he come here often, no more than that.' "

She filled the room with laughter, it came out in a burst, it made him sit up suddenly in his chair.

" I can't help laughing, my Captain, you look so—what shall I say—anyhow I told Labiche that you were simply a customer. I said, people are always coming and going, I rarely look at people's faces, this may seem strange in my profession, but it's a fact. Some nights perhaps, yes, it is often a matter of how one feels."

" I have seen him somewhere before " said Marius, " and I think he has seen me, too."

" You speak as though you were afraid of him. He is a harmless creature, I can assure you."

" If I could remember where I had seen him " continued Marius, " if I could remember——"

" Perhaps you have seen him when you have gone to the shipping offices, he is just a clerk, a petty clerk with the Heros people."

Marius struck the table with his fist. " You are right, that's where I have seen him. I wish Lucy would come back. She could tell me something."

Madame Lustigne drew her chair much nearer, she did not speak, but sat very close to him, smiling into his face.

The smile filled him with sudden horror, he drew back in the chair.

" You know ? "

" People are sometimes drunk, and sometimes they may talk in their sleep, but what is that, most often rubbish. How nervous you are, Captain, I sigh to see such a strong hand trembling, is there anything the matter ? Is it that you think we here may discuss the rubbish you shouted out last night ? You are something of a fool, Captain, I may tell you that because in a certain way I like you, I might not be so honest with others. Perhaps that is why you are now shipless. And think of it, the sea drying up all the way from Nantes to Marseilles, you are so slow, perhaps you are least aware of it. You are also a little clumsy, I have heard of your jauntings through the city in your admiral's uniform. If you like people to be interested in you, then that is the way to do it, people will always talk, if they did not they might go mad. You are in some distress. In your sleep you told Lucy that you had killed somebody at sea, that may be true," she gave a sudden violent shrug of the shoulders, "nevertheless, even if it were I should not give you away. I mind my own business. People are murdering each other every day, Captain, and think nothing of it, nothing at all. Hiding it up in you like that, letting it fester inside you, tear you to pieces, like a tiger grown there—you understand. You trust me ? "

98

" I do not even trust myself " he said.

" If it would ease your mind " she said.

" I will say nothing."

" In which case there is nothing more to be said " replied Madame Lustigne.

" I have someone else to tell " he said.

" Who ? "

" It does not matter " Marius said, he had turned his back on her and was looking straight at the door.

He heard her step behind him, felt his arm gripped, heard her say softly, " wait, sit down. I will go and fetch you a drink."

She went out and left him standing there, and he was still in this position when she came back.

" Your drink " she said.

She returned to her chair and sat down.

" Everything is all right, Captain," she said.

" Labiche is watching me " Marius said, " I knew it from the moment I first saw him."

" You are wrong, such a harmless person as that. Why, that man is not interested in anybody except himself, a most selfish creature if you ask me."

" He is watching me " Marius said stubbornly.

" I think you rather like being mysterious, Captain " said Madame Lustigne.

She crossed the room, took his hand, " for God's sake sit down " she said.

She pushed him into the chair, she felt she might have been pushing down some paper, some old clothes, inside this suit there appeared to be nothing at all.

" You are not ill ? "

" I'm not ill," he said.

" I say again, Captain, please, if it would ease your mind."

" I want to speak to Lucy."

" You have Lucy on the brain. I know what Lucy heard, I told you. She tells me everything, they all do, that is the one subject of our conversation. Men. Why, Captain, we haven't even the radio here, we make our own news, it is much more exciting. At this very moment you should be out looking for the ship you want——"

" Does Labiche come here every night ? "

" Well, no," she smiled, " he is a respectable man, sometimes he must be with his wife. You are getting Labiche on the brain. Indeed I think you are imagining things, Captain. Are you now afraid to go out ? "

He said " Can I wait for Lucy ? " and his voice had sunk so low she had to strain to catch what he said.

" You may wait."

She sat watching him.

" A poor, harmless clerk " she thought, " really—and then he is so mysterious, if he were honest with me——"

The silence had become suddenly unbearable. " You are so miserable" she said, " so miserable. Are you alone here ? "

" No. I have my mother, my sister."

" They live here ? "

" They followed me here."

" What do you want to do ? "

" Get away from here," he shouted at the top of his voice, " I want to get away from here."

" Have you money ? "

" A little ? "

" Something might be done, in that case you would leave them here."

" Nothing can be done."

" Now you are just being impossible " she said.

" I am unhappy " Marius said, he left his chair and went across to her.

" May I sit here ? "

" Do."

He sat down on the end of the bed.

" Why are you unhappy ? Because you have killed somebody, or because you only think you have killed somebody.

You are an intelligent man, Captain, you ought to make up your mind."

" I cannot get a ship " he said.

" Nonsense ! There are lots of ships."

" But I cannot sail them any more."

" You have Captain on the brain, too " said Madame Lustigne. " One must be humble, you have lost a ship, it is not easy, one is always falling down a rung or two, if you have legs you climb up again."

" You do not understand ? "

She could restrain herself no longer.

" I'm quite sure I do not " she said and laughed. " We seem to be talking for the sake of talking. You tell me nothing. What exactly is it that you want. You come here and have one of my girls, you get drunk, you come again, you get drunk again, we throw you out, but again you come, perhaps you are in love with my Lucy. Why do you come here at all ? "

" To forget myself."

" That is easy enough. But now you are wasting my time. I could say to you, 'get out' and you would have to go."

" It is Lucy I want to see " he said with maddening persistency. " This morning when I woke up I couldn't find my clothes, they'd destroyed them, my clothes, my own uniform— my——"

" Perhaps it is gone to the laundry, Captain. It was rather dirty if I remember rightly."

She got up and went and stood by the window.

" This man " she thought, " sounds a little queer to me. He has certainly got that poor man on the brain."

" But it was my uniform " he shouted.

She turned and looked at him.

" You may see Lucy to-night " Madame said, " it will cost you three hundred francs."

She crossed quickly to the door and opened it. " And now get out. You waste my time. What do I care about your misery, or whom you have killed. You are hardly a man at all, I suppose you are afraid to tell them the truth."

She stood waiting by the door. When he did not move she called out "Henri. Henri."

"Madame Lustigne" Marius said, he half rose from the bed, but promptly sat down again.

"Well?"

"I will tell you everything."

She waved her hands in the air.

"I don't want to hear a word" she replied, "I'm only waiting for you to go. Do you know what time it is? And think of the ship you may have missed, while you've been sitting here telling me how miserable you are. You're a coward, Captain, you are a spoiled child of your mother."

"I did kill him" Marius said, and he looked up at her, waited for her answer.

"I don't care who you killed."

"It was unfortunate," he said.

"Whining now" she said, her voice was pregnant with disgust, "you are hardly a man at all. I suppose you are living on *them*."

"I scratch along" Marius said, "do you mind if I smoke?"

She watched him fill and light a pipe, from which he took great long draws, as though from its stem he were sucking in some kind of strength. He stretched out his legs, looked up and said assuringly,

"I am sorry, Madame Lustigne, it is only that at the moment I am worried. Often I lie in my room and I talk, but there is no-one there, one cannot always be feeding on oneself. The others, they are as rocks. She is old, my mother is old. I did not say come, they came. They are there, alone, sitting, just sitting."

"Perhaps they are only waiting to bid you good-bye, Captain. Ships turn up when you are least expecting them."

When the knock came to the door she called, "all right, you may enter."

Henri came in.

"What is it?"

Marius studied him. He thought " this is her husband."

He saw a man in his sixties, grey, bearded, with tousled, dirty-looking hair.

" Is Lucy back ? "

" She has just come in " he said, he never once looked at the man on the bed.

" Tell her I want her."

He went out, banging the door after him.

" You see, he is no Labiche " she said.

Lucy came.

" This gentleman was with you last evening ? " said Madame Lustigne, a finger pointing towards Marius.

" Of course, what about it ? " asked Lucy.

Marius sat, steadily watching her. Her thick black hair made a violent contrast to the green of her dress, and he noted an even more violently green handbag hanging on her arm. She plumped herself down on the other side of the bed.

" Well ? "

The unchanging expression upon Marius's face amused her, she suddenly started to laugh.

" You see, Captain, Lucy is like that, she is always laughing, it's a sign of happiness at any rate. Now you may ask her what you wish."

" Here."

" Anywhere " Madame said.

She went to her desk and sat down, she ignored Lucy, had suddenly forgotten Marius. She took up some notepaper and a pen and began to write. Somewhere below she heard a child crying, and got up and closed the window.

" I am waiting for you to get out " she said, without pausing in her writing. She did not look up.

The sudden swish of a skirt told her that Lucy had got up. She heard her cross to the door.

" Close the door after you, please."

Marius listened to the scratching of the pen. Then he, too, rose and went out, closing the door silently behind him. He glimpsed Lucy going into her room, and followed. He opened the door and looked in. She had seated herself on the bed and was changing her stockings.

" It is only that last night when I was here, there was also in the next room a man by name of Labiche " Marius said, he looked down at the small bare feet.

" What the hell are you talking about ? " she said, she did not look at him.

" D'you suppose he might have heard what I said ? "

" What did you say ? "

" I don't know. I'm afraid I was drunk," he replied.

" Now you want me to remember your dreams " she said. " You want a lot for three hundred francs——"

" Did I mention the name of a man called Madeau ? "

She looked at him with a sudden disgust. " You're drunk *now*," she said.

She rose as he came into the room.

" *You* know " he said, advancing towards her, " Madame knows, you told her, you told everybody what I said in my sleep——"

" Am I expected to remember whatever rubbish you blurt out ? Am I supposed to lie awake listening for you, your little watch dog." She suddenly put out her hands and pushed him towards the door. " You're a bit crazy, that's what's wrong with you."

" You could tell me but won't " he shouted.

In that moment he seemed to grow, she could see him rising, she felt his strength as a pressure, she could feel her body being pushed slowly back, he had gripped her by the arms and had forced her against the wall.

" You bitch, you are trying to torment me. That pig Labiche is following me, I know it, even Madame's a liar, he's following me, she's put him on my track and so have you."

" Leave go my hair."

" What did I say ? "

" Are you mad ? Let go of my hair."

" What did I say ?."

She did not know, and she did not care. She was afraid, his

enormous hands had reached her shoulder, and, filled with a sudden horror that they might reach to her neck she cried out, " what did you say, I'll tell you what you said."

She felt the grip loosening, she raised her head, pressed it back against the wall.

" You said you killed a man, that's all, and then the ship sank and then you jumped into the sea, and I heard it and Labiche heard it, and Madame heard it, we all heard it and now, you bastard, you can get out."

She closed her eyes, her whole weight lay against the wall, and the hands were gone, she felt them go, something scraped upon the wooden floor, his feet. He must have drawn away, she hugged close to the wall, she was afraid to open her eyes. She was afraid of this man whom she knew must be mad.

She did not know how long she remained against the wall, but gradually a calmness returned, she breathed more easily, then, aware of the strange silence about her, opened her eyes.

Marius had gone. Through the mirror on the opposite wall her own white face stared out at her. She had drawn her hands high, and now they lay against each side of her head, as though she were pressing intently upon her ears, and standing thus she continued to look at the reflection in the mirror.

He said, " you are very beautiful."

He said, " you are so young, how old—twenty, you are happy—as this."

I said, " I am happy, I am very happy."

He said, " this sort of life—you——"

" This life " I said, " that is what makes me happy, I am like that."

And I laughed and he looked a bit surprised, and I laughed again, and went on laughing, he seemed to be a little frightened then, and I said, " what are you frightened about ? " but he said nothing and I went on laughing at him. Then he fell asleep, and after a while, I, too, and in the morning he gave me another three hundred francs.

She had moved away from the wall, yet hardly appeared to realize she had done so.

After a while she crossed to the door.

"Madame Lustigne. Madame Lustigne" she called down the corridor.

"Compose yourself, my dear child" said Madame Lustigne. Lucy lay in her bed and she sat beside her.

"I heard no scream."

"I thought he was going to kill me."

"Indeed. The ruffian. Well he has gone now, and I have told Henri to show him the door. You will not see him again. That Captain drinks too much, I was noticing how his hand trembled this hour ago, my best coffee cup, but I saved it."

"He pushed me against the wall and kept shouting in my ear. 'What did I say, what did I say?'"

"And you told him, he seems somewhat jealous of what he yaps out in his cups, but he is no exception. Is he, Lucy?"

She was full of concern for Lucy, lying there so listlessly.

"Come child, it's all right now. One day you may have worse than him. Who knows. Let me see you laugh" she said, "somehow it is not you when you're like this, you have had a bad fright. Now all this has come about because Labiche called and *he* happened to be here at the same time. He thinks that poor man is following him. Poor Mr. Labiche, if the truth were known he only wishes to help that Marius, he is a great helper of sailors, I know, he works for the Missions I have seen him of an evening going aboard the ships."

"He says Labiche is following him all the time."

"Probably for the good of his soul" said Madame Lustigne. "Drink this. I cannot have my best girl treated in this way—indeed——"

"He said he loved me. He wanted to take me away from *this*, said he'd marry me."

Madame Lustigne gave a high pitched laugh.

"They all do."

VII

WHEN MARIUS left Madame Lustigne's by the rear door, he turned off in the direction of the great line of sheds belonging to Transport Oriental. The sun was climbing and ravenous. He was glad to slip into an alley between two of these sheds. Here it was cooler. He stood there for a few minutes. He was struck by the intense activity going on behind the high walls. The noise of hoists, of rattling trucks, the endless shouting that split the air, it made him all the more aware of his own position, his in-activity, a growing sense of uselessness. He put a match to a cigarette, then moved down the alley and came into the light again. He dropped down on his haunches, leaned against a truck, he surveyed the scene. Loading ships, un-loading ships, ant-like men moving across decks, busy, puffing, important little tugs, a tall ship turning seawards, slowly moving barges. The whole world was moving.

" I feel outside it all."

The whole scene cried triumph at him and he hated it. He turned away with a feeling of intense sadness and started to walk towards the city, his thoughts ahead of him. He was already at the Heros, pushing in the door, walking up the steps, looking at the smug, self-satisfied Philippe, wondering what Follet looked like. Moving out again, further into the city, getting slowly lost amongst the buildings, he was at the office of Transport Oriental, the whole pattern of yesterday, of the day before, was clear to him now, it was simply a question of wearing out another day. He increased his pace, walked sharply for nearly a quarter of a mile, he felt strange in his new suit. Twice he paused to look in the mirrors outside shops, somehow he felt naked without that reefer, that peaked cap, those black trousers, it was like losing one's skin. Then he slowed down, and once stopped and turned round to look behind him. He had a feeling that somebody was following him, but all he saw were the faces of advancing people, who passed him by without noticing him, they were in a hurry, they had destinations to get to, they were doing something. For a moment he stood on the pavement, watching the screaming traffic tear past. He had turned his back on one sea only to find himself on the brink of another.

There was something merciless in this ever advancing traffic, this stream of people hurrying about their various businesses. Wherever he looked he saw huge buildings, on either side, ahead and behind him. He remained at the pavement's edge, hesitant, a little nervous, there was a defiance, an indifference in the very air, and always he was aware of the hugeness of things, high walls, hundreds of windows looking down on the avenue, shining like eyes, the swinging doors, the brightly dressed doorkeepers, and then the highest, proudest building of them all, Renart's.

Marius stood outside one of the long windows, stiff as a ramrod, the doors were continuously opening and closing, people coming out singly, in twos and threes, whole families, chattering and bustling, and behind him he could feel people very close to him.

Marius fixed his eye on a hat and kept it there. The laughing girls who came up so suddenly reminded him of Lucy, he saw their reflections in the glass, and they went on laughing and commenting on the hats in the window, whilst Marius became more and more aware of Lucy, she seemed so close he might almost put out a hand and touch her, smell the perfume, her flesh. He was afraid to move, he had become a part of the window, he was on view from the back, and for a moment he thought he was inside the window, amongst the hats, on show.

" My God " he thought, " how can I get out of this," for there was a pressure against him now, a feminine pressure, thighs, knees, bosoms, perhaps they were all staring at *him*, into his back, that weakest part of him. He felt their eyes focused on him, and madly, stubbornly he went on staring at the hat, so pale a blue, so delicate, something almost ethereal about it, except the defiant little feather, jutting up, cocking itself at the crowd outside.

In the midst of it all Marius felt lonely, felt cold on this hot morning, and as he lost his eyes in the blue of the hat he saw only his room, the small, tight, safe room, the window and the buzzing flies, the patient spider.

" Excuse me."

It made Marius jump, but he did not move, and he could not take his eye off the hat.

" If you *please*," and he was pushed and only then did he move, keeping his eye fixed on the window as he moved slowly along, and the next long window was full of books, he stopped again. He was afraid to look round.

He stared fixedly at one particular book.

A young couple behind him were discussing the author, he slowly raised his eyes and saw a young man and woman with linked arms. They were happy, Marius knew they were happy, their very presence, their voices as they talked were proof of it.

" I'm getting this Labiche on the brain " he thought, " and what the hell am I doing here, in my peasant's suit, Christ, I'd better get out of it," and he turned quickly, clumsily.

" Excuse me," he said and hurried away, pressing through the crush of people who had gathered about the entrance to the store.

It was a long avenue and it was like a battlefield. The pavements were crowded, cars pulled up, unloaded their passengers, who rushed off, disappearing through doorways, into restaurants. Lorries and vans were drawn up outside shops, a burly carter, great arms widespread and bared, carrying a hefty load cursed Marius when he bumped into him, and his " sorry " vanished uselessly into the air, whilst the carter's healthy swears followed in his wake.

Ahead he saw iron railings, a kiosk, a group of brightly dressed girls, a blue bus pulling up, he hurried past all these and turned into the park.

People were sitting on benches, children were playing on the paths, and Marius as he walked quickly past turned away his head, which lifted a little, he might have been studying the uniform line of trees. And then he saw a vacant bench. He was glad to sit down.

" Thought I'd be locked there forever. God. In the end I was glad to be pushed out of it, that hat—the way they pushed, that matron "—pressed against him, the feel of the big woman, that shattering backside—" I must have been crazy to stand there staring at a piddling little hat."

He lay back on the bench, he felt exhausted, a little frightened.

" I must pull myself together."

The closed eyes felt the heat of the sun.

" I've had enough of it. I must get out. In the end I'll stow away, buy my job, though I'll hate that, I have some merits, even if I have no papers," and the very thoughts were like shutters, opening up, another climate, another country, the little dream.

" The Black Sea—Greece, the Islands—Italy, Genoa, Leghorn, they weren't so respectable there, a man is a man to the very end. This place, I'm not the only bum here, at the end of my tether—and that man, Labiche, what's he after——I heard somebody say he's good, good people are a bloody menace...."

He opened his eyes to a silent, staring child, a boy, whose clear gaze at this tall thin man, made him at once embarrassed, and he looked away quickly.

" Hello."

" Hello " Marius said.

" Would you mend this wheel ? "

" Give it me " Marius said, not wanting to mend it, wanting to move again, wanting to get back, up the stairs, into his room, he could lock the door, shut the world out.

" There ! "

" Thank you, sir."

Marius smiled back at the satisfied child, and watched him go off and join another further down the path.

" If I'd married, perhaps—no, at forty-nine—now if I'd met Lucy—poor Lucy. Perhaps if I was younger I'd have married her, so young, I felt like a pig. I'll never forget her face when she told me she was happy—something stiffened inside me when she said it."

Here, inside the railings, one was free of the rushing sea. The noise, heaved up and down as waves. The cries and raucous shouts of children were tossed into the air as spray, themselves lost in the hoots of the passing cars, the dull roar of these drowned out by a loud clanging bell, and all commingling, to rise, clamorous, triumphant, the dominating, ruthless and ever thrusting voice of the city, beating against stone, and the high windows, and Marius seated comfortably on his bench could listen to it all.

He got up, turned towards the gate, stopped, went back to his seat and sat down again, but without knowing why. People passed and re-passed, lovers sprawled on benches, old couples chatted, read their newspapers, children played, it went on, it never stopped.

" I must get off " he thought, wondering why, to where, and quickly he was on his feet and hurrying down the path, seeing nothing, hearing nothing, feeling nothing, he was in the long wide avenue again, and this seemed endless, like that avenue to the Heros, roads leading nowhere.

Passing a huge hotel his eye caught sight for a moment of two huge brass bowls, one on either side of the entrance, filled with roses, and as he hurried past them he thought only of bunched fists.

The immaculate doorkeeper in one swift, disdainful glance took in the cheap check cap, the coat a little too short, especially the sleeves, the stiff trousers.

Marius slackened his pace, then fell into that wide, rolling gait, from sheer habit, and sometimes he was hard up against a shop window, and the next moment moving on the pavement edge. At street corners he stopped to look round, always careful of the traffic, standing there tense, nervous, waiting his opportunity to cross the road. Once he narrowly missed the wheels of a car and received the wrong kind of compliments from its driver. Against his own will he was falling into the pattern of this storming and thrusting life, he felt like a worn out cog, he fitted nowhere into the machine.

The Avenue was like a swiftly rushing river, he was being drawn into it, and as he crossed the road for the fifth time he thought, " I'll float anyhow."

He would sometimes fix his eye on some object ahead then move briskly towards it, only to falter at the last moment and ask himself, " what the hell am I doing amongst all this ? "

A bus approaching its Stop would make him increase his pace, as though he had decided to catch it, and the conductor seeing him would wait, and when Marius reached it he stopped dead and let it go on.

Once he turned back, went down the avenue for two blocks then returned by the way he had come.

" It hardly matters which way one goes " he thought.

A clock struck noon. The sun had climbed high, he began to sweat, and he could not get the hot, penetrating stench of petrol out of his nostrils, the smell seemed to lie congealed in the air itself. He felt sweat under his collar, between his thighs, he dashed a hand to his temples and wiped drops from it.

" I'm crazy, I'm walking too fast " he said to himself and averted the glance of a passing man who stared at him with some interest, and then passed into a café.

" I'm a fool. Rushing about in this heat, no wonder people stare at me," and before he realized it he had come to a queue of people outside the booking office of a theatre.

Marius paused. People were studying photographs of the company, and he joined them. He looked at the pictures of the actors, the actresses, he listened to the comments of others, and then he saw himself in the long mirror by the doors.

" I say, d'you mind carrying these bags down to the Rotunde, over the way there ? "

Marius swung round to face a tall, over-dressed, florid gentleman and an equally over-dressed and florid lady.

" What's that ? "

The man was offering him the bags.

" Yanks. Christ ! They take me for a porter " he thought and hurried away from the theatre.

He turned into the first side street.

" Ah ! " he exclaimed at the first Bistro, and turned in.

The bar was empty. Marius went to a table in the corner and sat down. The waiter bore down upon him.

" Good day, sir."

" A cognac, please " Marius said, then bawled after the departing waiter, " I don't care whether you bring it or not."

The waiter stopped dead in his tracks, swung round.

" The gentleman asked for a cognac, d'you want a cognac ? "

Marius sprawled, he felt tired, as though he had just completed a full day's hard toil. He eased himself up, one long leg was thrown up on a form, the other had vanished under the table.

" Well, damn you, can't you bring me the drink then ? " he shouted.

" What the hell am I doing down here ? " he was asking himself when the waiter returned with the drink.

" Your cognac, sir."

" All right. Leave it there," Marius said.

" There is the question of payment " the waiter said.

His nostrils quivered, as though this bird were high.

" Thank you, sir " he said, even before Marius showed signs of putting his hand to his pocket.

He stood quietly, hands clasped gently in front of him, waiting, and then he saw the man's hand go to the inside pocket of his jacket.

Marius put some notes on the table.

" Thank you " said the waiter, carefully extracted what was due, pushed back the remaining notes.

" Have it " said Marius.

The waiter's head lifted a little, " it is hardly necessary, sir, thank you," and he walked off down the long narrow room and left Marius fingering his cognac. But from the top of the counter he stood and watched him.

One got all sorts of people in this end of the city, all sorts of people in Ferroni's, but rarely a peasant.

"Smells a little" thought the waiter. "He'll probably end up by cadging a drink and then asking me to meet his wife."

He leaned heavily on the counter, he hummed to himself, a popular song, but never for a moment did his eye leave Marius, and suddenly he was calling again.

"Again."

"Yes sir."

He offered Marius a curious smile but this was not returned. And when he came back he offered the visitor another smile.

"Have you ever heard of a man called the Sailor's friend?"

"Me? No sir. I'm sorry to say that I have not. Why?"

"I was looking for him, that's all."

"Perhaps the gentleman is joking, nobody of that name ever comes into Ferroni's, besides you're in the wrong place. The sea is at the other end of the city, I believe, I myself have never seen it."

He leaned against the table, and he missed nothing of Marius, his eye drawn first to the powerful hands, the wrists, a small tattoo, the hairs between the fingers, a dead black, the brown skin, the untrimmed finger nails, the dirt. And then slowly up the sleeves of the coat, pausing at the neck, noting a collar almost hidden, a lean, hairy throat, higher to the chin, blue from the razor, and then he was looking over Marius's head. He could see more through the mirror.

"Why don't you draw the curtains," Marius said, "every time I move I see somebody looking at me," and automatically he handed the waiter his empty glass.

The waiter suddenly laughed.

"What the hell are you laughing at, I'll break your neck," and Marius made an effort to rise, but fell back again.

"It's only yourself, sir, you've but to turn round and look."

Marius looked round, saw himself in seven mirrors, himself laughed.

" Only me. Fancy *me* being scared of me," but when he looked up the waiter had already gone for the drink.

An old man came into the room, doddering, he might have been held together by string, and at his heels a stout, middle-aged matron, who kept a tight finger on his coat hem, and she said " steady there " in a low voice.

Marius looked up as the pair went past. " Tart " he thought, glanced at the old man, then again at the woman.

" Where's his leash ? " he asked.

The waiter was standing in front of him again. Marius turned and looked after the pair who had reached a top table.

" She's deaf as a post " he thought.

" That won't cost you a sou " the waiter said. " Are you hungry ? " He sat down opposite Marius and studied him closely. " I could get you something."

" You'll get me nothing. Here" and he paid for his drink.

" I have some manners left, thanks for the drink, but I can pay, and I'm not hungry. Did you ever hear of this man called the Sailor's Friend ? "

The waiter folded his arms, paused a moment, said quietly, " I only wish I had, so that I could tell you, but the fact is we never see sailors, we only see actors and actresses here. You look a bit like an actor yourself, that nose " he said.

" Were you an actor ? " asked Marius, and he lifted the cognac to his lips, " were you an actor ? "

" Only for three months, and that was too long. I felt like a virgin among them. I was too pure. Excuse me " he said, and dashed off to attend to the two new customers.

" God Almighty he thinks I'm a tramp."

He finished off his drink, called for another. The waiter did not answer him, did not move.

" Waiter."

Marius was ignored.

The two people at the top table paused in their conversation, lowered their glasses, looked at the man sprawled in the corner, smiled into each other's faces, then saw the waiter going down.

" You've had enough here, sir " the waiter said.

He picked up the empty glass.

" Not half enough " Marius said, he was on his feet, glaring at the waiter.

" Not half enough," closing in, his face almost touching that of the waiter, who now drew back a little, suddenly gripped Marius by the wrist, pulled him away from the table.

" I mean " the waiter said, "that you have had enough, and now you can get out of here. Your place is at the other end of the avenue."

With his hand in the middle of Marius's back he pushed, whilst with the other he gripped the man's neck, moving swiftly towards the door.

" Out you get " and Marius went staggering down the steps.

" He's right " he thought, " he's right, I've nothing left, nothing. One time I'd have put a man on his back for that, and now I'm like a dog with its tail between his legs, and I can go into a bistro and I can be insulted by a bloody flunky and accept it, and a kick in the arse into the bargain."

He sat on the bottom step, his hands clasped about his knees.

" The sea is at the other end of the city."

He was hearing the waiter again, looking at his woman's hands pressed flat upon the table, " for myself I've never seen it."

It dragged Marius back to his room again, he was there already, lying on the bed under the window, looking out at that impregnable Chateau d'If, the solid mass of the break-water, the restless, everlasting waters.

The waiter was right. Who the hell could see the sea from the Place de Lenche, if one believed in the sea one saw it from the top of the ant-hill.

" I'm on its second floor " he thought, " and perhaps I have the clearest, longest view of all."

He looked around as he got to his feet, but nobody was

watching him, and nobody cared very much, besides it was far too hot to notice anything except one's own discomfort.

" I could walk right back there. I could even take a cab. I could have what they've laid out, and I could sit and eat it with her watching me."

The very thought made his stomach itch, and coming suddenly on a fruit-seller he bought some apples, and went on, stuffing them in his pocket, and in the first side street took one out of his pocket and ate it. Then he came back to the Place and continued, his pace leisurely, aimless, his mind a chaos, his limbs dragging him relentlessly, in spite of a feeling of weariness and he longed for the night again, and for Lucy. The distraction, the wave that engulfed the hard facts, tore time to shreds. Suddenly he stopped dead in his tracks.

There before him, seated at a table was the living image of Brunet, Brunet of the Transport Oriental, he was sure of it. The small, wiry man in his sober black, his flashing watch chain, was seated at an outside table of Pelleron's. Marius sat down. He did not at once look at the man, who never glanced his way, or interrupted his slow, joyful sipping of the apéritif.

When the waiter came Marius hesitated, he couldn't decide what he wanted, but the waiter was patient, courteous, he was full of suggestions. His face fell when Marius asked for a beer, nevertheless he brought it and Marius paid him, his 'tip was generous. Marius drank, and at the same time he was carefully studying the other man.

Yes, this was the same man, he was certain of it, same build, same height, even the same dress. It made him think of the last time.

" You're a stubborn creature, you say you are a Captain and I ask for the simple proof of it and you cannot show me. I want your merit, on paper " Brunet said.

" It must be him " thought Marius.

" Excuse me, sir " he said, and the small wiry man turned round.

" Yes ? "

" You are Monsieur Brunet ? "

" I am not Monsieur Brunet," and he gave the other a withering glance.

" But I've seen you before at Transport Oriental " Marius said.

" I'm afraid you have not, sir " replied the other.

" Pardon, I was certain, sir," said Marius.

" And it is accepted," and the man turned his back on Marius and forgot him.

It came back to Marius like a fast running film. The scene in the office, the man behind the counter and the man in front of it.

" I only require to be taken on on my merits " Marius said.

" There is still the question of the proof of them " Monsieur Brunet said. " I'll be honest " thought Marius and he exclaimed shyly, " Monsieur Brunet will realize certain difficulties. If I say I have no papers, that is to say——"

" You have lost your ticket ?"

He had answered by a slow nod of the head, the very shame of it sent a rush of blood to his temples, he had stood there, helpless.

" Other men have lost them, one begins at the bottom again, sometimes it is difficult, sometimes it is not. But in the world of ships one takes no chances, if one does, one's broker may have one run in to the asylum."

" That " thought Marius, " that was the fifteenth time I had called."

He kept staring at the supposed Brunet, a suspicion had formed in his mind that it was *really* Brunet, that Brunet had recognised him, and was now completely ignoring him.

" I can't start at the bottom again, I refuse. By God I refuse. Back to the bloody ant heap again, no. I am a Captain of ships or I am nothing, and if I'm stubborn I'm stubborn, and too, I must hold on to some shred of my dignity."

The wiry man had long since gone but Marius had not noticed this.

He was travelling back years, back to the old days, the early climbing, the hard way, the smelly tramps, the Grecian floating grave, the Rumanian dungeon, all of them calling themselves ships. Back to the lodging-houses, the dossing shops. Already he had a whiff of it in his nostrils, he was lying between the dirty blankets again, log-like on the stinking, sweated mattresses.

" Begin again ? Never."

The waiter was standing just behind him, flapping his apron. He said casually, " the air is like a tomb to-day——"

" Yes it is, isn't it " replied Marius. " Have you the time ? "

" It is just past one o'clock, Monsieur will perhaps lunch ? "

Something in the very tone of the man's voice made Marius turn and look at him.

" And I'm not wrong " he said to himself, " only a person with a voice like that could have the gentlest of expressions."

" I will. I'll take that table in the far corner," pointing, " there."

And Marius went to it and sat down and enjoyed a hearty lunch.

" What's the damn use of calling anywhere any more " he thought, and hurried out of the restaurant so quickly that he did not hear the old waiter's emphatic thanks, his " come again, sir."

It was two o'clock. He dropped into the first cinema and sat down.

He saw nothing, though he heard all too clearly the rampant, strident music screeching round the auditorium. He deliberately shut his eyes, his head had begun to throb. Anyhow it was much cooler here.

At half past two an attendant woke him up, didn't like the look of him, nor did the people behind him who had complained of his loud snoring, and within a minute Marius was in the Place de Lenche again.

" I'll tire myself out to-day, and then perhaps I'll have a good night. Life to-day was made up of walking, and moving from one place to another for the simple reason that you kept on walking. There was something interminable about it," the Place de Lenche was growing longer and yet longer, and Marius began to wonder if he would ever get within view of Port Vieux again.

"At least that Labiche hasn't got this far" he thought, "I wish I knew what the hell he wanted of me. All the same I'm going back, down, far down, and then that bloody climb again into the Rue des Fleurs.

"If only that Follet would have seen me once, just the once, twenty years ago he knew my father, I could have explained, he might have helped. Or must I really dive to the bottom, get half pissed one night and be shanghaied somewhere."

He hailed a passing tram, whose toothy conductress failed to notice him, ran after it, clung desperately to the rail, swung himself aboard, and the tram rattled on, and he gave his body willingly to its wild lurches, and let the shrieking horn penetrate his ears.

He had no ticket. Where did he want to go?

"Anywhere at all?" he said.

The toothy conductress smiled.

This tram was not stopping again until it reached the Place des Treize Coins, and then it turned sharply and stopped by the cemetery gates. Perhaps Monsieur wished to go to the cemetery.

Marius was holding out a filthy note, and she took it and gave him his ticket.

She was leaning over him. "Where d'you want to get to?"

"I told you. Anywhere you like."

She grinned. "As Monsieur wishes then."

The tram, as it careered its way down the Place seemed to shake the very foundations of Marseilles, but it eventually came to a stop, and one or two people got up from their seats, Marius among them. The conductress looked him over as he got off the platform and said as she turned away, "perhaps Monsieur is on his way to a wedding after all."

At that moment a funeral procession had reached the gates. Marius went across and stood by the railings, noting the shade under the plane trees, the little white church with its belfry, its tiny tower and sturdy black clock, which at that moment began to strike. Marius moved along slowly until he stood just by the gate.

The procession had formed up, the hearse had drawn away past the gate. He turned round, and something made him suddenly bear up, he stood stiffly, his hands hanging at his sides. A girl passed him, glanced shyly at him, went on, a man passed, paused, looked at Marius.

Without hesitating a moment, without realizing why, Marius turned and followed the man through the gate, he had become a part of the procession. He walked by the tall, heavily built man.

" A sad day, Monsieur " the gentleman said, head forward, hat held tightly in his hand, great beads of sweat standing out on the big florid face.

" Yes " Marius replied, and kept pace with him. There were only three people here, the girl, the man, Marius. They were suddenly at the graveside.

" Your son ? " asked Marius.

" Hers."

" Your daughter ? "

The big man shook his head. No, he was only the undertaker. She was the only one. He looked sympathetically at Marius, laid a hand on his arm, the lightest touch, " so good of Monsieur, it helps to make it look a little proper."

Marius hardly heard. He was standing staring at the girl. The moment she noticed him she lowered her eyes. The tiny coffin went down. The undertaker offered Marius the plate, he took some soil from it and flung it down.

The bearers had gone, but in the background stood the one whom nobody could fail to recognise, the digger.

Marius suddenly saw the priest shake hands with her and walk away. She turned round and faced the bearded man who had been standing mute behind her. Marius watched her take out a worn purse, extract from it what looked like a single franc note, saw her hand it to the gravedigger.

" Be kind to him " the girl said, and turned and moved away, came over to Marius.

" Thank you, Monsieur."

Marius was unable to speak. The undertaker had touched his arm.

" I can take Monsieur to his destination ? "

Marius shook his head. " No no, thank you, no no."

His hand had caught that of the girl, he had gripped it, looked at her. Neither spoke.

He stood watching her go, remained standing long after the sound of the wheels had died away, and he found he was still staring at the grave.

" It's like a dream " thought Marius, " the whole thing, its like a dream."

He gave one last glance at the still silent, still motionless gravedigger and walked out of the cemetery.

He was in the middle of the sea again and a storm had begun. Buildings everywhere were disgorging people, the pavements became more crowded, the cars roared louder, the bicycles whizzed past him, shop doors were banged and locked, he heard rattlings of chains, ringing of bells, wild toots of horns, and over it all the air, smell laden, burdensome, the grind and sweat and energy of the day had borne upwards as a cloud bears upwards, to hang like a pall over the sun drenched roads.

Marius seemed to grind his way through the throngs, slowly, ruthlessly, and twice he had endeavoured to cross to the other side, but half way over had taken sudden fright and hurried back again. The city frightened him, he longed for the descent to be over, to apprehend the smells, the feel, the very rhythm, and sight of the toiling Vieux Port. Never had he longed so much for the sight of a ship. It was as though he had crossed an endless and arid desert, been lost in a strange and un-navigable country, gripped in the centre of thousands of people whom he had never seen before, would never see again, who had no meaning for him.

" One is safe in the muck heap."

" I'll never venture down there again, God, the whole thing scared me," remembering the waiter at Ferroni's, the cancer face of the apple seller, the shy, beautiful, yet terrified features of the girl who was burying her child, the Americans who took him for a bagman, the woman's hand that gripped like iron and flung him down those steps, the child with the broken wheel, the walrus-like teeth of the tram conductress, they were passing to and fro across Marius's vision as he walked quickly, and yet more quickly down the long, relentless hill.

At the first Bistro he almost burst through the door.

" Black coffee " he called.

He sat stirring it for nearly five minutes before deciding to drink it.

" What a fool I was to think that that shrimp of a man could ever be Brunet. God ! I'd give my eyes to be upright again, walking up a gangplank, full of authority, taking her out past the Chateau d'If."

There was a grinding of brakes outside, sudden shouts, then a party of six people, all young men swept in and past Marius like a wave. Shouting and laughing and gesticulating they went far up the room. After much creaking of chairs there was silence.

" Another coffee " Marius said.

" To-morrow morning promptly, at nine o'clock I'll go down to the *Clarte*, I'll go aboard her, I'll beard Manos in his cabin, I'll sink my bloody pride."

He stirred and stirred the coffee but never drank it.

" I'll find Follet's private address, why the hell didn't I think of it, of course, I'll go to his house to-morrow evening——"

" Lucy said she'd take me to a man named Jacquette, what a name, sounds like a girl-man to me, hangs out at THE TOMB, there's a waiter there named Varinet, knows everybody, she told me—yes, I'll do that—— even a Greek cockleshell is better than nothing after all."

All the time the spoon was moving round and round

and round in his cup, but he had quite forgotten it, he was uplifted by a wave of resolutions, but these reached momentum and fell heavily, vanished like trickles of water in the desert.

He got up and left the un-drunk coffee and went out.

" I'm scared, that's what I am. Scared. If they hadn't followed me here. They know, of course they know, they only followed to drag it out of me."

" Can't you mind where you're walking ? "

" In the end I'll tell her, I'll tell her to-morrow—be done with it."

" Look out man."

Marius, unheeding pushed on. He was glad to see a sight of the fountain, he felt safe now, and moved in under the trees. The whole of humanity seemed gathered here and at last he felt he was alone. He sat on the corner of a bench on which two old men were chatting.

" I'm a little drunk " he thought.

He huddled up, never looked in the old men's direction, stared down at the ground.

" I could climb up Accoules this moment, disappear into the warrens and never come out again. Christ, what's the good of that. I must find my clothes. Yes, I must find my clothes. I don't believe she burnt them at all, hidden them, wanted to humiliate me. And she calls herself a Christian——" he felt in his pockets, turned quickly.

" Have you a match ? "

A beardless face, hammered by age, turned towards him. Marius could not see the eyes, which were almost lost beneath the bushy brows. He leaned towards the old man. The eyes seemed colourless, lay far back in the head, half buried by years.

" Have you a smoke ? "

Marius felt furiously in all pockets.

He shook his head, he was sorry, he hadn't a cigarette either. He took some loose coins from his pocket, handed them to the old man, got up and walked away.

" The people I'm meeting to-day."

A church clock was striking the half hour. He went on, he was making for the Quai de Belge.

" It may be that Follet doesn't even know I've called, asked for him, day after day, that swine Philippe, he's got under my skin, blast him and his correctness, his colossal opinion of himself, happy in his little cage, thinks of nobody but himself, hasn't even good manners, I might have been a pig."

The moment he heard the rattle of the winches his spirit lightened, already he could feel a light breeze, the petrol stink seemed far away now, and there were no mad, thrusting crowds. There was the *Bergerac*, still there, would she ever sail, her decks deserted, her derricks neatly laid home, a quietness settled over her as though she had resolved never again to turn her head seawards.

" A lovely thing " thought Marius, " now if I could take her out——"

The great quay had about it the calmness of a lake, only a single winch went on rattling, and as he walked slowly on, he watched the day's debris blow about his feet, old newspapers, cigarette packets, ends, bits of string, yarn, a matted bundle of old lading bills. Ahead were some timbers.

Marius sat down. He did not look at the sea, but watched attentively at the bits and ends of litter as it went by. A half sheet of old newspaper came his way, anchored at his heels and he bent down and picked it up, began to read. All the ships of the world, all the ports and docks and quays seemed centred on this soiled sheet as he slowly read. Names of ships and their movements. He cried in his mind the names of *Hercules, Avenger, Orleans, Triumph*.

" If " said Marius, " if ", but there were so many of them, and he dropped the paper and watched it slowly blow away. He felt that if a gust of wind strong enough had come along, he would have been blown after it.

" What's the use."

An exhaustion was pressing upon him, his head began to nod, his body sagged, fell heavily back upon the timbers.

" I feel filthy " he said.

The heat of the long day, the grind, the traffic roars, the voices, the smells in the air, all seemed harboured in his person. He heard the winch stop suddenly, raised himself and looked towards the *Bergerac*. Beyond it he saw a single man move away down the for'ard deck. She was a small ship and her bow was facing him, but he could not make out her name. " If somebody came along this moment and said 'are you ready' I'd get up at once and I'd say, ' I'm always ready ' and I'd go off with him, I'd ascend that gangway and the moment I touched her deck I'd grow, I'd rise up, I'd climb out of all this," and his hands moved slowly down the length of his body.

" Pull yourself together," he said.

" Go home."

But he did not stir.

He fell asleep.

VIII

"DAYS CRAWL over me like bugs."

In the hot, sweltering night he lay naked on his back, the iron bed drawn up beneath the high, narrow window. For half an hour he had been looking out, and through it had come the dull, monotonous roar of distant breakers, it made him think of some kind of animal prowling upon night and air. The darkened room was slowly unburdening itself, the piled up heat of the day rising from corners, out of the cupboard, from underneath the bedclothes, falling away from his own flesh, rising and vanishing through the window. He imagined that if he put out his hand he would be able to feel the darkness itself, like a skin, and to Marius, even this seemed to sweat. But always, over the dull roar, clamant and as remindful as struck blows, the steady tick of the watch by his pillow.

"That Lustigne woman's right. The moment we're out we're watched, somebody following you all the time, one's only safe here."

He turned over in the heat-clinging bed, then he jumped out, crossed the room and turned the key in the lock. He returned to the bed and stretched out again.

"I'll plan. I'll get out of this dump, into the Black Sea, anywhere there, if I could get to Greece, the Islands—Italy perhaps, Leghorn, Genoa——

"Ah! If I could have seen that Follet now. Just the once. There's a man of understanding, I could tell him everything, everything. I'd sink all pride, forget my merits. Merits. Jesus! Look at them? Rusting away, falling to pieces. I only want the broad deck of a ship to walk on, no more than that, God, its not much to want, feel it moving under me, to be away,

away. Ah, Follet, trying to see you is like trying to see a bloody Emperor. So precious is intelligence, so rare the under-standing, you battle to reach it. Through what ? These bloody men, damn them, say I'm a Jonah, spread rumours about me, won't sail with me. It's those bastards who draw up the gang-ways, block the doors, glare at me through the windows, turn up their noses. They pick and choose their Captains like they choose their tarts——"

" If by some effort of the will——"

He was staring up at the window. There was something not quite right about it.

" It's those damn flies, they've gone " he thought, he won-dered where.

" Been to five offices to-day, boarded three ships, sat in half a dozen Bistro. That waiter Varinet. Lucy said that Jac-quette man frequented the place, never turned up, hoped like hell he would. Can't count the number of walls I leaned against, and that man Labiche, following me, saw him three times to-day, what the hell does he want anyhow ? He scares me, he really scares me. I've been to a funeral, too. Took coffee in a café, stuck twenty minutes outside Renart's, couldn't move, stiff as a ramrod. Couldn't budge. All those people rushing in and out, the mad Sales were on, it's unreal, can't believe I was there. Can't believe all those rushing, shouting, laughing people were happy, pushing past you as though you weren't there. That girl, alone, sitting in the park. And now I'm here. Another day."

He sat up with a sudden jerk, put his head in his hands.

" It's this place, too. This bloody house."

He sat motionless, as though listening. The dead silence of it screeched at him, an intense, persistent spirit was about, Marius could plainly hear it in his ear, " not satisfied, not satisfied."

" That Philippe. The swine. I could kill him. So smug, so correct, so *good*, a wink from him, a finger held up, just saying yes, change everything, get me out of here to-morrow. . . ." and a ship was blowing, a tug hooting, cranes roaring, winches rattling, men hailing and hurrying, the ship's engines first heavy sounds, and then the steady rhythm of them, everything moving, and it made Marius move, he was on his feet again, pacing the floor.

" Knew my father in the old days, if I could see him, *if* . . . by God, I'll visit him at his home, why the hell didn't I think about that, why didn't I ? It's in the Directory, of course, easy . . . fool—you're a fool . . . but that Philippe, day after day after day, his very goodness makes it hurt, see him smiling now, covers you with slime, see him talking to Follet, hear him, ' that Nantes bum was in again to-day '. One is deaf after that, I never hear what Follet answers."

He stopped dead in the middle of the room.

" Who's there ? "

He waited, but there was no sound, and then he was off again, up and down, up and down, round and round.

" How happy Lucy is, I can hear her laughing," and he gave an odd little chuckle himself, he could hear her talking, her warmth all round him.

" Be really sick, Captain, it'll do you good, she was in ballast for Algiers, what's ballast ? "

He was back on the bed again, he was listening to the sound of his own voice.

" Lucy's got ballast, there's iron in poor Lucy."

" I should never have arrived, that's the trouble."

Through shut eyes he saw himself carried high by a single wave, right across a sea, the sound of which was now roaring in his ears, and there he was, landed, in the murdering town, fighting his way through the jibbering, incoherent groups, Royat back somewhere, away back somewhere, lost. There was the station.

" All lighted up. Mad."

Sometimes it was difficult to remember. Flinging himself into the train, rain hammering on the windows, the darkness outside, and there on the opposite seat the old man, silent, frozen with horror.

" Are you flying, too ? "

The stupid face of the old man, hugging and hugged by his terror, bewildered.

" Everybody's flying, don't worry."

" I wonder where he is now " thought Marius, " that poor old man," then he shouted, " Ah, France, you took some mighty kicks in the arse," and the sounds seemed to split into fragments and scatter everywhere, the quiet house was deluged by them.

" The things I've seen."

" Who's there ? " he shouted.

He was at the door again, rattling frantically at the knob.

" Who's there ? "

There was no answer.

" I thought I heard somebody. I must be going crazy."

He got out of bed and drew the curtain across the window. The darkness was final. And somewhere within it were the soft, continuing padding sounds as of a moving animal, and this was Marius, on his feet again, naked, the closed window forgotten, the heat of the long day always rising. Sometimes he stopped and listened, glancing towards the locked door, and heard only his own breathing and the tick of the watch. It was at this moment that he heard the voice calling and following in its direction walked quietly into the sea.

Ships moved in utter darkness, the sea was full of ships, slinking through the night, like petty thieves, like murderers, fugitive ships, determined ships, ships already lost before they had veered away from the quays, and he was there in the middle of them. He was on the bridge and Berriat was there, and Jean, too, both there, and silent.

" At ten Gasse'll come up. He won't say good evening and I don't want it, we know where we are. He'll watch me all the time, *I* will be the fool, *I* will make the mistake. My orders are explicit, final. A reduction of speed at twenty three hours, not an inch more, we're moving towards a minefield. Madeau isn't here, I'll wait."

There it was. Five bells, loud and clear.

He watched the reliefs come up, Gasse, his nephew. He waited a little longer. Then he crossed the deck, stood watching him there.

" You all right, Jean ? "

" Yes uncle."

How clear the youthful voice in the night air, strong, beautiful.

" Sure ? You know what you're about ? "

" Yes."

" Not unhappy, not afraid . . . no ? "

" No. I'm not."

" Good ! Steer well."

He could feel and smell and touch this moment.

" Should never have gone, never, I went below, yet I knew, felt I shouldn't, my feet held so hard, forced myself to it, how tired I was, nervy. I was in the cabin, fell asleep—Christ, I fell asleep. . . .

" I woke, by God how sudden I woke, perhaps I wasn't asleep after all, dozing . . . and then I saw that watching eye, that Gasse. And I sat on my bunk and I looked at my watch. How we hated each other. His eye. Never see an eye like it again, never. I had slept too long, it was done, too late, knew it, knew it running, falling over in the darkness, how she heaved. . . ."

Marius stood still in the middle of the room, clenched his hands. He felt the sweat drip from his forehead, and was so still he heard their minute drops. And risen high above him on the darkened sea, as clear as day, the ploughing ship. He felt again the odd shiver of her timbers, as though this living ship realized she had been caught in the trap.

The steady pulse of the engines rose from the depths, sounded as thuds. And beyond, in the darkness, others, blind, groping . . .

" Gone ! They'd gone. I swear to Christ we were alone,

that hammering, what the hell was that, like great fists beating at her hull . . .

" There's something wrong."

" There's nothing wrong " the man at the wheel said.

" Blast you for a fool, what course is this ? "

" The course as ordered " the helmsman said.

" Swing her back at least three degrees."

He saw Gasse, tall, sphinx-like.

" D'you wish to sink us ? I'll put you in irons. . . ."

Gasse did not stir, not a muscle of his face moved. Marius stared, felt weakened, was helpless before those eyes.

" It's *you*, you're wrong " Madeau said, " Monsieur Gasse is correct, uncle. . . ."

Marius felt himself go suddenly limp, he dragged himself across to the bed and slumped there.

" Fell where he stood, struck him, never even looked at him. It *was* Gasse. I flew at him."

" If she strikes, then by the living God I'll see to it you're dead before I am."

He threw his arms behind his head, stretched out his legs, he seemed to be waiting again, listening. He heard her strike.

Some monster, some giant perhaps, unseen in that darkness, and darker still that great confused mass of water.

" It was like somebody struck a match, it flamed and it went out."

" At a single blow, one blow, there he was, as he had fallen, stone dead, I knew I had also killed myself. Poor little Jean. I was mad with rage. . . ."

Marius watched himself turn and fling himself towards Gasse, meet nothing save the onrushing sea. In a matter of minutes, gone. A whole living world wiped out. In four minutes.

" That time he looked at me I knew I was finished."

He began frantically searching under the pillow for his cigarettes, the matches, his hand gripped the watch, it ticked *at* him, and he flung it across the room, and he listened to the smash.

" Where the devil are they " still madly searching, aware of his hot tainted breath upon the pillow, the stickiness of the sheet.

The bed creaked a little as he searched.

A match suddenly blazed and went out again.

" Phew " Marius said, puffing out smoke.

He drew up his knees, clutched them, lowered his head until he could feel chin bristles rubbing against tenderness of chest. Marius spoke in barely audible whispers to Marius.

" My arm was too strong, and I was far too proud, but I wasn't going to drown, not even for France."

He saw, very near to him, suddenly, powerfully there, Royat. The deck-hand, the simpleton, the poor boob who knew not left from right, the disaster seemed more hideous with him there, the sea more terrible, this harmless, useless creature flung into it.

" By somebody's mercy it was, only that. Picked up."

" I didn't care any more, about anyone, about anything, I was alive, I felt the different parts of my body, kept feeling them, I was alive. . . ."

Marius broke down and wept.

Behind the closed door she heard him, had heard it all. She turned the knob, pushed, the door refused to open.

" Eugene," Madeleine said, " Eugene."

He did not hear her footsteps moving away from the door, the steps on the stairs, did not hear the sudden barking of a dog, a far distant wail as of a fog-horn, nor hear her ascending the stairs again, the key in the lock on the other side, his own fall with a clatter to the bare wooden floor.

" Eugene."

He heard steps across the darkened room. The light came on, a blinding flash, and she saw him, naked, sitting crouched on the bed, haggard, huddled.

She went across to him, sat down on the bed by his side, she put a hand on his shoulder.

"I thought it would never stop," Madeleine said, "that pacing, it went on and on, *she* heard it, it wore her out, she's gone to bed."

He did not answer, and did not look at her. As she rose again his head rose, he opened wide his eyes to stare at her, she had gone to the window, drawn aside the curtain, dragged open the window, the dawn seeped down into the hot, tight room. She returned to her place, again her hand was on his shoulder, feeling it hot, sweated, strong, she let it lie there.

"Eugene."

He leaned towards her, and she withdrew a little, but her hand lay cool on his shoulder. She had the smell of his hair, and then in a half frightened, half shy confidence, he said, "I nearly got away."

Still naked he got up and crossed to the fireplace, and from its tiny, narrow shelf he picked up a heap of letters, and in his sudden hurry to get the one he wanted, the others fell in a white cloud to the floor. He came back to her.

"Look! Transport Oriental. Skipper for the Arabian. Wrote at once. Look what they said."

He began waving the letter in the air.

She took this from him and read it.

"Give it me" and he tore it from her hand.

"No vacancy. Never was. Wanted a deck-hand," his voice louder, words rising like froth, "wrote again, I'll have it, give it me. No answer.

"*Silence.*"

"Ssh!" Madeleine said, "ssh! For heaven's sake. You'll wake her, she's fast asleep, not well—she's failing—that strength—it's a lie—ssh!—ssh! You'll wake her."

"I can crawl like a bug myself" Marius said, and his curious smile frightened her.

She saw a snake lying flat between elbow and biceps, the eye travelled the full length of this arm—her gaze immobile, rapt. She could not move this eye, nor close it, nor turn her head, but went on staring at the arm, saw its whole length live, rising, high, then falling.

She turned from him quickly, pressed the flat of her hands to her face, she wanted to be sick, a wave of feeling was rising in her, she felt she would drown in it.

Through her fingers she said, in a low, husky voice, trying to hide her desperateness, "you've been out all day, you haven't eaten, I'll get you something," ordering her body to rise, to drag itself away, and then she was through the door, leaving it wide open behind her, groping her way blindly down the stairs, their every creak sounded like shots.

She stood in the kitchen, hesitant, a little stupefied, she wondered what to do. She saw the clock. It was turned half past four.

"It's Sunday" she said, "it's Sunday morning," and went to the tiny pantry. Her hands shook, she put the wrong things on the plate, and was half way upstairs when she noticed what was lying on it.

She could hear the long, trembling snores from her mother's room.

"I've got the wrong things."

She went down a second time, and stood in the pantry again, the empty plate in her hand, her eyes searching about, she had forgotten something, she couldn't remember what it was, but it was there in front of her.

"That terrible arm" she said.

Then quickly, like a good orderly housewife she had gathered up bread and meat and the bottle and was on her way upstairs again.

"You'd better dress" she said, she felt like a nurse, a doctor, a mother once more, "you'd better dress."

She put the things down on the little table. For a few seconds she looked about her, she saw his "things", the sextant, the old telescope, the brown paper parcel, the little pile of letters which she had gathered together again, whilst he put on his trousers, his shirt, hid from view that snake, the hairy arm.

" Eat " she said, her back to him, she was standing by the window, and there it was again, the sea.

" Madeleine."

She heard the noise then and she gave a jump. The wine bottle had fallen from his hand, and the liquid was spreading in a thin red stream across the floor. The bread had also fallen, soaking it up. She saw him sitting stiffly in front of the mirror, gazing at himself.

" You're ill."

Through the mirror she watched herself place a hand on his shoulders, saw the eyes steadfast in their stare, and in them an expression of melancholy, something beyond her, something she could never reach.

" Lie down, Eugene " she said.

The body was so erect, so taut, she felt this as upthrusting rock, and when she put a hand on his head she felt it there also, as though in a moment the whole body had stretched itself and frozen like ice.

" Do lie down."

She tried to move the head a little, from side to side, it had the resistance of iron.

" I'd better wake her " she thought, " God help him, something is happening," and she lay her head heavily on his shoulder and in a low voice kept saying, " Eugene, Eugene."

The sun had thrown a ray of light across the floor, and under it the wine shone and grew warm.

Below, a workman's heavy boots struck hard upon stones, and his shrill whistling cut clean through the air.

In the corridor beyond the open door some plaster fragments fell with a patter and a fine dust rose, spreading into the room, and this she saw through the mirror.

Marius had half opened his mouth as if on the point of speaking, and it remained so, as though he had suddenly forgotten what he had to say, as if the words, crowded and confused in his throat, could not come out.

The warmth of the big shoulder had oozed through his shirt, and she felt it against her face, and like him, she was now

136

motionless, but out of her mouth the three words had finally broken.

" God forgive you " she said.

" I—— "

" Enough " she said, hand upon his mouth, " enough."

Far out, beyond the house, beyond the quays, a mist was rising slowly towards the sun, far stretching, formless. The light falling upon the greyish-white mass gave the impression as of golden rain striking the surface of the sea. The night was splitting into fragments, life struck out with the breaking day, struck everywhere. Unseen, towering somewhere at the horizon line, the ship, whose syren now burst brutally upwards and for some seconds one could hear the reverberations rolling swiftly inwards like some iron ball, moving towards the waking city.

The two figures, staring at each other in the mirror had not moved, were so still, so fixed and held, it seemed as though life itself had stopped.

" Are you ill ? "

For a moment or two she seemed not to realize she had spoken, and then she saw his hands rising, high and back to the shoulders, felt them pressed flat upon her own, he pressed hard, he drew her head down over his shoulder and leaned his own heavily against it, she felt the rough palm stroking her cheek.

" Don't cry " he said, tenderly, " don't cry," to her who was not crying, who could not cry.

" It's me, my fault, I did it, I was mad, I killed him."

" He loved you " she said.

The surface of the mirror was clouded by the vapour of his own breath, but she yet saw that his eyes were closed, as if only at this moment he had realized she was behind him.

" Let me go " Marius said, who was yet clinging to her, and he heard her say with a quiet voice, " you are free."

She drew away from him, he got up and crossing to the window, closed it again, drew the curtain, came back and stood behind her, saying quickly, " somebody watching, somebody outside. That man. Been following me, watched him, three times last evening, won't leave me alone."

She took his hand, led him towards the bed.

" Sit down, Eugene " she said.

Obedient as a child he sat down, and she sat by him, held his hand.

" It doesn't matter " Madeleine said. " It's too late."

He turned towards her.

" Don't look at me again, and don't touch me " she said.

" Drink this."

She had retrieved the bottle from the floor, offered him the dregs of wine, which he took, and his head went right back to drain it, she saw the muscles of his throat moving, listened to the gurgling sound.

Then she took the empty bottle from him and offered him some bread.

" Eat it " she said.

He ate the bread.

" It was there, all the long day, lying on the table, you never came in."

He remained silent, he was listening to the heavy, distinct breathing from the other room.

"She's fast asleep, she doesn't care, it doesn't matter, nothing matters now," he heard her say.

His fingers tore at the remainder of the bread.

" D'you remember " she began, then suddenly stopped.

It didn't matter, she was back there already, it was years ago, they were sitting together in the wood, sitting just as they were now, she could hear him laughing, looking down at her, saying, " how very simple you are."

" I'm still simple " she thought, " here I am, sitting by him, now."

" Don't go " he exclaimed, " don't go," but she only got up and went and shut the door.

" There" she said.

From time to time he turned and looked towards the window.

" There is nothing there, nothing at all."

" There's the Angelus " she said abruptly, " I must go," and she was in the other room, watching her mother wake, the whale-like movement as she stretched and yawned, and then as the bell's tones rang in her head, the lumbering movement to the floor, upon her knees, the first prayer, and the sharp voice saying, " Madeleine, Madeleine. It is time to get up."

" Don't go, don't go " Marius said, and she could not move, he had fallen on his knees, his head buried in her lap.

She was still in the other room, this head was felt only as weight, he was mumbling into her skirt, weird, confused sounds.

" No, it could not be that, he would never cry."

" I must go " she said, " I can hear her, she's awake. Eugene, let me go."

He clung to her.

" There's nothing I can say."

" Madeleine ! Where are you, Madeleine ? "

She could feel his hands clutching her knees, " Madeleine, Madeleine."

" There's nothing I can do."

" It's like this " he said, " like this," and he was jabbering into her lap, speaking so rapidly that she could not catch a single word, and above the continuous mumble she heard the sharp blows of her mother's stick upon the bedroom floor.

" I must *go* " she cried, " I must *go*," feeling the stick's hammering in her ears, pressing there, " let me *go* " trying to free herself, hearing the old woman's shouts, " are you deserting me, are you running away from me."

" I'm coming, mother " she shouted at the top of her voice, " coming, coming. Stop hammering."

The very floor seemed to vibrate under the falling, metal-studded walking-stick.

" You *are* my brother " she said, and with her calm hands stroked his hair, " oh Eugene, Eugene. If you'd had but one drop of the spirit of my heart-happy man—don't be frightened nobody will harm, nobody—I swear."

When he raised his head she could not bear to look at him. And as though he had sensed this momentary terror, this revulsion, he quickly lowered it again.

She was aware of the cessation of the blows, from her mother's bedroom, and she called out sharply. "Coming, mother! Coming."

"Listen" Marius said, "listen," she felt the breath from his mouth upon her knees, he was babbling again, he seemed to vomit words, her ear strained to them, and now and again a certain word would rise clear of the stream of incoherent sounds.

"Gasse. It was Gasse. Been up in the main-top looking for a light. Loom of a red light, no light there, never was. Never see a light I said, never see it, bring her up to windward, bring her up to windward—head up higher to the wind, higher, *higher*—HIGHER—he was on the lee side of the bridge—I was there, he fell——"

"Stand up" Madeleine said, she hardly realized she was free, his body grown so limp beneath her.

"Stand up."

It seemed to her that this was not a man, but something nameless, something she had never seen before, something that could not rise and remain upright.

"Stand up."

"Look at me. Look straight into my eyes, Eugene" she said.

The door was flung open. Madame Marius stood there, tall, dishevelled, hair streaming upon her shoulders, a single breast bared to the light, the long gown swept the floor, her very stature made her magnificent.

"What is the meaning of this? I ask you? Are you mad?" Then she strode in through the door.

Not hearing her, not thinking about her, Madeleine, put a hand behind her brother, led him towards the bed, she felt she was taking a child with her.

" Lie down."

At first he knelt with one knee on the bed's edge, then slumped down.

He did not speak.

" Be quiet. You're ill."

The voice spoke to him, but more powerfully to her, it sank inwards with the searing touch of ice.

" Main-top " she thought, " why, that's a sailing ship—what's he talking about ? " and could not answer the question she had put to herself. Something had foundered.

She covered him with the blanket.

" Lie still."

Madame Marius watched all this in silence.

" Go out " she said, not looking at Madeleine, nor at her son, her eyes were centred on the chair at the bed foot.

" Get yourself ready. You know I hate arriving after the First Gospel."

She remained quite still until the door closed upon her daughter. Then she picked up the chair, stood it in the centre of the room, and sat down. She looked at the man on the bed.

" Are you ill then ? " she cried.

There was no answer. She was struck by the inertness of the figure, and, as she stared about her, by the disorder of this room. There came vividly to her mind the one and only occasion she had been taken down into a malodorous foc'sle. The movements in the nearby room she had ceased to hear, she was aware only of the silence by which she was surrounded. She looked from object to object, the piled bedclothes, the empty wine bottle on the table, his clothes in a bundle beside it, she noted the large stains across the white floor boarding. She looked up at the high window, then down at the man.

" You look composed " she said, " even peaceful, which shows this to be your natural place. It's three hundred or more miles from where we came, those awful train journeys, but you never lost your sense of direction. It may not be the last, or even the first. That is your affair."

She found herself staring directly at the great toe of his right foot, it stuck out from beneath the blanket.

"There is a man in this city, who, twenty years ago was engaged to and then deserted your sister. You came here to see him, you thought he would help, and you would crawl to him. I hope you will spare us that final humiliation."

The chair creaked as she got up. She then left the room.

"What were you doing in *his* room?"

"*Please*, mother," still edging her gently towards the bedroom. Quietly she closed the door.

"Something has happened to Eugene" she said.

"And nearly time. If you're to be at the first mass you mustn't stand about, and neither must I."

"You don't understand, mother."

Madame Marius was dressing, and she was not listening. Once or twice she paused, threw down a garment, as though she were uncertain about it, then picked it up again, but finally she was dressed and had left the room. Madeleine, was struggling into the same old black dress as of yesterday, and all the other days since first they had come. Then she, too, went downstairs.

"I can't find my prayer-book" Madame Marius said, "where is it?"

"*There*. You're looking at it," and she pointed to the book on the window shelf.

"I heard you get up. What does he want of you?"

"Nothing" Madeleine said, "nothing now."

"In that case—— There's the bell" Madame Marius said.

She fussed about in the sitting-room, looking for her hat, her black gloves——

"My stick, my stick," and Madeleine said, "here" and pushed it into her hand.

"We'd better go" her mother said, "I hate to arrive at the church after the first gospel."

" There's a time to speak, and there's a time to be silent "
Madame Marius said as they went out into the street.

" Ah ! " she exclaimed, pausing a moment to take in a great
breath, " after that house—how splendid the morning is.
Come along, Madeleine, have my old feet to run you to
shame," and she went forward with spirit, with determination,
she would not be late, who was never late.

" It must be a holy day," thought Madeleine, glancing
over the crowded church, and then she was separated from
her mother, she had to take a separate bench. She knelt, but
not for long. Feeling sick she sat back in her seat again. She
remained seated throughout the first Gospel and the last,
and to her mother's horror did not rise and go to the rails
as was usual, but remained tight in her seat. She stared
straight ahead, at the altar, at the chalice, through the chalice
and through the altar, she was back in the room with Marius.

She saw his bared right arm, his man outside the window,
his sailing ship, circling round in its feverish sea.

" She does not understand."

The man at her side blessed himself, left his seat, genuflected and went away. Someone had taken his place. Madeleine's fingers, holding the dangling beads, were now encircled
by other fingers, and they gripped her own, hard, she winced,
looked aside, her mother was there, kneeling, saying quickly,
" you did not go to the rails."

Madeleine took no notice, and again Madame Marius said,
" you were not at the rails."

" Leave go my fingers, mother. I was not at the com-
munion, I felt sick."

" We all of us feel sick sometimes " her mother said, but
the words carried no sympathy.

They knelt for the blessing.

In silence they walked back to the house.

" Make the coffee " her mother said, left Madeleine in the
kitchen and went straight upstairs to her son's room, but
was down again almost before Madeleine realized she had
gone.

" He's gone, off on his sotting expeditions. Have you made the coffee."

" Yes mother," Madeleine said.

" A man who can leave a house the moment your back is turned is not very ill. I wish you had never spoken to him. How weak you are. It would have come time enough, he couldn't hide it forever, it would have come out like vomit, the whole miserable story of it, the incredible lies, and that was how I would have had it. But no, he was ill, you couldn't, and then he crawled to you and you forgave him. That's how it was. God in heaven ! The things that are asking to be forgiven, we're living in a madhouse. Coward. I suppose he brought up the war as an excuse, they all do. You think perhaps I'm a hard natured woman, but you are wrong. I admired your courage, my child, and the silence with which you took your blow, and now that blow and his filth are on the same level. Drink up your coffee. I wasn't angry because you had not taken the Sacrament, but only because I had found you in his room.

" Sometimes I have watched a peasant beat unmercifully at his horse, or at his oxen, and it had been so unbearable I have wanted to scream. There is no great distance between the peasant and us, Madeleine."

" Mother ! "

Madame Marius held her cup in mid-air. " Well ? "

" Do you really love me, mother ? "

" I have always loved you, sometimes I've thought you foolish, silly and sentimental, nevertheless my daughter is always my daughter——"

" Will you listen? "

" There is somebody knocking, go and see who it is " Madame Marius said.

Madeleine did not move.

" Eugene is ill, I know, something has happened—— I mean——"

" The door, that knocking is getting on my nerves."

The old woman dipped her bread in the coffee, soaked it

well, then lifted the sodden mass with a spoon and sucked it. She heard the door close.

" The post."

" Give me the letter. Thank you. I would like some more coffee, Madeleine."

" Yes mother."

" I followed him here to get the truth out of him, in justice to you, Madeleine. Life is not some rag to be torn up, we are not toads to be trodden on. It was his duty to speak out, to be honest. Are we to be left to drag it from him that he murdered your son, as much my flesh as your own. If it had been *my* son I would have followed him to the edge of hell and made him speak. Look where we are to-day, it is justice that we should remember what we have been, to where we belong."

She was slowly tearing open the envelope.

" My spectacles " she said.

" Clear away now " she said.

She had read only a few lines of the letter when she looked up, but Madeleine had gone out.

" We're on the rocks " she thought. " He will not come now. No, he won't come now."

" Are you there, Madeleine ? "

But Madeleine was already on the stairs, Madame Marius's hand fell to her lap, the letter dangling from her fingers. The footsteps she heard seemed to her only the beginning of another journey.

" Madeleine, Madeleine " she called, she shifted her great bulk and moved to the door, " Madeleine, come down " she cried.

She had the open letter in her hand when her daughter came in. She embraced her.

She said quietly, " sit down, Madeleine, there, sit there, by me. No no, don't speak, just remain quiet, I must read this letter, just a moment ago a curious dread took hold of me, I heard you climbing the stairs, and I thought, My God ! She's walking away from me, out of my life. Wait, let me finish this letter. There's something I must say directly."

She patted her daughter and smiled at her. Then she resumed her reading.

" I would never leave you, mother, you know I promised you that. I told you I would always stay with you, you *know* that. . . ."

" And I believe you, Madeleine, I believe you," the old woman said, not looking up but intent upon the letter she was reading.

" Eugene is ill, I know he's ill. . . ."

" We are all of us ill, something has laid hold of us. Will you please allow me to finish reading this letter. It is most important that I should do so. It is from Father Nollet. He will not be calling to-day as was his promise."

Some parts of the letter she read aloud, " and others have taken account of it," and from time to time she looked across at her daughter, and her quick intense glance seemed to say, " good, you are still there, you are with me, you won't desert me. . . ."

" What does he say, mother ? "

" In a moment or two you may read the letter. It is a terrible letter, nevertheless you shall read it if you wish," and her head lowered still further so that she was now bent forward, her spectacles trembling over her nose, her fingers shaking as she read on.

" Perhaps he is right, perhaps I ought to go after him " she said.

" Who, mother ? "

" My son. But no, I'm not sure even yet—this man of God—he is good, I have no doubt, but there is right and wrong. Goodness alone is not the power to decide such a question. It is too big. I will read you the letter."

In a strong, clear voice she began :

Dear Madame Marius,

                I am writing you this letter, since, though I had meant to call and see you again, I now find, and regret that I cannot do so. I am called away for some ten days by my Bishop, and I feel that the situation in which you find yourself, and it is at once the situation of your children, should be resolved, not perfectly, and not finally, since this could never be so. We have all of us our limitations, we accept them, and under them we do the best we can. I will try to do so. First things first.

I regret to say that I cannot now advise you to take the step you contemplate, and that is, after all, your reason for seeking my advice. I have given the matter much consideration, so that the decision I have come to has not been easy and it could never be ignored. I feel that were you to take this step you would leave behind you something far more corroding than the filth you effect to despise, and also that you would vest in yourself complete authority over a life to which you are not entitled. It is not yours, and you cannot own it. I say this after having had a long conversation with your daughter, and she has told me much. She has taken, with a splendid resignation, a blow far greater than your own. I have pointed out to her the possibility of her re-marrying again, even though she has been some years a widow, for at forty-five one is not old.

But she has said plainly enough that there can never be another Madeau. That may be so. I respect her sentiments. Such creatures carry in their hearts a certain gayness, a curious kind of joy, it is difficult for me to find the right word to describe it, but always it lies there as the prey of a terrible innocence of soul. A heart so blind with trust is struck but the once. She will never take another blow. If she has accompanied you here, it is simply because there was nothing else that she could do. You followed your son, and she followed you. One can understand that, even appreciate it, he, after all, *is* your son, and will remain so to the end. Nevertheless I feel it was very foolish of you to have torn up your roots and left your home, for at seventy they remain the only roots you will ever have. You felt that you had been disgraced, and you placed a high price upon your respectability. You treasured the memory of your husband, who I'm sure was a good and honourable man. But your decision is an act of cowardice. My advice to you is to return from whence you came, and resume your life together where you really belong. I have taken the liberty of writing to your Father Gerard, informing him of my advice to you.

Your daughter has made up her mind and will not alter it. She will remain by your side and will not leave you. In your declining years you may accept that loyalty and the grace that goes with it. But Madame Madeau must not be looked upon as some kind of faithful cow, to go on yielding to the dictates of your selfishness and pride. And here we get to the root of the matter, for it is only of yourself that you are thinking. In so doing, it would seem that you are making an exception of your case. Life is not as exclusive as all that. There is always somebody on the rack. It's an echo of the selfishness you bear. There are *always* others. Often it is good to remember this.

You have followed your son here for no other purpose than to strip and wreck him, who is already wrecked, and there are some who have taken account of it. Madame Madeau has also told me that since his return home you have not addressed to him a single word, and she was under your orders not to do so either. I refrain from comment.

I now come to the question of your son. Your daughter has shown me a letter from a man named Royat, who, with your son, survived, when their ship, in ballast to North Africa, ran into a minefield. In that letter he accuses your son of murdering his nephew in a fit of temper. Some terrible argument had arisen between your son and his first officer as to the course they were taking and it seems that your grandson took the side of the Mate against your son. It is not my purpose to say, even to venture to say, who was right or who was wrong. The fact remains that, according to Royat your son felled his nephew at a blow, and accused him of siding with the First Officer, a man many years older than your son, who, I gather hated serving under a Captain so many years his junior. As I say one cannot pronounce on this, but your son had once had a suspension of his ticket by the authorities. It may be that he realized that if he *were* wrong in his navigational calculations, it was the end for him.

But all this with reserve. I notice that the writer of this letter gives no address upon it, and moreover, writes from behind the formidable barrier of some three thousand miles of ocean. It is certain that he has talked, perhaps to old shipmates, who have carried this rumour across the seas. It has had its results. Your own silence can cause your son little pain, compared with the silence of others—I refer to the shipowners who ignore him, the agents of the sea who say No. The closed door is the measure of their indifference. They are not concerned with murder, but only with their own boats. The survival of tonnage is important to them, as it is to their brokers. Your son is paying for errors, rightly or wrongly.

Madame Madeau has told me of certain things, and I accept them. Royat and your son were picked up by a fishing boat and landed some fifty miles down the coast, where in the great confusion of France's bitterest hours, they finally lost sight of each other. They had been under way only three days. He did not report. He *could* not report. In that respect I accept what he says. When he arrived everybody was departing. Authority had dissolved, France was on her knees, France was bent in two. It was a matter of skin for skin. His own master, who owned this single ship had disappeared together with his own buildings. There, I think, authority ended. In those poignant moments when he arrived on the threshold, and alone, to deliver without word or sign the full weight of a blow to your daughter, in those moments it is wise to remember that whole cities, and whole generations of men were vanishing. We need go no further than that.

At this moment, whilst I am writing to you a good man is endeavouring to get in touch with your son, to help him in what little way he can, and not least to relieve him from the burden of a terrible illusion. Your son thinks that he starts again where he left off, but this is not so. Life is split clean in two.

He cannot be a Captain again, and he is too old ever to start afresh. When one has struggled and kicked, from bottom upwards one does not wish to fall again, and he may well have a horror of so doing, even supposing he were given the chance. It is sad to think that your son is frightened of a good man. My advice to you would be to speak to your son and relieve his mind of the horror that lives with it.

I recall something that you said to me at our meeting. You said that if it were possible you would go and see this man Follet yourself, and ask him if he had a ship that would take your son off the face of the earth. I would advise you of this. Your son will not sail again, and may never get beyond the frontiers of this city.

He is a miserable, unhappy man, and you have your duty to do.

And having done that, I would again say to you, go away from this place and take your daughter with you, and endeavour to take up the broken threads of your life. One must live with one's errors. Forget your terrible pride, which in the end will destroy you. Do not worry about your son. No one is ever quite alone. The peace of God be with you, and with your own. Yours sincerely, Dominic Nollet.

Madame Marius folded up the letter and replaced it in its envelope.

" We will pack," she said. " At once."

IX

MANOS had gone. It was Philippe's firm opinion that the final blast from his syren carried back to the Heros building something more than a formal farewell. He felt it also had a rude message wrapped up in it. So much did Manos think of all land, all landsmen, all shore establishments, all ship-owners, their brokers, agents, runners and petty clerks.

Secretly, Philippe was happy. Indeed he hoped that Manos and his ship would get bogged down somewhere in the Black Sea and remain there for a long time. He had never liked Manos, he could manage the other Captains, but Manos, no. There was something about Manos—that terrible *maleness*, that fierce independent spirit, that courage, that indifference to the conventions. Philippe always saw Manos moving about the world like a shout.

" Perhaps " he once reflected, " I'm jealous of a person like that."

Sometimes he wished he could be like Manos, but that meant breaking out. Manos in port meant chaos at the Heros, in little ways, since Philippe's mind could only harbour the minor matters. Manos meant banging doors, doors left wide open, mud on the carpets, cigar smoke everywhere, torn papers, cigar butts and match sticks all over the offices through which he had to pass, and it also meant a short, stocky little man striding past the reedy man named Philippe as though he weren't there, as though he did not exist. Only once had Manos ever addressed M. Philippe, whom he knew as Follet's right hand man.

" Ah ! You stink of flowers " Manos cried, and that was the end of that.

The building had settled down to dead rhythm, doors would

not burst open, footsteps thunder in and out of rooms. It was nice to be quiet this morning, you could even hear the Heros clock ticking, and once or twice Philippe had taken out his little gold watch, just to see if Heros time was correct. He loved watching for slips, he loved to adjust. Casualness in a person, was an affront to Philippe.

It was natural that he should have a secret warm corner for the dwarf-man who sat so diligently at his desk, and whom he could now see through the window, from the sheer comfort of his own seat. He liked watching Labiche bent over his desk, adding and subtracting, collating, going forward and doubling back, checking, bent forward again and again, the whole of Labiche absorbed in his task, so close to his time sheets, so that the minute and the sou should not by accident roll off one of the precious pages.

Liking diligence, punctuality, faithfulness, scrupulous attention, all the conventional virtues, Philippe found room in his odd-shaped heart for Aristide Labiche.

Seated at his desk, elbows anchored and chin cradled in long, bony fingers, Philippe told himself that, Follet not coming in until after lunch, the usual Monday procedure, he might tap on Labiche's window, and ask him to come along and have a coffee with him at Grandmother Dernier's place.

He could see the whole thing at once, the scene lighted up immediately, as for a theatrical producer. They would sit down to wait for their coffee and for the first few minutes conversation would be quite formal, discussion about the weather, Follet's week-end on the farm with his grinding old father, Manos's departure and the excitement and relief of it, that absolutely merciless Toulon man who wanted the earth in return for a small service, the state of shipping, the Governmental position, the possibility of another German kick from the rear.

Eventually, the atmosphere becoming more friendly, and less business-like, Philippe would gaily introduce the news of a new grafting in his flower garden, and Labiche would discuss souls, flowers and souls being the magnet, the fulcrum, the two circles around which the lives of Labiche and Philippe centred.

Yes, it was quite on the map that Labiche was in the act of saving somebody, and quite on the map that he, Philippe would not be greatly interested.

" To shock Labiche " reflected Philippe, " you've only to tell him how bloody absurd life is."

He got up and walked slowly across the room, and stared through the window. He wondered how long Labiche would remain so bent, so absorbed. Surely he would notice. But he did not, and Philippe tapped gently on the window, and at once the large, mis-shaped head rose and the brown eyes were looking across at Philippe, and the expression upon the face said, " yes, Monsieur Philippe, what may I do for you ? "

Philippe shouted through to him, " let's have a coffee, the old boy's never in until after two," then he turned his back on the other and went across and took his hat from its hook, and his stick, for always Philippe was accompanied by a stick and never seemed quite complete and set up without one.

He stood watching the little man put some papers away in his desk, dutifully lock it, and pick up his own hat.

He met him at the top of the iron stairway, amongst the smells, by the be-mapped wall that so much needed a new coat of paint. And that little coil of manilla, was nobody ever going to remove it.

" Good " he said as they met. " Let's go."

The door swung to behind them. Philippe paused for a moment to look up at the sky, this morning the very heavens seemed ablaze.

" What an ordination the sun really is," he exclaimed, " sometimes I find myself wishing that the Heros headquarters had transferred themselves to one of the Polar regions."

Labiche offered his companion a wide, toothy smile, and then the tall and short of it set off for what Philippe termed " the hole in the alley."

Sparing with his confidences, aware of his superiority at the Heros, Philippe yet found himself so relieved after this latest visitation from Manos, that it was impossible for him to keep his satisfaction to himself.

"I always feel more like myself the moment that Manos is away from the quay. How'd you get on with him—Spaniards are difficult, and how they talk their heads off . . . but of course, how stupid of me, you have no dealings with our doughtiest Captain."

"He has spoken to me on occasion, sir" replied Labiche, and Philippe stared as though this were some kind of warning.

"What d'you think of him? Reminds me of a playful elephant——"

"I found him a tolerable man" said Labiche.

He part walked, part trotted, it was difficult to keep up with Philippe's long legs.

"Here we are."

And there they were, seated opposite each other in a shady corner.

"This morning" began Philippe, "something seemed not quite right to me, and for a while I couldn't make out what it was. Then I found myself instinctively looking at my watch and discovered that the Heros clock was nearly ten minutes slow. That cleaner is not doing his job thoroughly."

"Imagine that," said Labiche.

"Another thing I noticed was that that bum never showed up last Friday. . . ."

"Nor Saturday" added Labiche.

"Of course. You see him like I do, but you are tucked away and are only an observer. I have to face these bums, and what a lot of them there are. Extraordinary tribe, sailors. But this fellow, he'd the stubbornness of a mule, I hope he doesn't come again, began to get on my nerves. Sometimes he'd walk in and just stare and say nothing. . . ."

"I noticed that, poor man, I felt sorry for him. And I did not think him such a common person. A little distinguished if I may say so."

"It sounds like an echo of your patron Saint" said Philippe, and he laughed. "Personally I like to see a man washed and clean shaved, and with some presence. This chap often looked as if he'd been out on the tiles with the cats—the scruffier they are the more you like them, Labiche. No offence of course. It's a fact, isn't it?"

Labiche sipped at his coffee and said nothing.

"You won't see him again" he said, he did not look up, but remained staring at the table.

"That's splendid. I expect he'll land on his feet some time or other, poor swine. But what could I have done? What could anybody have done? Sailors, ten for a franc, that's how it is, and then look at the riff-raff here that call themselves sailors."

"He may not have liked you" ventured Labiche, his finger making circles round the cup rim.

"That's frank enough anyhow" replied Philippe. "You'd be sorry for him at once, I know you, Labiche, and I admire you, but being sorry . . . is that helpful, the poor bastard wants a ship, we'd no berths, they're very few to-day, the war's shot holes in everything, no sense of security any longer—besides look at his record?"

"Have you seen it, sir?"

"Hadn't got one to show. We had a line on him, those Bilter people, too, and they weren't the only ones—sailors talked, too, sticky past they say . . . however fair's fair. If we'd had a berth and he'd a decent record, Monsieur Follet would have considered him for a job."

"You won't see him again" said Labiche.

"Good. You've told me that already" replied Philippe.

He had finished his coffee and pushed away the cup, his watch was out, he checked up with the Dernier monstrosity which had the tick of ship's engines, he would be back in his office in three minutes.

"Finish your coffee" he said.

Labiche put down his cup and stood up. From his great height Philippe looked down at him. If Labiche hadn't been in one of those St. Vincent de Paul moods, he supposed he would have laughed at the sight of him, stood there by the table, looking right up at him, there were comical sides to Labiche, one could not always ignore them.

" The last thing I want is a moral sermon from him " he reflected, yet could not avoid remarking " how you do *love* lame dogs, Labiche, they magnetize you. Quite extraordinary. And so many of them, even good people must pick and choose. Only the other morning Monsieur Follet said to me, ' Labiche is sharpening his claws. . . ' "

" He said that ? "

" He did indeed. You were asking him questions about this Marius. He told me. You were no doubt interested in him. He looked so sad, so lost, so miserable."

He put his hand on Labiche's shoulder, there was something almost fatherly in this gesture, and he smiled down and said, " Labiche, I admire you—how I'm repeating myself this morning, but the world contains a vast sea of misery, there it is, looking at you, and my God, if you're going to have any sense of proportion at all, then I say all one can afford is a hard squint, and I mean just that."

Labiche remained silent. He did not once look at his companion. He could hear him calling out the time of day to passing friends, people from neighbouring offices, and with such a light-hearted spirit that Labiche realized at once that Philippe had already swum right through this sea of misery and come out safely on the other side.

" Monsieur Philippe " he said.

" You were saying. . . ."

Labiche caught Philippe's coat sleeve, " speaking as man to man, Monsieur Philippe " he began. . . .

" *Man* to man " thought Philippe, he could hardly conceal a smile, " I just love that. . . ."

" Yes, Labiche ? "

" Captain Marius is a sick man, and I could help him . . ."

" Then do, good lord, what are you waiting for, Labiche,

by all means—poor swine, how'd you know, been following him I suppose. . . ."

" He is at the end of his tether . . ."

" So many are, Labiche . . . oh, these headlong hearts—these headlong hearts, and what's especially attractive about Marius that you wish to save him, it's his soul, isn't it, for by some miracle or other he's saving his own skin. . . ."

" He believes he's a Captain still. . . ."

" He drinks too much, to say nothing of whoring, sailors will always be sailors. We must get back " said Philippe, " just look at the time."

" It was nice of him to ask me to have a coffee " thought Labiche, " the second time in ten years."

He heard Philippe say good-morning to somebody, then the door shut, and when he glanced up Philippe was in rapid conversation with this gentleman, and like Philippe, he was tall and lean. Labiche stood quietly by the table, he wondered if he should go, if he should sit down and wait. How tall these men were, they existed on another level of air, and suddenly Labiche's mind travelled back over twenty years. He was a boy, he was in the hideous little house behind the Quai de Belge, he was nine or was it ten years old, but a year hardly mattered. There he was, standing in the kitchen, looking at his mother. She was seated on a stool near the hearth, she was feeding his youngest sister. He remembered how calm and peaceful his mother looked as she held the child, as he remembered the big breast that jutted out from his mother's blouse, he had stared at it wonderingly.

" What are you staring at, Ariste ? "

" Nothing, mother, nothing."

" Then stare at something for a change " she said, but he could not take his eyes from her.

" Poor Ariste " she said, " you'll never be anything but half a man."

The scene came back to him clearly now, as he stood rudely diminished by the two tall men, he could hear his mother's voice, " you'll never be anything but half a man," and it had the solid weight of a fist in it. He had never forgotten it, this first painful morning of his childhood, and now he felt its echo.

He could see himself hurrying upstairs to his box-like bed-room, bursting into tears as he flung himself on the bed, how miserable and lonely he had felt. He remembered being roused by the sound of his father's heavy, clopping footsteps on the stairs, how he had sat up quickly when the door opened, a little puzzled and frightened and ashamed, and the man straight back from the fishing had stamped into his room to exclaim:

" Ariste ! What the hell are you doing here, get down to your supper at once."

He had gone to his father and thrown his arms round one knee, clutching his trousers, looked up at him, and into his nostrils had come the dense fish smell.

" Father ? "

" Well ! What now ? "

" Is it true that when I'm grown up I'll only be half a man ? "

" You'll be half a man all right, son, but you won't grow up. How can you ? Comes to the same thing. You're half a man *now* and you'll remain so till your dying day."

He could heard his father's loud, coarse laugh.

" Probably put a bit of fat on, they all do."

" Come along, Labiche," Philippe said, and he was standing there waiting, the other gentleman was already enjoying his coffee, his head buried in the morning paper.

" Come along now, I only gave myself ten minutes " said Philippe.

" I cried myself to sleep and I knew I'd never grow up," and then he felt a tap on his shoulder, and there was Philippe, the table, the other people, the sunshine on the pavement, the door bell ringing, the big clock ticking, and Philippe waiting, stiff and business-like again, and Labiche said, " sorry, sir,

I'm coming " and together they walked down to the door.

" Day dreaming, Labiche ? "

" Thinking " said Labiche, and then they were out on the avenue, ringed in the bright sunlight.

Again Philippe paused, surveyed the scene, and then remarked, " makes me think of the country, a day like this. By the way, when d'you go for your holidays ? "

" November 15th " Labiche replied, and at once Philippe exclaimed, " Ooh ! " feeling the cold.

" Poor Labiche, you simply can't avoid the sackcloth and ashes," and seeing the little man colour up he patted his shoulder and said kindly, " well well, no offence Labiche, none at all, just my manner, forget about it. Sometimes, I must confess, I look at you through my window and I ask myself if you are happy, I never hear you laugh, Labiche, but I suppose you are, really. How's the family? "

" They are quite well, thank you."

" One day we must go out to lunch " Philippe said as they reached the entrance.

" Thank you, Monsieur Philippe. To-day I shall eat sandwiches with my family, under the plane trees, it's always cool there."

" How nice."

They separated the moment they went through the door, each to his own desk. A moment later the sheet of glass had divided them.

" I've never seen Philippe so sociable " thought Labiche, as he sat down to begin his work.

Then the telephone bell on Philippe's desk rang out and it raised a solid wall between the two men. Labiche forgot Philippe. The little man remembered only the coffee, he had enjoyed it because Philippe had been nice this morning.

But now, business was business, and a door in his mind shut the other man out. He had forgotten him, but not the moment in which he had stood at the Dernier table, that hand on his shoulder, Philippe looking downwards. The shadow of a smile crossed Labiche's face.

" A look of lofty commiseration " he thought.

" Are you packing ? "

Madame Marius stood at the foot of the stairs.

" Yes mother," replied Madeleine, but she was not.

She was standing in her brother's room, and she knew she had seen the last of him. She was like a boat, helpless against the pull of the tide. Leaning against the bedroom door she looked without interest at the objects in this room. The bed he had slept in, the chair, the table, the personal objects, the dark wine stains on the floor board, his pipe fallen there, an old cap.

" You're very silent up there " her mother called again.

" Where are we going ? " asked Madeleine of herself as she stood there, staring into the deserted room. "Why are we here, what does it mean ? "

" All right, mother, I'll be down directly " she called below.

She closed the door noiselessly, and something in her very action brought relief, shutting out something she had never understood. This dreadful hatred of her mother, this iron determination to pursue her brother to the bitter end.

" D'you want me to pack in this old shawl ? "

" Why not. Pack everything, I said so, didn't I ? "

" Very well. But where are we going, mother ? "

She stood at the top of the stairs, but Madame Marius had not answered. Madeleine could hear her busy at the task, and something of the old woman's energy, her determination, seemed to flow upwards to her. She went into their bedroom and began to gather the personal belongings.

" Don't be up there all day, will you ? "

Madeleine called loudly, " I told you, mother, I'm packing."

" I thought you might be slobbering in his room " replied Madame Marius.

In the sitting-room the old woman was bent over a large black trunk, and into it, neatly folded, she was laying her things. There was something almost forbidding in the rude energy with which she packed, somehow it did not belong to age.

Sometimes she would lift up a dress, a pair of shoes, pause, holding them aloft against the light, and then fling them down into the trunk like a riddance of something hateful from the hand, as though she were piling into the slowly filling trunk, weight upon weight, the burden of stone to be dragged into the world and to another place.

On the table behind her, there lay a letter as yet un-sealed, the ink still wet upon its page. Naked to the light one could see the bold handwriting, even from a distance.

Dear Father Gerard,

Thank-you for your kind letter. It gave me a sudden lift of the heart, but I must admit at once that it's pure nonsense to say that we should return. There is something crawling about mercy and I want none of it. A good man here, a Father Nollet, you may know him, Father, has said almost the same thing. But there is a contradiction in what he says, and he does not face it. How can one live among good people any more? We're all tainted. If I came at all it was to drag the truth from my son, and nothing more. To get it from that mouth is satisfaction, something finished, final, done with. But hiding the sin behind mercy, it's beyond me. Yours sincerely, Genevieve Marius.

Madeleine had come down, was in the room, standing by the trunk over which her mother was bent. The old woman, absorbed in her work, and in her thoughts, had not heard her come in, yet felt she was there. She was on her knees now, arranging the contents of the trunk. After what seemed a long silence, she exclaimed, without looking up, " perhaps you could assist me instead of standing there so helpless."

Madeleine knelt down by her side. And more and more things were pressed into the trunk.

" Where *are* we going, mother ? I have the right to know."

" We've seen a bit of the world, we may see a bit more."

" But Eugene, he's ill, mother."

" I forbade you to speak to him, and you broke your word to me. I am his mother, and I'm the person to be told what must be told. Do you take me for a fool ? D'you suppose I came hundreds of miles just to watch him at his drinking and whoring, his bouts of misery, his self pitying hours up there, hiding away in his room like some horrible old woman who has thrown her skirts over her head just because the mice are there."

" But he's ill, mother, please believe me, I know, he's ill."

" In time he would have told me. That's all that I wanted of him. Nothing more. To hear him say it, to see him open up, to see it flowing out, all that dirt, those lies, that beastly horror inside him. He didn't drown like a man, he couldn't. That he should have dared to raise a hand against that child, all that innocence, for his selfish ends.

" On his knees, that's his place, on his knees, he's entirely without shame. Do we have to acknowledge the good and the bad in the same breath. In the name of the good Christ what are we coming to ? You know nothing of him, I do. I've travelled with him, every mile of his bone, I know. Rotten from the beginning. Are you asking me to forgive him ? Where is your son ? My name ? My God ! You're half awake, child, and that's the truth of it."

She had risen to her feet, and leaning over the trunk, she put out her hand, appealingly, offering it to her, and Madeleine took it and held it.

" That priest was right, Madeleine, that Nollet man, there is something in you, and it shuts ruin out."

Then she withdrew her hand. " Go and see the time."

And when she came back and said it was nearly noon Madame Marius said casually, " then make ready the lunch, such as it is. I do not intend to be here to-night and that is all. I won't see the darkness fall and neither will you."

" And Eugene ? "

" He has never loved us. That is an answer. Go and get ready the lunch."

" I'm breaking up " thought Madame Marius, " I can feel it, it's like being blind, losing one's footing, unsure of it."

She was standing near, and facing the wall, the big black bag in her hands, which she kept clasping and unclasping, putting in her hand and drawing it out again, opening it wide to the light and peering down into it. She stood hunched, holding this tight to her body, as though behind her, eyes were spying upon it.

" Lunch mother."

" I'm coming."

" If I'd the proof of it I'd give him up, and that would be just " she thought, as she made her way to the kitchen. She had put the black bag in the trunk, drawn down the big lid and locked it.

Madeleine had laid the table and was already seated as her mother came in. The old woman came slowly.

There was the chair in which he had sat, facing her, the stains and cigarette burns at his end of the table, a shiny patch where his elbow had used to rest. She could hear the noise of his drinking, see the fist that might at any moment crush the glass to shreds, hear the crunch of the high-smelling onion.

" A whiff of him " she thought, and only then appeared to see her daughter.

She then sat down.

" We will say the grace " she said, folding her hands.

" Fish " she exclaimed, " one is sick of fish," but she started to eat the mackerel that Madeleine had cooked for them.

" You're certain the man will call for the bags at three o'clock ? "

" He promised faithfully " replied Madeleine.

" Then that is well enough."

" You've still not said where we're going, mother " and Madeleine looked directly into her mother's eyes.

Madame Marius paused in her eating, " At forty five she's

still a child. It's I who am looking after her, not she tending me" the old woman thought.

"There is the place of the Evening, that calm time of the day" said Madame Marius, "for old souls, the door is never closed, and they say the nuns are kind."

"You should write to Father Nollet to thank him, mother."

"He requires no answer from me" said her mother.

"He was kind."

"Are you instructing me?" asked Madame Marius, and then went on with her meal.

"No mother, I only said he did his best."

"We all do our best, Madeleine, everyone of us. We are not completely stupid. Life isn't a fairy-tale, we know that already. We don't have to be told. Our eyes are open. There's goodness, but there's horror, too. But some people think that just by being merciful the difficult situations are resolved. Rubbish. The mercy of men sometimes adds flames to the horror. Noble gestures with shut eyes. Father Nollet supposes that if I follow my son and embrace him the matter is ended. It is not so simple as that, Madeleine, you poor, innocent child."

She pushed aside her plate, saying, "actually, I'm not hungry. Bring me some water, please."

Taking the water from her she drank.

"I was thirsty" she said.

"It was strange this morning" she said, "Kneeling by my bed, beginning my prayers, my beads suddenly turned themselves into railway lines and I was on a train again, rolling across deep and silent country, and then I was back where I belonged. I was sitting in a white chair, under a fig-tree, giving suck to you. It was so quiet a morning, I could hear the tiniest stir of the leaves, and the sky was so blue, so deep a blue, and so overwhelming, that I closed my eyes, and then I could feel you warm in my arms, strong against my breast. Father Gerard got off his bicycle and peeped in over the gate and saw me and we both smiled, but he said nothing and went off again. The morning grew, and it was still peaceful, still silent in the garden, and there you were, snug in my arms, and I thought of your father a thousand miles away, in an ocean, and somehow he seemed to speak to me across the distances.

"And in the afternoon I was sat by the stove in the kitchen, and it was still silent, still as peaceful. Annette had gone off for the day, and I found myself knitting in the chair she used to sit in, by the stove. A long day and it seemed to have no end. There, in the bowl were the flowers she had cut from the garden, and from the table the smell of the fruit was powerful. That was what came into my mind this morning, and as suddenly as the pictures came, so they also vanished, and there I was, on my knees, in this place, asking myself how I came here, and why did I kneel and go on kneeling, in this hateful house."

"Poor mother."

"Leave me alone" her mother said.

Madeleine got up and left her, and left the room, and the house, and walked far away from it. She walked quickly and with resolute step. She took a tram and was borne inwards. She alighted and walked half the length of the Place, then turned, and dived out of sight. And at the third building in this alley she paused to look up. Behind the long high windows she saw cars and bicycles, rubber tyres, nuts and bolts, and looking higher, she saw painted upon the window of the second floor, "The Society of Saint Vincent de Paul. Branch office." And she went in and climbed the stairs. The sign on the door said, "Please enter", and she opened the door and went inside.

There hung upon the facing wall a large framed picture of the good man, and below it some flowers in a vase, which Madeleine saw at once were faded, and she was of a mind to go behind the counter and clear the dead flowers away, and to refill them with fresh cuttings from the shop below. Instead she lifted the pen, chained to the desk, dipped it in the dust-covered ink, and upon a sheet of paper drawn from the box, she wrote,

" Dear Sir,
          My brother Captain Eugene Marius is ill. Please see that he comes to no harm, for the love of God. Madeleine Marius, Rue des Fleurs 47."

There seemed no life in this office, the air was still, nothing moved, even that door had opened noiselessly. Madeleine folded up the note and placed it on the counter. There was a bell at her left hand, and she rang it. It gave a weak tinkle, and she waited. There was no response. The office was empty. Perhaps the secretary was out to lunch. Perhaps that man upon the wall was watching over it in his absence.

Madeleine wrote " Urgent " upon the envelope, and then, " To the Secretary of the Society of Saint Vincent de Paul."

She left the building and caught a tram on the corner, and was borne outwards. Then she walked back to the house.

Madame Marius had not stirred in her place, and was sitting a little back from the table, hands flat in her lap, head a little forward, she seemed to be contemplating these hands. She heard an outer and an inner door close.

" You were out ? "

" Yes mother ? "

" Were you looking for him ? "

" No mother."

" Do you think I'm cruel, Madeleine ? "

She stretched the little finger of each hand towards the thumb and pressed, suddenly loosened them, she twirled all her fingers, she turned her hands over and lay them flat on her knee, stared at the wedding ring upon her third finger. With the tip of another finger she burnished the stone in it.

" Did you find him ? "

" No."

" You have well considered this step you take ? "

" Yes mother."

" You are sure of that ? There is then nothing in the world that would draw you out ? "

" Nothing."

" You realize that I shall stay where I go."

" I do, mother, I do."

" You realize also that you are free to do as you wish. I am not forcing you."

Without waiting for the answer she went on, " do you think that if we went back from where we came, we could carry on as though nothing had happened. Or that if I followed that Father Nollet's advice and we all three were together again, that we would go on as from that time. . . .

" You understand that I am asking you some questions and I would like to hear what you say."

She glanced up. Madeleine was seated at the table.

" Can't you speak ? "

" It was the sailing-ship that frightened me," Madeleine said, " the ship he never put foot on."

From the sleeve of her blouse Madame Marius withdrew a handkerchief and handed it to her daughter.

" Wipe your eyes, child " she said.

She put a finger under her daughter's chin and raised her face, and looked at her and said, " it is bitter for me also. I'm going upstairs to dress and be ready, then I shall lie down and wait for the man to come. You're sure he will be here at three?"

Without waiting for a reply she went out and shut the door behind her.

" One clumsy lie behind another, now he's pretending that he's mad, no end to the devilry."

She entered her bedroom and flung the door to with a sudden rage.

Into a red and blue basket she packed the few objects that she wanted. She sat down in front of the mirror and started to arrange her hair, she tried on a hat, and with this on sat looking at her reflection in the mirror, and then Madeleine came in.

" I look terrible in this hat " Madame Marius said.

She took it off and put it down on the table. She gathered her coat, and her gloves and laid them across the chair. Then, fully dressed she lay down on the bed.

" There'll come a time " she said, " when he will be glad to tell me, his own mother. Lie down, Madeleine and rest yourself, we shall hear the knock."

They lay side by side on the bed.

" The nights we have lain together " her mother said, " ever since we came to this place, night after night, just you and I," she felt for Madeleine's hand, " I'm afraid," she said, " being alone, Madeleine, I couldn't be alone, ever, I'm too old."

X

LABICHE folded up his surplice, and as he picked up his coat the note fell from the pocket. He opened it and read :

" Dear Labiche,
                    I have a Requiem mass in the morning at eight o'clock, and I wonder if you can come and serve me. Sauret is taken ill. You know Sauret. He is a man I like very much, and indeed, if it were permissible I would have none other behind me at the altar—your good self excepted—but I have never been in favour of too young boys serving at the Mass. I hope you can manage to come. Also I have some news for you. Yours sincerely, Dominic Nollet."

Labiche put the note in his pocket. Then he closed the heavy drawer of the great oaken chest, the shining top of which threw up a blurred reflection of himself. Father Nollet passed him by, on his way to disrobe, and he patted his altar-boy on the shoulder and said, " don't be long, Labiche, breakfast is ready."

" No Father, I'm coming directly."

This was Labiche's world, and he was happy on its threshold. Kneeling behind the priest and giving out the responses he felt he was singing out his own peace and contentment, his whole being rose to receive the single acknowledgement. He passed through the vestry and at the door of the dining-room knocked, and went in. Housekeeper Morell was already serving breakfast.

" Sit down, Labiche " said Father Nollet, and indicated his chair.

His voice seemed somewhat grave, as though he were not quite beyond the threshold of his own high hour. But when the housekeeper went out, closing the door softly behind her,

Father Nollet smiled across at the man and said kindly, " Eat well, Labiche."

Labiche remained silent for a moment or two, his head bowed. The priest was looking at the small, soft, almost hairless hands, the fingers holding lightly and nervously to the immaculate linen cloth. He looked up and smiled at Father Nollet.

" It was good of you to come " Father Nollet said.

" I was pleased to do so, Father " replied Labiche. " My wife would have liked to have come also, but at the last minute, Blanchette, who sometimes looks after our children, could not come."

" What a shame. I hope your family are well, Labiche."

" They are quite well, thank you, Father."

The priest leaned forward in his chair, looked steadily at the dwarf-like man.

" Labiche " he said, " do you know you are a very good man ? "

" No Father " Labiche replied, and he looked straight into the other's eyes.

" Then I am glad of that " said the priest.

" And now I have some news for you," he went on. " It has now been decided, and at long last, that you should be permanent secretary of your branch of the Society. For this reason it will no longer be necessary for you to serve with the Heros people, but the decision is yours entirely."

Labiche paused in his eating. Father Nollet refilled his cup with coffee.

" Why, of course, Father, I am only too glad to accept it, but——"

" There will be a salary, Labiche, you will be a paid, full time secretary, there is no reason to worry about your family. And I feel sure that this is your real place. You are that kind of man. May I congratulate you, Labiche."

They held hands over the table.

" I have known you since you were a boy, Labiche " began Father Nollet, and then, " eat your breakfast, man, have some more coffee."

For a moment or two Labiche seemed unable to speak, then he said, "thank-you, Father," and resumed his breakfast.

"I remember your father" Father Nollet said.

Labiche looked up. "It's a long time since I was a boy, Father."

"Your father was very ill, and I had come to anoint him. You had just left school. I remember your showing me your prize for the composition. You showed me your little essay."

"I can't recall it, Father, it's a long time ago."

Labiche seemed nervous, embarrassed.

"You called it The Glory of France" Father Nollet said.

Labiche dropped his bread, spilt his coffee.

"For a fourteen year old boy" said the priest, "it was a very good essay."

"I have quite forgotten it" Labiche replied.

"The box on the Marne has burst, Labiche, and the spirit of the man is flowing all over our country, like a sea."

"Yes Father" Labiche said, and he was still shy, bewildered.

Suddenly he shouted excitedly, "well yes, Father. Of course. I still have the photograph over my bed. I remember the morning it came, from Paris. I nailed it on the wall. He was my hero."

"Peguy is moving strongly" Father Nollet said.

He got up and pushed in his chair, and Labiche immediately stood up, but the priest waved him back again, saying, "the other matter I wished to see you about, Labiche, those two women in the Rue des Fleurs. Did you call there? The——"

Labiche sat down.

He said quietly, "those people, Father. They're gone."

"Gone."

Father Nollet was standing looking out of the window, his back to the other.

"You mean away?"

"Yes Father. I called there last evening. I had, after much trouble, got Monsieur Gallois to take an interest in Captain Marius. You know the name, Father. Monsieur Gallois is a great help to our Missions in Africa. But now he is going into shipping, and he will see this man, papers or no papers. He is a man like that. No words. Deeds only. It is Marius's one chance. Other shipping firms are sick of the sight of him, and they have not forgotten the reputation he had years ago. Still I do not myself think that the worst ships attract the worst of men, Father. But now he has not been seen for two days. . . ."

" When did the Marius women go, Labiche ? Why it is only a few days since I called there, and only a few hours ago I wrote the mother a letter advising her on a matter of some importance to her."

" It was the lady next door who told me " continued Labiche. " It was the third time I had called trying to see the man, but always for some reason he was running away from me. That Madame Lustigne for instance, she told me that Marius thought I was an odd lot from the Sûreté. I was at her place twice, but he has not been seen, and Madame Lustigne seemed almost glad to hear that he had at last got lost, as she termed it. He had become known in certain Bistro also, but they have not seen him. There was one chance, the quays. But I was also unlucky there."

Father Nollet walked back to the table and sat down.

" What made you interested in this man, Labiche ? There are so many others, I mean——"

Labiche interrupted quickly, " If the Heros had been civil, Father, if that Philippe had said Yes instead of No, but the once, perhaps I would not have noticed so much . . ."

There was a sudden silence, and through it Labiche had passed. For a few moments he was back at his desk in the office. He was absorbed in his work. He was hearing the opening and shutting of the Heros door, hands on the bell demanding attention, Philippe coming out of his cubby-hole.

There were always people calling at the Heros, all conditions of men ; commercial travellers, agents, brokers, the busy bees of shipping, but mostly sailors looking for work, and sometimes in their absence, their wives. Out of this assembly, that grew with the days Labiche had lifted clear the impression of a single man. A tall lean man, wearing an old uniform, a dissolute-looking person, haggard, with a curious mistrustful eye, who, day after day called and asked for Follet. Like Philippe he had come to regard a certain stroke of the clock with the act of looking up, of seeing him there, grown yet another day older. He remembered when Philippe had barely looked up, though he heard the door open, the steps across to the counter, Philippe waiting for the parrot mouth to open.

" My name is . . . I would like to see Monsieur Follet."

He, Labiche would look up, at Philippe and at the man, then bend to his work again. But now, day after day he anticipated the arrival of the tall man, the same question.

The Vincentian finger was pointing, " this one."

Labiche looked straight at the priest.

" It was just like *that*, Father " he said, " I knew he needed help. Something made me interested in him " . . . he paused. " He looked desperate " he said.

" One does what one can " thought Labiche.

Vincentian fingers were pointing everywhere, the arm was ever out-stretched, opening a door, stifling a cry, revealing a hole, unveiling a man, drawing aside a curtain, opening a window ; this all-embracing arm, was to Labiche, as real as his own.

" They are all of them lost " Father Nollet said, " they are complete strangers here."

" I have since found out " said Labiche, " that our Monsieur Follet did indeed have some acquaintance with the Marius family, some twenty years ago, and perhaps Marius had come all the way there to get help from him. I am only guessing, but I have never seen such stubborn-ness, such persistence, day after day, asking for the same man. . . ."

"But surely, Follet himself must have known he was being enquired for, the man ceaselessly calling there. . . ."

" Nevertheless to my knowledge, Father, Follet never once saw him."

" He may have had his reasons " the priest replied.

He rose from his seat, looked at the clock, then at Labiche. It was the sign for him to go.

" If you can find this man, Labiche, I would like you to bring him along to me."

He accompanied his altar-boy to the door, shook hands and said good-bye.

" Good-bye, Father. Thank you for my breakfast."

As he reached the end of the gravel path he half turned, waved to Father Nollet, and was gone. And in ten minutes the green bicycle had landed him outside the Heros. He placed it in the shed, then went into the office.

He sat down and began to drag from the desk yesterday's unfinished work. Looking across to the other office he noticed that Philippe was not there. There was nothing unusual in this, and Labiche began his work. A few minutes later Philippe came in.

" I say, Labiche " he exclaimed excitedly, as he shut the door and went and stood over the little clerk, " d'you remember that bum who used to come here day after day asking for Monsieur Follet ? "

Labiche held the pen in his teeth, he glanced up at the other man.

" To-day he is going to see him. Think of that. After four months. . . ."

" Why now ? "

Philippe shrugged his shoulders.

" You're asking me " he said. He smiled, " perhaps like you, Labiche, he has had a vision. But he arrived five minutes earlier this morning, an unusual thing, he is generally that much late. He seemed in such good humour, too. I thought, ' maybe that father of his has died and left him all his money, not to mention the farm. . . .' "

" Well ? "

" If that Nantes bum looks in on us to-day " he said, " I'll see him in my office. But I will not see anybody else to-day, Philippe."

" He stopped coming two days ago, why should he suddenly look in now. And think of the efforts before, melting like ice in the sun."

" There it is. Monsieur Follet has had a change of heart in the night."

He leaned over Labiche, " but also " he said, patting the other's shoulder, " you have prayed, too. I've no doubt of that, Labiche, no doubt at all. It may be the answer to your own prayers. A special prayer for a special bum."

As he went out he said over his shoulder, " and what a surprise for the bum himself, after four months of it, crawling about looking for a job. Been to any amount of shipping people. You know I think Monsieur Follet put them all wise," he turned to smile at Labiche and then went out.

" What Philippe does not know " thought Labiche, " will certainly do Philippe no harm."

He counted eleven visitors up to lunch-time, but Marius had not appeared.

On his way out Philippe said, " you watch. Just before five that bum'll turn up. A little lapse of memory. Never forgive himself for forgetting us."

The door had been wide open. Labiche had walked straight in. Approaching it he had sensed that it was empty ; he had stood across the road and looked at it. A miserable place, a house all points and corners, a flat, dingy, ugly little house. The rear door was as wide and gaping as the front one. And once inside there were more doors and these were open. Labiche had stood inside the front door, had called out twice. There had been no answer. He listened to the clock's tick, looked at the cheap curtains, walked across to the stairs, called again. His own voice answered him. It was as ugly inside as out.

" Even the house seems to have rheumatics."

He sat on the kitchen table, then called again. A pity that Madame Touchard had been out. He would have called on her first, he knew her husband, he had a fish stall in the market.

There was nothing on the table, cupboard doors stood wide, but these were empty. It made him think of ransacking, a hurried flight. He hesitated at the foot of the stairs. Should he go up? Instead he went to the rear of the house and stood at the door. He saw what they had seen, the distant sea, riding ships, a roaring noise from the quays.

"What a place to have come to, to have brought such people" he thought, and returned to the stairs.

To make quite certain he put a foot on the first stair, making a noise, then called again. Receiving no answer he went up. Bedroom doors were open. On the landing he stood, looking downwards. The sheer emptiness of the house gave him a chill feeling, as though life had never been there, his the first breath drawn, the first foot upon the stair, the first voice.

Number 47 Rue des Fleurs gaped at the world. He went into the first bedroom, moved straight to the window and looked out, then down into the untidy back area. He shut the window, turned and stared about him. The bed seemed monstrous, but what struck him at once was its untidiness, it gave the appearance of just having been left, perhaps he might find those tumbled blankets still warm, and he crossed the room and put his hand on the bedclothes.

In amongst them he found tiny fragments of what had obviously been a letter. He gathered them together and held them in his hand. Furious fragments, insensate fingers, the scene was coming clear, he could now see the letter being torn, and then he noticed the pillows.

"There has been a struggle on this bed" he thought, "a struggle for a letter," and at once he saw them, the old and the young woman, grappling, fighting to get possession of the letter. The unlovely shapes of bodies struggling in a black moment, the creak and rattle of the old iron bedstead, the raised voices.

"My imagination is running away with me" he thought, but then he looked at his hand, the gathered fragments, back to the tossed bedclothes. "I wonder why they've flown?"

Suddenly he walked out of the room and closed the door

behind him. It was like shutting out the wilderness. Labiche paused at the next room.

"I've seen worse things" he thought, "the old, fighting, old, old, women, the Massier sisters—dreadful."

He walked into Marius's room.

A closed window and a drawn curtain, an untidy bed, things scattered about the floor, a crowded little mantelshelf. He saw the old binoculars, the sextant hanging by a piece of string, a pile of letters, Marius's pleas, Marius crawlings, Marius whinings, hopes, threats, but he did not look at these. Instead he took the brown paper parcel and opened it and sat down and looked through the charts. And for the first time Labiche hesitated, quickly folded them up, wrapped them in the brown paper, then let them lie on his knee, these, the sacred relics, humbly wrapped, zealously guarded. Marius had often sat on the bed and opened them likewise, and had stared and stared at them, the red and the blue dots, the straight lines and the wavy ones. The seas that had dried up, the ships that lay rotting, the rivers carrying nothing, the lighthouses without lights.

Labiche got up and put the parcel back on the mantelpiece.

"Perhaps they've all gone" he thought.

"And every day he set out from this room, went down those stairs, and walked and walked and walked into days and through weeks, and Follet was very busy."

He could see Marius walking out of the Heros offices.

"I suppose he did in fact walk everywhere."

Moving the single pillow he saw the tobacco plug lying beneath it, and flung it back again. He picked up the empty wine bottle, held discarded clothes in his hand, saw bread crumbs upon the table. No altar here, as in the other room, no night-light, nothing but Marius, and his dead seas, and some faded flowers in a vase.

And as he descended the stairs there rose in him the same

feeling he had had when approaching the house, he had paused for an instant to stare, its gaping doors seemed to say, " come in, gorge yourself."

For a few minutes he sat in the kitchen. He remembered a large peeled onion lying on the drain-board, some evidence of cat in one corner, flies on the windowpane, peeling wallpaper. But wherever he now looked he seemed to see only the big iron bed and the women on it. When he opened his fist he found he was still holding the now sweated fragments of this letter. He stepped off the table and dropped them into the firegrate. It was then that he heard the key in the lock, a woman's voice. He went out. Madame Touchard had just returned.

" Good afternoon, Madame " Labiche said, he raised his hat and approached her. " I hope Francois is well."

Madame Touchard was short and wiry, and might have been draped in grey granite. She frowned at Labiche, and he noticed the cast in her right eye.

" Who are you ? " she asked, the hand holding the key suspended in air, "what is it you want? Have you been in there? "

" My name is Labiche, your husband would know who I am. I have been next door but there is nobody about. I found all the doors open."

" They're not mine to shut " Madame Touchard said. " The church mice have flown. If the owner is interested in her property she should call and lock it up."

" Have they left you a key ? " he asked. " Strange that they did not close the doors. Do you happen to know where they've gone, Madame Touchard. I am trying to get in touch with the man."

" They have gone to the station. I saw the taxi call. Will you come in, Monsieur ? "

" Thank-you."

Labiche went inside.

This house was small, clean, orderly. He sat down on the proffered chair. " Once or twice that man has rolled past our window and I have heard your name mentioned, Monsieur.

Very late at night. Do you know them? They are strange people. They never spoke to me, though often I was abreast of them on my way to Mass."

" Were they always at home? "

" Always."

" What did you think about them? "

" I thought they were swells, down on their luck, until I saw *him*. After that you could think anything, and never be surprised. We're glad they've gone."

" You saw them go? "

" No, Monsieur, I did not. I did see the taxi-man arrive, and he could get no answer to his knocking, he came to me and asked me if they were in. I joined him outside. Then he looked up to the bedroom window, hearing raised voices, he saw the old creature with her back to the window. She was quarrelling with her daughter, or perhaps the man——"

" The son, you mean."

" A man anyhow. The taxi-man got into the house. I heard him shouting up to them that if they didn't hurry their train would be gone."

" They came down then."

" I did not wait to see. I had to meet my husband. When I came back they were gone. The house as you see it. It is not my house, it is no business of mine."

" Did the man go with them, Madame? "

" No. Indeed if you move down to the quay you will probably find him. The children often come upon him there, asleep. They have stolen some money from him when he has been drunk, Monsieur."

" Thank you very much, Madame. I am glad of the information. Like you, I do not know them, they are strangers here, but the man I have often seen in our office, he is trying to get ship out of here."

Madame Touchard nodded, she had no comment to make. Labiche went away.

" Father Nollet advised them to return to their own home. They may well have done so."

Labiche paid his bill, and from the restaurant he bicycled down to the office in the Place de Lenche.

" If I could once talk to this man " he thought as he climbed the stairs.

There was no sound in this office but that of Mademoiselle Moreau's knitting needles.

" Good-day Mademoiselle " said Labiche.

She raised her head and smiled. " Good afternoon."

After a pause she said, " there are one or two messages. There is a letter marked Urgent. Left here in my absence. There was a telephone ring from Madame Lanier's daughter. Her husband died in hospital last night."

" Poor Lanier " Labiche said.

" Poor *Madame*, you mean " said the assistant, " oh, and this note from your home, Monsieur Labiche."

" Thank-you" he said.

He sat down with his back to her. She never moved from her chair and her knitting needles made odd noises in Labiche's ears. He tore open the note from his wife.

" Dear Ariste,
                    I will be away until seven o'clock, I am taking Madame Sorel to her doctor."

" Of course " he exclaimed under his breath, " this is her day."

He opened the note marked Urgent, read it, put it in his pocket. He looked at some other letters, he marked some, tore others up, handed one to Mademoiselle Moreau, the technique of mercy was at work.

" Well, I must be off " he announced, turned to the spinster in the chair, and somewhat surprised her by his expansive smile. But he did not inform her that from next week he himself would sit in her chair.

" He hasn't gone and I'll find him. He'll be certain to return to the house. If I could get him along to the presbytery I feel certain that Father Nollet would do something."

How strange it was that this Marius should imagine that he, Labiche, was an agent of the police.

"How curious" he thought, "that I should match him against the mountain of misery in this city," and he saw the children in the gutter, Madame Sorel with her mask of affliction, the Massier sisters tearing at each other over a will, Lanier in the long white ward, and the frightened eyes turned to the ceiling. Madame Lanier lonely and life turning cold.

"And even at that Madame Lustigne's—he might have taken that little girl. . . ." the very thought gave Labiche a shock.

"I will call at the house this evening. If he is not there, I shall wait. I feel that this man only wants to see a hand held out to him, to feel the warmth of it, a frightened desperate man, about whom many rumours are flying about, a tired, miserable creature who crouches through his days."

Labiche could see the stairs again, and Marius climbing, the silent women below.

"It is hard to believe, yet she told Father Nollet that if she once possessed the proof she would give him up to the law."

"There must be blindness there" he thought, "blindness without limit. A mother giving up her son. I wonder what is true and what is not. I wonder why the women followed him here?"

"A proof of what?"

He saw again the squat ugly house, the disordered bedroom, the tossed bedclothes, the sextant on a string, the scattered fragments of a letter. Labiche thought of the quays, Marius lying against timbers, the sound of a syren tearing through his brain, the childish hands at his pockets, the sea smashing against the breakwater, and over all, the sun in splendour.

XI

Marius came out of the Bistro, and as he walked down the road he could still hear them laughing. He had asked for a drink and they had given it to him, but when they had demanded payment it was awkward. He searched in his pockets, but he had no money. He did not speak. The people in the bar had watched his frantic search with some amusement. Nobody had offered to pay. When he looked at the barman he saw him laugh. As he turned away, leaving the untouched drink on the counter, the others joined in. It was growing dark as he approached the house. The door being wide open, it looked like a large eye in the white wall, and as he drew nearer he looked about him, stopped, stared up at the house. He walked straight in, but closed the door after him and locked it. He had not seen the man standing on the corner, who, as soon as he saw Marius enter, walked round to the rear of the house. Marius struck a match and held it high, and looked about him. He went to the table and put his hand on it. The match went out.

He called out, " hello ! "

There was no answer. He struck another match, he went to the corners of the room and stared into them. He continued to strike matches. It had not occurred to him to switch on the light.

" Hello ! "

When the matches ran out he groped his way into the sitting-room. This room was empty and silent. He found the small cupboard high in the wall, and took from it another box. He started striking again. It was difficult to understand. The two chairs in the window were empty. The sentries had gone. He sat down on the one nearest the door. He felt the seat of the other one. He called again. " Hello ! "

His own voice answered him. He sat motionless on the chair. The darkness increased. He could no longer see the door. Each time he called he would sit tense, listening. After a while he got up and struck another match. He left the room. At the foot of the stairs he called, "Hello!" The house kept its mouth shut.

He climbed the stairs. In the larger of the two bedrooms he went first to the window. This he closed. Turning towards the bed, the small flickering light, the red glow from the bowl, frightened him. He rushed at this, and in an excess of fear blew violently upon the night-light, and this drowned in its own oil; it gave off a sharp, acrid smell. But the light itself that had burned for four months before the altar, had gone. Marius put his hand on the bedclothes, began turning them over and over, he felt about in the bed.

Stretched across it, he called " Hello " and listened, his head turned towards the door. He left the room. The silence made him feel chill, he descended to the kitchen, and instinctively his hand went to the switch. The room flooded with light.

The place was swept and clean, the corners were empty. Nothing on the table, not even a crumb. He felt along shelves, he bent down and looked under the grate, into the fire that had never been lighted. Nothing. Not a scrap of anything, an old bone, a scrap of paper, an envelope. He switched out the light and returned to the other room. He talked to himself. Through the window he stared at nothing. But every attitude was that of a waiting, listening man. He called again, but this time in a low voice, then he went out and started to climb the stairs for the second time. He found his own door, opened it, he went on talking to himself. He shut and locked the door. He closed the window and drew down the catch, he drew the curtains across it. He struck no match, switched on no light. He sat on the chair at the foot of the bed, hands gripping his knees. He listened. His own boot scraping the floor made him jump and he said quickly, " hello, hello there ! "

The house that had been silent so long, was no less silent now.

It had been a strange day. On the quay, lying under the keel of a rotting boat, he had felt something crawling about him, things with claws, crabs perhaps. And in the late evening he woke, shivering a little, he could not remember leaving the house. He tried to remember a dream. The eyes, fish open, were staring towards a large object that looked like a crane, and then like a house dissolving, and he had dragged himself to his feet and walked towards it. Nobody had appeared to notice him, walking across a short gangway that spanned two ships, two ships so close together their plates might be congealed.

No sound. No winch, no crane, no voice. No rattle of chain, whisper of steam, no pulse of engine, no bell, no footfall. Marius had walked the length of the *Bergerac*, tossed up by an ocean, bound to the quay, buried in mud and slime, a ship dying, discarded, ransacked, the last wave broken under her vitals. He had walked for'ard, climbed to her foc'sle head, leaned far over her rail, perilously hung there, staring at the brass letters of her name, the light upon them falling as the sun withdrew. Staring down to darkening water, thickish with its skin of refuse, the water hemmed in by the pressure of the plates. Things moving, an old greasy cap, a salmon tin, orange peelings, old papers, scattered invoices, lading bills, all moving to the slow stir of this dead water, the plop and blob and chug against steel.

Marius had turned, gone down the ladder, run the length of her well-deck, cupped his hands, shouted, swore, called the hands. He had then climbed to the bridge. Upon it he stood erect, his hands behind his back and clasped tightly, he stared at the piled city. *Bergerac's* head was turned from the sea.

He pulled hard upon her port telegraph but this had refused to ring. It was strange indeed. And speaking rapidly, nervously down the tube the engineer below had refused to answer him. He pulled again at the telegraph handle. Then he clenched his fist and struck hard upon the stout teak of her bridge rail, and swore and left the bridge, pausing with each step upon the companion ladder, to listen, to wait. But only silence. Nothing happening. Life flat upon its back. He ran down her starboard alley way, passed through the steel door, and this clanged behind him, began to descend down three staircases of shining steel. Below, something that looked like silver and shone brightly, and he cried as he went, " hello ! Hello there ! " And then he reached bottom and stood and stared at the things that shone.

But it was unbelievable—he had been hours in the engine-room. He had first toyed and felt the stationary wheel, the stiff piston, and then in incredible rage had pulled and tugged and heaved and hammered, sat down and reflected and sweated, risen again and turned and twisted and pulled, but nothing had happened. The engines would not start. A most stubborn ship.

He had been fore and aft, and for'ard again, below and aloft. Even her syren had refused to budge. Perhaps in the darkness a hand had risen from the river and gripped it, torn and destroyed it. He had stood at the foc'sle door, bawling them out, cursing, he had gone to the cabin of the chief engineer, sworn, and beat upon his door.

Marius's world was full of doors, and these were closed. He returned to the bridge. Again he grasped the telegraph, moved her over to SLOW-AHEAD. He began to pull it backwards and forwards as though he would drag up this stubbornness by the roots. Wearily he had turned away to lean on the bridge rail again, and stare raptly at the far off horizon. Nobody had noticed him board her and nobody had noticed him leave.

As he slowly walked her deck there came to him more clearly the sound of his own footsteps, striking hard upon the iron surface. But this could not disturb her bones, whose head was turned from the sea forever. He had paced her bridge and her decks, whilst all around him the world was in motion.

He sat very still. Always he listened. When the chair creaked again he got up and went to the door. He turned the key, unlocked it, turned it again, he continued to turn it. He heard this sound, and he heard other sounds. He heard the doors at the Heros being closed, the blinds drawn down. The

Bilter Line doors were closing, too. Somebody was behind Marius, counting the thousands of steps he had climbed. Men were counting them in offices, and writing the figures into their books.

A dark cab, drawn by a lame grey horse, had pulled up outside the Heros building, and Monsieur Follet had come out, head bent, body wrapped against a winter journey, and he had entered the cab. Philippe had followed down the steps with a wreath of his own roses, and he entered after the other. Then the door of the cab had closed, and it moved slowly away. Another man had rushed from the building, crying, " wait," and he had climbed on to the back of it. He was small and thick-set, with dark, penetrating eyes, and he hung on, and the cab vanished into the fog.

Marius held the key in his hand, the hand in the air, he was looking at this, holding it very close to the eye, and it glittered. He smiled at the key. All down the street of ships the doors were closing, he heard the keys turning in the locks and hurriedly he pushed in his own key, and quickly turned it. Then he threw himself hard and close to the door, and all endeavour of muscle and bone were behind him as he pressed forward. He heard the gangways pulled down, ship after ship was losing contact. The great gangways were rolled inwards, and rumbled through towering steel doors, and these too, were closing with noises like gun-fire, and the last gangway was rushing forward to the final door.

The dying *Bergerac* gave a lurch, pulled clear of her companion, turned over, sank from sight into the mud, the locked water moved, was swept up in a wave that washed swiftly inwards, as though to swallow the quays in one great gulp. Then, in the same instant this wave rose high, as towers rise, smashed down, and at once Marius saw the huge mass of water turn again and move swiftly towards the horizon, and then there was only the mud, the desert, and beyond it the quick-moving sea, rolling further and further, far beyond the quays and beyond the breakwater. Watching, he saw the mountain of water tearing past the great Chateau.

Marius now pressed with all his might against the door of his room. He heard the sea, and saw it break, move forward again, and he heard the closing of the last door; this was far out in the Black Sea, the night like pitch, and Manos, bearded and drunk, placing his body against the cabin door before the sea should strike.

Marius's body was moving, gradually, slowly, as melting snow piled to the wall breaks under the sun, until he was on his knees, and the key in the lock and his hand to this. He cried feebly, " hello ! "

" Hello ! "

He stiffened.

" Hello ! " Marius said.

And the voice said, " hello ! "

Then silence.

" My name is Labiche. Aristide Labiche. Do not be afraid. No harm will come to you."

Labiche could hear the heavy breathing behind the door. He had entered the house by the back, and in the darkness found his way to the top of the stairs. He now sat on the top stair, his head turned towards the locked door. He had listened to the rallentando of the key in the lock. With another kind of eye he was trying to ascertain where in the room Marius was. Behind this door ? By the window ? Sat on the bed ? Sprawled on the floor ?

" Your sister Madame Madeau has left me a note. She says you are ill. I would like to talk to you " he said.

Listening intently, Labiche thought that in this moment even the man's breathing had ceased, he felt he could cut this silence with a knife. He rose to his feet.

" May I come in ? I am not from the police, as you appear to think, as you mentioned to our mutual friend Madame Lustigne."

He knocked gently on the door, and waited. Hearing a step behind it, he thought instantly, " here he is," but there was the silence as before.

Marius had gone to the window.

" Nobody who comes to this city is ever refused help, and nobody who comes to us will be turned away. We are not the Heros, nor the Transport Oriental, and we are not the Bilter Line, and we are not the Messereau concern either. Father Nollet would like to speak to you. I have a friend, a good man, and he will help you. No questions asked."

Noiselessly he returned to the top stair and sat down.

Labiche lit a cigarette and drew greedily, pleasurably upon it.

" It's getting late " he thought, and fished out his watch. By its illuminated dial he saw that it was nearing ten o'clock.

" I will tell you his name. It is Gallois. He is a gentleman who has been a strong arm to our society, which is that of Saint Vincent de Paul. There are no limits with us."

After a pause he said quietly, " Marius, you are not lost," and the intense silence within and without the door gave a frightening audibility to these quiet words.

" We are not concerned with the things that have been done. The debris they leave behind, that is our concern."

He drew heavily on the cigarette, and for a moment his thoughts winged clear of the house.

" It is getting late. I have a wife and children at home and they are waiting for me. It is so very simple, Marius. You get up and open the door. I will come in. Or I will go out with you. Perhaps you would share black coffee with me across the way. Perhaps a vin chaud higher up the street. Your mother and sister have gone away. Father Nollet, parish priest of this district wrote your mother a letter and advised her to return from whence she came. She may have done so. Your sister, Madame Madeau has left me a note. That is why I am here."

Labiche stood up. He began a slow, leisurely pacing of the landing, his thumbs stuck into his vest, in the manner of a man who has oceans of time in front of him, one who was totally indifferent to the total darkness that surrounded him. He wished only to draw through the door a sick, and miserable man.

Within the room something had fallen to the floor. Labiche paused by the door, took the handle in his hand and rattled it.

" It is a sin to be miserable " he said.

He stared downwards at the banked up darkness.

" I sit on the lowest stool at the Heros office, you will have noticed me whenever you called, as I noticed you, on that first morning, on all the other mornings, and it was the Marius who had gone out who interested me. I would say to myself, where will he go now? What will he do? He will go to other shipping offices, climb their stairs, get his answer, climb down again, he will walk about in a dream and he will end up where they all end up, on the quays. You are not the first who has come to this city, and I don't suppose you will be the last. The others had no illusions whatever, and now they are gone, Marius. But you remain. You are not cunning enough to be wise."

Labiche threw down his cigarette and stamped it out. He tried the door handle again, but it refused to give.

" Please open the door, and I'll talk with you. We help, not hinder. Many people come to us, and we have gone to many others. Some felt no shame in their coming, and others fooled us, some bit deep into the hand. Can you hear me speaking to you ? "

There was no answer, and for a moment Labiche fancied that all the time the man was asleep. He went to the top of the stairs, stood there with a hand on either rail.

" I must get him out of here " he thought, " the man is very ill.'

He heard a long scraping sound within the room and turned quickly round, he was certain now that Marius would open the door to him, and he stood by it and waited.

" Are you there ? " he asked.

He grabbed the knob and rattled it again. " It is important that you should remember you are a man," he said.

" I know why you came here. You came to see Monsieur Follet. He would not see you. Not because you were without papers, but because he himself would be embarrassed. We know that much."

He lit another cigarette.

" I say again, Marius, if you will trust me, we will help you. Of course we do not solve *all* situations. For instance we do not make people happy. If all a man requires from life is simply happiness, then that is only another way of killing oneself. Will you open the door ? "

He knelt down and spoke through the keyhole.

Marius had suddenly recognised the voice.

He had carried the chair to the window, under which he now sat, his hands pressed to his knees. And out of the voice had risen the man. He saw him at the Heros, standing up to stare when Philippe had been so rude, saw him following him down the road, sitting opposite him in a Bistro, smiling and saying good-evening to that Madame Lustigne, the man who was everywhere, the man with wings. The man who was following him. Now he was outside the door. There he was, speaking again.

" I am only another creature like yourself " Labiche said.

For the third time he knocked gently on the door.

The smashing of glass sounded like thunder throughout the house. Labiche jumped.

" Marius."

He began a tattoo upon the door. But there was no answer, and the door would not give. He heaved his weight against it, and the shaky lock broke clear, the door was wide, and he was in the room. He felt for the switch. The lighted room revealed nothing save the open window. He ran from the room and down the stairs.

Marius was already running down the street.

" Poor man " thought Labiche, as he rushed to the rear of the house.

Outside he found nothing, and the glass made a sharp crushing sound under his feet. For a moment he leaned against the wall.

"If he'd understood" thought Labiche, "running away from me. I'm completely harmless," and then he hurried quickly down the street.

Marius had reached the end of the street, and now stood against the wall, his hands to the collar of his coat, hugging this, pressing his head against the brick. A single light from the bared, and dirty yellow bulb threw curious shadows upon it, and Marius's head grown huge in shadow seemed to be climbing roofwards. Beyond this the darkness, wall upon wall of darkness. Marius remained perfectly still, listening. Footsteps sounded in the distance, drew nearer, grew louder, passed by. He moved from the wall and ran on. He passed through patches of light and darkness, the air was suddenly cold and chill. He kept close to the buildings, the doors, the walls, fugitive sounds struck at him as he ran, a voice from a doorway, somebody laughing, the clink of glasses, somebody hammering.

Stepping off the kerb he tripped and fell, got to his knees, at the moment that the light came, stabbing the darkness, drowning him, he was unable to move. The car pulled up with a screech, its horn tore at him, he could not remember reaching the other side, but beyond this light was darkness again, darkness itself reeling, darkness as fluid and flowing as the sea itself.

He flung himself to its shelter and ran on. He stopped dead in his tracks, he seemed to sense the oncoming protection, and threw himself into the doorway of the empty shop. He crouched, shivering, put out a hand, drew back in horror, exclaimed, "Labiche!"

"You ought to be ashamed of yourself" the old woman said.

The voice was drowned by a greater sound. Marius thought them the footsteps of a man. He stiffened by the darkened window.

" Labiche" he said.

Labiche was everywhere. The sounds drew nearer, resounding stampings, he saw sparks fly up from the cold stones, and then they ceased. He could not move. He stood listening for the sound again. But here darkness and silence held tightly. It was as he began to move from the window, slow, furtive, forever turning his head and looking to his rear, that the shape loomed up. Marius stood in the middle of the road. He shut his eyes.

The great horse was stood quiet against the kerb, the sacking across its magnificent shoulders. It drew breath, it reared its head, it sensed silence, sensed air, sensed the strange stillness of this dingy street, its shops shuttered, its warehouses sealed. It reared its head again to the chill night air, it stood serene and powerful, beyond the frontier of man himself. Behind it there glowed a tiny light, a bluish white light, and past this its master had gone, and it heard his dragging foot steps before they died away in the depths of the Bistro.

Marius did not move. He was aware of darkness, aware of this curious shape that seemed to rise before him as upon another level of air, and then he heard the curious sound, the single giant stamp of the hoof, saw fire struck from the stone. Into the long narrow street there poured out through the bared teeth the single neigh.

" Labiche."

Marius turned and fled by the way he had come.

The sound of a syren held him for a moment, and frantically he looked one way and then another, as though he were searching for its direction, as though he were smelling out those swarming, protecting quays. He found himself once more leaning against the high wall, and the dancing shadows, the naked light swinging ever so slightly near the roof top drew his attention for a moment or two, and he pressed the flat of his hands against this wall and rested there. Always he was listening, always he was ready, waiting for the footsteps. When the light suddenly went out, leaving him hidden against the wall, it was as though he had reached beyond the barrier of the feet.

The light might never have gone out, Marius yet pressed to the wall, and, for a second or two shut off his own breathing. From the opposite corner Labiche was watching him, he had never lost sight of Marius. He walked when Marius walked, stood when he stood, ran when Marius ran. He saw the light go out.

"Poor creature, he thinks he's making for the quays, he's wrong."

Through the darkness Labiche could see the quays, to him they were as clear as daylight.

The hawsers, heavily hanging, trailing over slack water, climbing to hawse pipes, under deserted decks, the yawning hatch, truck tops buried in the darkness, a dampened flag sagging in the upper air, winches powerless and cool. A reflection upon water that gave it skin. A conglomeration of smells rising from trampled ground, rising from the heat and hum and litter of that day, as though the whole earth had suddenly closed in upon this mysterious port, and powerful above these, the smell of pitch and rope. Life burrowed inwards, Labiche knew, who sometimes came at night to the quays, and once saw, pressed close and riding easily upon the slow stir of water, the sleeping gulls. Labiche *knew*. Eyeless, he could point anywhere. The map quivered under the hand. He saw the feet driven into the piled grain, sharing warmth with the rats, the exposed face, white against timbers, the head lost in the sacking, a late stupration in the rotting boat, bewildered creatures moving in from all compass points as darkness drew down. The hideous collapse of ferocity and desperation. God-frightening, powerless in sleep. Labiche could read clear upon his map, Magnificent and Bestial.

He heard Marius shout.

A lone gull sweeping low over the roof cut off his thoughts.

"It must have scared him" said Labiche to himself, and looked towards this frightened and miserable man. And as he looked he felt the priest behind him.

" Nothing is good, Labiche, until it is loved, nothing evil until it is hated."

When Marius moved, he moved.

Suddenly he began to run. Something at last had smashed through the darkness, rode as high as heaven and he saw it, something like a great tower. As he moved swiftly towards it he thought it moved. He stopped, raised his head, the eyes stared at the height, as quickly were driven downwards as though drawn by some magnetic power of the light below.

Marius did not know it was a door, did not know it was open, yet went slowly forward. The moment he stood within it he saw the stars.

This church had ship's shape, and the stars shone through the large rent in its roof, legacy of fiery and demented nights. Marius stood very still, he heard himself breathing. And then he lowered his body and finally sat upon the marbled floor.

Beyond him there were other lights, one on either side of the altar, at whose foot was knelt a priest, old, bent, and farther behind him, in one bench and another, as still as stone, other figures. Marius was conscious of sounds, they rose from the foot of the altar and soared upwards, and after a moment their echo swept up from the rear of the church. Marius uttered no sound, but stared fixedly at the lights ahead of him. The great bowls hung motionless under the flickering lights.

Labiche, in his dark coat, his hat pressed almost flat upon his head had come into the doorway, and now leaned there, and saw the seated figure, three benches up in the centre aisle. He entered, blessed himself at the font, then tip-toed quietly to a rear bench on the left hand side of the church, knelt and watched. He was aware of the murmuring sounds at the foot of the altar, but against these he heard the deep, sonorous ticking of the clock above his head. He turned to glance upwards towards the choir stall. Darkness had curtained it off. Even whilst he looked Marius had risen and was walking slowly up the centre aisle. Labiche rose, moved slowly after him, and sometimes he stopped at a Station of the Cross and prayed there, and then went on. He saw the scattered figures, heads bent, he could not tell whether they were men or women, they were still, rapt, and as he moved farther and farther up the aisle, he glimpsed the single tall candle burning in front of the statue of Saint Francis. He had moved beyond the clock's sounds, and the priest's words came clear to him.

" Passer invénit sibi domum—"

And Labiche said under his breath, " Confiteor deo omnipotens deus," moved again as Marius moved.

Once he saw Marius turn right round, look down the church, his attitude that of one waiting, and always, listening. His footsteps rang clear upon the marble, but he did not seem to hear them. His whole attention was drawn by the two lights.

There they were, partly hooded in their bowls, port and starboard, the ship ploughing steadily forward under the stars. For a single moment the sound of the sea rose to his ears as he drew nearer the lights. Passer invénit sibi domum, et turtur nidum, ubi repónat pullos suos; altária tua, Dómine virtúitum, Rex meus et Deus meus; béati qui hábitant in domo tua, in sæculum sæculi laudábunt te.

He stood quite still listening to the sounds.

Labiche had stopped moving and now leaned against the pillar that hid him completely from sight. He saw Marius move into a bench, he counted the benches from the top, as he saw him walk sideways along this, suddenly stand and stare at the pulpit. As he came out into the narrow aisle, he passed within inches of Labiche, who heard him breathe. As Marius reached the next bench a figure stirred, appeared to rise as from nowhere, a woman, who, as she blessed herself dropped her beads, and these fell with a slight scraping sound upon the floor.

" In the name of the Father, and of the Son, and of the Holy Ghost, Amen."

Marius pitched forward as though these words had struck him in the back, and then he was running up the steps to the pulpit. Labiche hurried after him, waited by the tiny oaken gate.

" Clear away aft " Marius shouted.

He stood, his back to Labiche, hands cupped to his mouth. " Away for'ard."

The words rolled like organ notes around the silent church.

" It is as well " thought Labiche, " it is as well."

He walked quickly to the top of the church, genuflected and turned, and drew near to the still kneeling priest.

" Excuse me, Father."

The priest did not move. But from the bench on the right a man withdrew, he had seen the small man go up to the altar rails. He touched Labiche. " Ssh ! " he said.

" Ssh ! " said Labiche, gripped the man's arm, drew him from sight.

" Ill " he said, " very ill, that is to say——" and still pulling at the man's arm he drew him far down the church.

" Let go for'ard."

" Terrible " the man said, " blasphemy " and Labiche said under his breath, " it is understood, please come outside."

The man shivered a little in the cold night air.

" Ill " Labiche said, " terribly ill. An ambulance had better be sent for."

This was done.

XII

LYING back in this small white bed, Madame Marius had never felt so cool and so comfortable. She hoped her daughter, in another room, was equally so. She felt cleaner. It was as though through the night hours body and mind had dripped clean, the noise, the confusion, the harsh voice of that city, the clinging heat; even Madame Touchard's mongrel dog had ceased to bark. The litter of days, that had gone. She looked at the room in which she lay. Bare and clean. Bare walls of palest blue, a single white-painted chair, the plain scrubbed floor boards, a cleanliness in the very air. No mirror, no pictures, no radio, no curtains, no carpet, no table. Life simplified. No rubbish. No clock ticked. She wondered what time it was, and looking through the window saw the light reflected upon the great belt of poplar. This bed on which she stretched yet reminded her of the other, the last few hours on its lumps and flock, she shut her eyes as with some disgust, she refused to see it. What could not be shut out, too warm and flushed with life, were the memories of that journey. This refused to fall clear of the mind. The train jogged remorselessly back by the way it had come. She saw the rolling fields dissolve to outskirts of city, and then to city itself. The taxi, the station, every sight and sound and smell, moving in their order, controlled nightmare, the creature at her side, the afternoon madness.

"That she should have had hidden at her very breast, that letter from Royat, all those weeks—I would never be less than just to her, never."

She moved on these words, as on wheels, she was rushing to the station in the taxi, Madeleine close and warm beside her. The memory gripped and held. The whistle of the train was sharp in her ears.

His name was Despard. He got out of his seat, flung out their baggage, cried a porter, followed them in, right to the booking hall.

" Forty francs " Despard said.

" Robber! Thirty," replied Madame Marius.

" Forty francs " he said, parrot-like, final, his eyes fastened on the redoubtable black bag, he felt he could strip it open by a look.

" Wretch."

He saw the black bag open, his fingers itched, time was pressing, it always did. Behind him he felt pressure of other passengers endeavouring to get to the booking-office window, and in the distance there were the shouts, the hiss and stink of steam. And of the voice at the window, barking like a dog.

" Where for, Madame ?

" I said, Cassis" Madame Marius said, her eye on Despard, and beyond him, at the entrance, the monstrous taxi.

" Here " she said, counting.

Another voice. " Are you for Cassis ? "

" Of course I'm for Cassis, I said so, how stupid everybody is, what an accursed place——"

"You will excuse me, Madame, you have three minutes only."

She heard the croak in the voice, the slight whine, the porter was lost behind the beard, his fingers had gripped their trunks, and, Hercules-like, he shouldered them.

" This way, Madame."

She passed through an avenue of shouts, steam, rushing trucks, slamming doors, people running.

" Come Madeleine " her mother said, gripped tightly on an arm, went forward, head held high, dismissing age, " hurry."

The platform, the train, the chatter, and then the frontier of things.

" If I remain here I will give him up to the police " she said.

Madeleine was silent, but Madame Marius saw the tears

start to well up in her daughter's eyes. She lowered her voice a little.

"You may do as you wish. Whatever you feel it is your duty to do."

Madeleine was staring at the enormous clock in front of her, it's long, rusty iron hands jerked minutes round and round, the strokes of a silent hammer. She kept her eyes fixed on the large white face. Her hands rose to her own face, for a moment partly covered it.

"I don't know," she said, "I don't know."

"There is not much time" her mother said, the voice seemed to come as from a distance as though she were now stood at the other end of the platform.

The whistle blew.

"Which carriage, Madame?" enquired the porter with the beard.

Ignoring him, Madame Marius said quietly, "we are on the verge of departure."

Madeleine, looking directly at her mother, did not speak.

"All his life he has had the devil's own luck" her mother said. "He is too cute to suffer."

And after a pause, "come dear," taking her hand.

"You are pitiful" she said, and then she boarded the train, and knew her daughter was behind her.

The carriage was empty. Madame Marius sat down. The doors were slamming shut, porters were running beside the train, and now it threw off a warning burst of steam, the wheels heaved forward the train gathered speed. A porter ran parallel with their window, into which he flung a curse. Madame Marius had forgotten to tip him.

She watched the platform swimming past, people standing like statues, a guard waving a flag, a child high on its father's shoulders, she saw this child as a burst of purest joy. Then the set rhythm of the train. Winking lights in the tunnel, a sudden darkness, smoke blowing in through the window, a rush of air. Light.

Madeleine sat in a corner, and she did not stir, but looked

thoughtfully out of the window, and in the expression upon her face was locked her own secret.

"There is no need to be dumb" Madame Marius said.

"There is no need to talk" replied Madeleine.

"I covered my face with the newspaper."

Madame Marius rose in the bed, arranged the pillow behind her head. Somewhere there was the tinkle of a tiny bell. This came from the small chapel at the end of the building. Looking out through this window she could see the rolling landscape, a great belt of poplar. The quality of light clothing them gave the old woman a sudden sense as of Spring. Suddenly she saw, black against the blue of wall, hard, predominant in this clear light, her black bag. The shock of surprise was over, the dream broke. Dumb, inanimate it yet spoke to her across this room.

"That evening I went to the Benediction by myself, and after the Blessing I went into the vestry, and I saw that good man. I said to him, 'I have in this bag, Father Nollet, money I no longer require. Would you please accept it for any purpose that you wish.'

"And he said, 'thank-you, Madame Marius, but I do not want your money.'"

She was back in the carriage again, hidden behind her newspaper, the bag rocking gently upon her knee.

"What is it that I hold. Rubbish? Filth then?"

The newspaper had fallen to the floor, she could not read it, and now she looked across at her daughter and cried:

"He refused it, he would not take it."

"Who? Take what?"

"The priest, he would not take what I offered. It was like being killed."

"You slept well?" Sister Angela said, as she walked towards the woman in the bed.

This room was no different from any other, bare and clean as bone.

"Yes sister, thank-you" Madeleine said, who had not slept, who had tossed and turned through night hours, had got out of bed and knelt, and prayed for him. Sister Angela sat down.

"I have seen your mother" she said.

"Yes, sister. She had a good night?"

"She says so, yet looks drawn, tired."

"She is breaking up" Madeleine said.

"Of course. Her age. Breakfast is in twenty minutes," and as she bent forward a tip of the fine, stiff linen touched Madeleine's hand and its touch was cold and clean.

"Have you plans, my child?"

Plans? Wide-eyed, Madeleine stared at the nun. She might well have said, "have you ever walked down a corridor of the moon."

"No, sister."

"But you will make plans. Our order—well, you will understand—you may rest here a while, there is another place for your purpose. I will write to the Mother there."

"Thank-you very much, sister."

"You have a story" Sister Angela said, "there is always a story."

"I was born at Nantes, I was happy there. I am not at Nantes, I am not happy, sister."

"You are married?"

"I was."

"There are others perhaps?"

"My brother, sister."

"Where is he?"

"In Marseilles. He is waiting for a ship."

"A sailor then?"

"A sailor, sister" Madeleine said.

"What will you do?"

She studied this face before it fell from sight, passionless, remote, no man and yet no woman looked out at her.

" You are unhappy, child."

Madeleine had buried her face in her hands, she did not answer. The words that had come to her were soft, flowing as water, as light tipped fingers moving in, feeling for it, stroking hurt away.

" I was happy once."

" You will be happy again " Sister Angela said.

She raised the head from the pillow.

" I have no will " Madeleine said.

Sister Angela stood up, and said, quietly, " it is understood," and she left her and went out.

" There is a matter for the Mother Superior," she thought.

There was at this long, well scrubbed table, Madame Marius and her daughter, who faced each other, a blinded soldier, a girl, two ageing women, who looked like sisters. They did not look at the new arrivals, but concentrated entirely on what lay before them.

There came to the door behind them, a short woman, round and red of face, whose chubby hands were fidgeting with keys, hung from a silver chain about her waist. Her eyes were of a periwinkle blue. She was fat and solid as butter.

" Good morning " the Mother Superior said.

One after the other, heads turned, they said " good morning, Mother Superior."

" Eat well " she said, closing the door upon them.

They ate, slowly, carefully, gravely, as though this were some exactment risen from the very atmosphere. Nobody noticed or cared that the old woman who had arrived the previous evening with her daughter, made coarse noises as she supped her coffee, and into it placed lump after lump of bread. And nobody noticed Madeleine. All would be on their way this evening, to-morrow evening, they were passengers upon a ship whose horizon was boundless. The blinded soldier rose, his delicate fingers feeling for the chair back, and the girl rose and led him out. The sisters leaned their heads together, whispering. By the side of the smaller of them lay the contents of her little blue bag. Her beads, her scapulars, her pamphlet on Therese, the tiny sheets of thin paper that announced a Plenary indulgence, the Pontifical edict, a fortnight's Retreat, a request for prayers: A little silver cross, the bundle of letters tied with string, the photograph of the forgotten family, a small plaster saint, flat upon his face, the bric-à-brac, the sacred furniture shoring up the rapt, the devoted mind.

Their heads lay close together, and as they rose they seemed as one person; one thought of aged trees, gnarled, pressed close under winter blast. Carrying their little bundles of belongings, they moved slowly out of the room, and looked, both in the same instant at the two remaining figures, seated at the top of the table. They did not speak. The door closed.

" I was wrong, child," Madame Marius said, " and I cannot think how I came to be wrong, the Poor Clares are not what I had in mind. I can't think how I made the mistake," the tiny protest in the voice, as though she had never been wrong ; she might strike her breast at the very thought.

" I know already. Sister Angela has told me. This is for casuals. We leave on Friday."

" Another hundred miles " Madame Marius said, " I will be glad when I have finished travelling." She clutched her daughter's hands, " you won't leave me, ever ? "

" I will stay with you to the end."

" You think I am right ? " her mother said.

" I cannot answer what is right and wrong, it is too difficult," Madeleine said.

" Perhaps you would yet like to return to Nantes, have your pride yoked."

Madeleine did not answer. She got up and went to the door.

" I am going into the garden, do not come near me, I want to be by myself."

But she did not reach it. In the long, silent corridor the Mother Superior was waiting for her.

"Madame Madeau" she said, smiled for a moment, put a hand lightly on her arm. "There is something I wish to discuss with you. Please come this way."

Madeleine followed her to the end of the corridor, entered the tiny office.

There was here a large brass crucifix upon the wall, a deal table, two chairs, a small desk, a calendar hanging over this. The door closed.

"Sit down, my child" the Mother Superior said.

"I have been talking to Sister Angela," said the Mother Superior, and Madeleine looked up.

"Yes Mother" she replied, and for a moment seemed to see this nun stripped of her clothing, cowlless, and, apron-ed, she sat in a farm kitchen a fat, practical house-wife, and around her there was a soft, white cloud of feathers. She was plucking a goose.

"You are in a situation, and it is not resolved" the Mother Superior said kindly. "Do you understand what you are doing, Madame Madeau?"

"Yes, Mother."

"You intend to retire from the world?"

"Yes, Mother."

"You are un-happy?"

"I have had some happiness, Mother."

"Your mother comes of good family at Nantes, and has left that place, and will not return there owing to some disgrace brought upon her by your brother? Where is your father?"

"He is dead since the First war, Mother, he was on a battle-ship."

"And you have left your brother now, alone in Marseilles, looking for a ship. You think he will find one?"

Madeleine hesitated, then replied, "I hope so, Mother."

"And I understand your mother has sold up her property and intends to give the money to the church."

" Yes, Mother " Madeleine said.

" And thinks that her situation is resolved by doing this ? "

" It is her wish " Madeleine said.

" What is the wish of one, may be the hurt of another. Has she discarded her son ? "

Madeleine bowed her head in reply.

" Why ? "

She saw the muscles of the face contract, the lips start to tremble, she turned her head away and glanced out of the window.

" I will not press you."

" I cry so easily " Madeleine blurted out, " please to forgive me, Mother, I am like that."

" Your mother looks as though she had never cried in her lifetime, perhaps if she did so she might be happier than she is, strength is not everything. Why has your brother been discarded, I use the word that fits best."

" Sometimes " stammered Madeleine, " sometimes I dream about him, I think, one evening he will, as sailors sometimes do, come in on me."

" Your brother ? "

" My son."

" He was lost then—at sea ? "

" He was murdered " Madeleine said.

" By whom ? Do you know that ? "

" By my brother."

" This is true ? "

" He has told me. But still I do not believe. He talked of another ship, a strange ship, I could not understand, a ship my son could never have been aboard, I clutch madly at an error."

" I will talk to your mother, child " said the Mother Superior.

As she rose to her feet, Madeleine rose also, they drew close together, the nun placed her hands on the other's shoulders, their faces almost touched.

" An error is not a strong hold, child, and will anchor no-where. What are you trying to tell me ? "

She felt the body slacken under her hold, and gripped harder, she led her to a chair and said, " sit down."

She put a hand in hers.

" Rest there. Quiet yourself. When you are calm again go to your room."

And as she reached the door, " I must talk to your mother."

Madame Marius sat on, and only when the young novice came in with a large tray and began to clear the table, did she rise, and as she went by the girl smiled and said, " good-morning, Madame," and the old woman replied, " good morn-ing " but did not glance her way and went out of the door and returned to her own room.

She took a chair to the window and sat down.

" Another chair, another window, I seem to spend so much of my time sitting in windows, looking out, thinking.

" *What* a lovely garden it is " she said to herself as she stared about the unfamiliar ground, drowned in sunlight, the flowers wide and abandoned to the warmth and light.

" I could rise up from here, this very moment, collect my things, travel back by the road I have come, my child with me, go back to where I first drew breath, touch all the things I knew, see the old faces, sit in a garden again . . . no, it is done with—snaring happiness, what use is that ?

" I could go back to that horrible city, become swallowed up in it, watch him falling to pieces—I could delude myself."

She got up and opened the window, she leaned into the garden, all the scents were strong to her nostrils. In the dis-tance she saw the passing whiteness of nun.

" It is a peaceful place " she thought.

" Who is to set himself up in authority and to say that my pride is destroying me ? Look at the world without it. A beautiful spectacle. Forgive him ! Why should I forgive him ? Who is to question my deepest feelings. He has done a terrible wrong, to both of us. Mercy ? Rubbish. Perpetuating the horror. One cannot help what lies in one's bone, and I thank God I have some pride left."

Madeleine came in.

" There you are " Madame Marius said, " do bring the other chair over here," and Madeleine brought the chair and she sat in the window with her mother.

" Did you have a good night, mother ? " she asked.

" Fair enough, my bones ached a little when I got up. A beautiful little chapel they have here. You did not go to the mass, I noticed."

" No, I slept late, I was very tired. Have you seen the Mother ? We must go on Friday morning. . . ."

" I know that. We're going to Lyons." She suddenly exclaimed, " you wish to say something ? "

Looking at her daughter she had divined in an instant a momentary urge, and then a sudden hesitation, " what is in your mind ? "

" I was thinking " Madeleine began, but Madame Marius never found out what it was, for the door opened and the Mother Superior was coming towards them.

" Madame Marius."

The old woman rose and gave a short, stiff bow.

" You wished to speak to me, Mother Superior ? "

" Yes, there are some matters I would like to discuss with you " she replied.

" Madeleine," her mother said.

" She need not go."

" I would rather she did " said Madame Marius.

The door closed.

" I have here a letter, Madame Marius, which you may hand to the Mother Superior when you reach the Home at Lyons, but before I hand it to you it is necessary that you should answer me a single question."

Madame Marius looked up.

" I do not question the step you wish to take, that is under-stood, but does your daughter—is she of like mind. Is it her wish to do this ? "

" It is."

" You are not forcing her against her will ? I do not question her loyalty."

" She is all I have, all I have ever had, we are terribly close to each other, it is difficult to explain. Also I am now old, and I dread being left. . . ."

" But you have left your son behind you who is ill ? "

" It is so simple " said Madame Marius. " He is a sailor, he is unlucky, he cannot get a ship, he gets depressed, he drinks heavily, it is that kind of illness . . ."

" Madame Marius, will you call in your daughter ? "

Madame Marius walked slowly across to the door and opened it.

" You may come in now " she called.

The Mother Superior walked straight up to Madeleine and asked, " is it your wish to join with your mother in her inten-tions ? "

" Yes mother. I have promised. . . ."

" I am not asking what you promised. Do you wish to retire with your mother ? "

" I do."

" I am glad of that. These things are not simple."

She handed the letter to Madame Marius.

"There is a train at nine-thirty in the mornings, and in the afternoons there is one at four-thirty," the Mother Superior said. " You will be given a meal for the journey."

" Thank you, Mother " the old woman said.

And when the door closed upon her she went to her daughter. She put her arms round her.

" Think " she said, " a meal for the journey, we have been reduced to tramps."

" It is how they think, mother " Madeleine replied, " char-itably."

" I do not wish to stay here " said the old woman, " I would like to move on, we will go this afternoon. You still wish to come with me ? They think here that I am forcing you against your will. That is not correct. You are free to do as you wish, to go . . ."

" Where can I go ? "

" All the same you are free, Madeleine " Madame Marius replied.

" I have never been free, and now I would be frightened of it " Madeleine replied.

XIII

"LABICHE" called Follet, the moment he heard the clerk's door open, he hurried to his own door and looked out, " and be quick about it " he cried as he went in and slammed it after him.

And hearing the tap he roared, " come in, come in."

He swung round in his chair, " Sit down."

Labiche sat down.

" What on earth has come over my right hand man " said Follet. " One does not mind five minutes, Labiche, not even ten, after all, things happen to people, illnesses, sudden deaths, traffic hold-ups, but almost an hour, so unlike you, most punctual man we've got . . ."

" It's like this, sir "....

" Yes yes, explain yourself " Follet said, he picked at his finger nails, refused to look at Labiche.

" I had a call from the Director of Administration at the hospital, sir, and I had to go, and when I got there I found myself in the line . . ."

" My God ! I thought that affair was finished, done with. You've done what you wanted to do, Labiche, you've saved your man, what more do you want, there is work to be done here, much work, and I have to rely on everybody, take them on trust, I can only say it's quite unlike you, Labiche. You can go back to your work," and Labiche had gone. That was yesterday.

To-day, the Heros calendar standing on Monsieur Follet's desk showed Tuesday, Fifth, the Heros clock showed a quarter to one. Follet had made some notes, was still making them when Labiche knocked and came in. He had been expecting this all morning, he had not liked it, but here he was, what could he do about it? Nothing. The best clerk he had ever had.

"There you are, Labiche" he said, and did a thing he very rarely did, he got up from his desk crossed the floor and shook hands with his clerk.

"This is damned bad news, Labiche. We're sorry to see you go, I suppose there's nothing I can do now—it has come as something of a surprise. And you suppose that a Secretaryship of a charitable organization will pay you enough to live on? As I pointed out to you only a month back, there was Philippe's place, he retires soon, it would mean a big increase in your present salary . . ." and suddenly he stopped, turned his back on his clerk, went to his desk, sat down, picked up some notes, read them through.

"I couldn't stop him," he thought, "nobody could, what's the bloody use, the man's a crusader, a zealot, it's the work he wants, almost cries out for it. I'll just have to content myself with somebody else, but blast it, he'll have to be trained. How difficult people can be. Ah well!"

He dropped the notes on his desk, sat back and looked at Labiche.

"We're all sorry about this, Labiche, everybody here, but I shan't try to persuade you, it's the kind of work you want, and good luck to you. But we shan't see anybody as reliable as you for a hell of a time, I'm afraid. By the way I was thinking over that matter last evening, and I can see no harm in your leaving a collecting box here, it can stand on the desk in the receiving office. From time to time you can call for it."

"Thank you, Monsieur Follet . . ."

"And of course I'll personally see to it at our next director's meeting, that a bonus of some kind is given you."

Labiche stared down at his feet, his mind was far away at this moment, stretching out as far as Lyons . . . "er—thank, you, sir."

" How is he ? " asked Follet. " What a strange thing."

" He has crossed the border " said Labiche.

" You mean crazy ? "

" He is probably happy, certainly safe " Labiche said.

Follet sat up in his chair. " Did you find the women ? "

" It was difficult at first. Madame Touchard—that's the woman next door to where they were living—she did not even know who the taxi driver was who had driven them to the station. However she was helpful and we went to the station together. We found him. Chap named Despard. He was the only person who could have helped me. I was able to discover that they had gone to Cassis. The Administration have already written her about her son."

" But imagine leaving him like that " Follet said, " you can't account for people—they must have positively hated him, or else they were scared to death."

" I saw him this morning " Labiche said, " he is calmed down a little, perhaps he is safely wrapped in his dream. But I shall not forget the night in the church, it is difficult to describe . . ."

" I'm sure it is " replied Follet, whose fingers had begun to drum upon the desk.

" I think the doctors are hoping he will recognise them. I hope so, too. I would like to see reconciliation. They have also sent for his clothes . . ."

" Yes, yes, of course. Perhaps I might have seen the fellow " Follet said, " but you know how difficult everything is—and there are bums all over the place. Sometimes I think a great clean up is necessary. What do you think ? "

" It was very sad " Labiche said, " nor could I under-stand. . . ."

" Yes " shouted Follet, " what is it ? "

The door had opened. A boy stood holding the cable in his hand.

" A cable from Manos, sir. . . ."

" Yes yes, all right, bring it in, can't you ? "

He grabbed the paper from Marcelle's hand, and Marcelle got out in a hurry. Follet in a temper was best at long range.

" Blast and blast and blast this bloody man " cried Follet, he had jumped to his feet, waving the cable in the air. " My God, just look at this, one thing after another, Labiche. You come and tell me your leaving, now I have a cable from Manos, bad news, he's held up at Leghorn, repairs, think of it, and cables me to say that the *Clarte* will have to lie up some days, Heavens above. And how I told him to ram it down Duvenet's ear that he must *nurse* those engines, and now look, the bloody engines have begun to whine. And of course the Heros will pay the crew for sitting on their useless arses, doing nothing, no questions asked——"

Follet rolled the piece of paper into the tiniest ball and hurled it into the grate. Then he flung himself into his chair, grabbed the telephone.

" Get me Corbat."

" Hello hello hello—that Corbat, no, then for Christ's sake get me Corbat, yes at once, what d'you take this place for, a morgue," and then Follet lowered his voice, and muttered and swore under his breath.

" Hello. Corbat ? Good. And not before time. What the hell are you people paid for, what—I've had an S.O.S. from that damned Spaniard—I'll pitch him out—he's getting old— hello, yes, can you hear me, take this down for immediate transmission to Manos——"

Still holding the receiver Follet swung round and looked at Labiche.

" All right, clear out, Labiche. I want those *Clarte* files on my desk, immediately after lunch. Understand. Good. All right, clear out."

And Labiche cleared out.

Seated at his desk, Labiche gave never a thought to the files. He was thinking of Marius.

" It will be sad for them when they see him, and when they are no longer able to be silent, it will be too late, there will be nothing to understand."

" On Saturday I shall be gone from here because the world

is too big, even for the Heros, and beyond this place there
are things to be done."

" To think " reflected Madame Marius, " just to think that
I have not to travel any more. It's wonderful. And there, in
the laundry is Madeleine washing clothes. There is something about the place that slowly induces in one that feeling
of resignation. I can feel it."

She knelt down by her little white locker, opened it, took
out a bottle of wine, filled herself a glass, corked and put back
the bottle, then returned to her chair.

" Of course, I'm not used to living with four people in a
room—one will get used to that—they are an odd lot."

Madame Marius sipped her wine, with pleasure, with
content. The recourse to the locker the moment the other
women went out for their morning walk, had become a ritual
with her. But once they returned she never went near the
locker for the rest of the day. Even the replacing of the empty
glass had become ceremony, and as she put it back on the top
shelf, she saw, as she always saw, the black bag stuffed back
on the bottom one.

" I offered them this money, which I did not want, and they
refused it. It hurt. If they had given their reasons. But
since it is not wanted I will henceforth sit on it."

" They do not know where I come from, and they do not
worry me with questions."

Rising she walked the length of this room and back again,
suddenly flung her hands into the air and exclaimed :

" The calm, the peace of it, it makes one wonder what one
is doing outside at all. I am at last content. I need not write
anybody, and there will be no more letters and I am glad of
that. I have had a fairly long life, some of it was so happy
I shall treasure it away, and always guard it. A good husband,
a faithful daughter, a good name, yes, thank God, Marius is
still my name."

She wandered idly about the room, stood for a moment at the foot of each bed, once she picked up a shawl hastily discarded by Madame Bazin as she hurried to join the others in their walk. The old woman had carried it to the light and carefully examined it, studying its colour and pattern, the quality of the wool, and she saw how poor a quality this shawl had, then quickly she had flung it back upon Madame Bazin's bed, thinking of lice. There were people who sometimes harboured them, and they were Madame Marius's horror.

" Why they don't sleep altogether in the one bed I do not know " she thought.

She had never seen women closer to each other than these four, she wondered what they thought of her. She could see them in a slow, doddering line, moving off down the drive, their terribly used bodies muffled against sharpness of morning air, moving down the tree-lined avenue towards the park.

" I would have paid for a room for us both—but no. One gets used to things and life here is levelled flat. It is peaceful, what more does one want. Soon I shall get so cushioned in this peace that I know I will once more take up my knitting and my embroidery, something I have not done for a long time."

In the corridor one morning she had passed Sister Therese, the head of the laundry and had spoken to her.

" You think my daughter is content, Sister, happy I mean ? " she asked.

" She's very quiet, barely speaks, she works well."

" She was always like that."

" It's difficult for anybody to say what happiness really is " Sister Therese replied. " But she is a good worker, Madame Marius."

"In the end" the old woman told herself, Madeleine would forget.

" And I will forget. I have shut the world clean from my mind. And I will keep it out. But I will hold tight in me what I have been, such things mean much."

" Here they are now " she exclaimed, as through the window

she saw the quartette returning. As they advanced, she studied them.

The crippled Madame Berriot, the foreshortened right foot, heavy and clumsy and burdensome to so slight a body, which seemed to Madame Marius to have been bent double from birth. The bland features. The arms that never swung freely, but were held always in front of the body, and giving the impression that at any moment she might embrace you. The shoddy coat and skirt, the tiny gold ear-rings, the mouse-coloured hair, perilous as fluff, the whole might blow away at any moment, leaving her bald. Always on top of Madame Berriot's locker there lay a motley heap, beads, holy pictures, pamphlets, blessed flowers, a crucifix, Madame Marius had already christened it " the sprite's little mountain of prayer".

And Mademoiselle Gilliat, so tall, so terribly lean, with her curious hunted-looking expression that seemed graved upon the face, the eyes like beads, small and hard and black.

Taller than her companions, she moved quickly, lightly, she might have been the possessor of wheeled feet, moving on oiled springs. Periodically Mademoiselle Gilliat would burst into song, for no reason at all, and always they were snatches of song, they had neither beginning nor end. She sang in a high, penetrating, flute-y soprano, a razor-edged voice that cut through the air like a knife. These bursts came suddenly, wildly, as though they had been forced from her body by sheer pressure, yet never once did the pale face light up, take colour from words or melody.

Sitting beside her at the lunch table, at the close of a hot morning, Madame Marius had been struck by the fact that Mademoiselle Gilliat was wholly odourless, she seemed non-human, she had no animal smell.

She could now hear the sound of their feet upon the gravelled path. And wasn't that Madame Bazin on the outside? Of course. Always on the weather side, a buffer. But what a fool she looked, and at her age, with her grey mass blowing about her ears, that terribly induced hardiness, that, thought Madame Marius, would end up in one, quick, final shudder.

" And serve her right. Older even than I am, and imagining she's a young girl. Factory written all over her. Look at the hands. Leather."

Their voices broke on the air, but Madame Marius could not catch the gist of their conversation, and they were all looking inwards, towards each other, all smiling, except of course that Gilliat creature.

A sudden loud laugh broke in upon Madame Marius's ears as a cruel reminder that Madame Lescaux was still here, and still had to be lived with. Yes, she could see her now, that short, sturdy, thick, emboldened body, that large head that seemed to rest on no neck at all, but weighed heavily entirely upon shoulder, those short legs that were shapeless.

" I will " she thought, " get used to them all. I must learn to live with others. It will be hard, but I will do it, I have not come here without using my intelligence.

" Madame Lescaux laughs at nothing at all."

She heard the door opening, the voices in the hall, the approaching footsteps, then the room door burst open and they came in together, their closeness at an end, they broke as waves break and scattered to their various beds. They did not speak to Madame Marius, did not even notice her, each was pre-occupied with her own thoughts. And they sat on their beds and they waited for the bell to ring.

Madame Marius looked up. There was Madame Bazin, actually throwing that awful shawl over her shoulders and saying to nobody in particular, " if there's anything that comforts me at all, then it's a good shawl, I've had it years, it was a present from my poor daughter, God help her."

The bell ringing, it shut off Madame Bazin's threatened reminiscences.

It was at the ringing of this bell, when Madame Marius rose from her bed, that a silence grew within the long, low-ceilinged, and narrow room, with its bone white walls, broken only by the hard black of crucifix and its polished wooden floors. As one after another they rose and approached the table, the old woman towered above them, by physical height, by a certain grossness of presence, by the carriage of the head. The features, thrown into profile for a moment and catching the direct light of the sun, showed the greater encroachment of marauding lines. The fine nose, the well shaped nostrils were menaced.

Madame Marius dominated yet without being aware of it. And as she sat down to table, and made herself easy, the quartette seemed to be sitting very uncomfortable indeed. They said the grace.

There was a moment when the old woman withdrew into herself, when the door opened and the beautiful young novice, over-burdened by her heavy tray staggered into the room, and the steaming soup, the bread and the water was laid out upon the table. The air shook with a spontaneous chatter, reminding Madame Marius of a sudden descent of sparrows, a group of close-headed children pressing against a window, anxious to catch a sight of the procession that was passing. In this rapid fire exchange of opinions and observations the old woman was just a silent listener. And not always did she understand.

Their pleasantries struck oddly upon her ear, it was like endeavouring to catch, to understand the words of some new language, outside her own, somehow she had not the key to this. Sometimes she would ask herself where these women came from, tried to envisage the kind of life they had left, wondered about their characters, their families, their histories, what substance lay behind these outer masks. She had noticed a certain deference, and, even in Madame Bazin's case, a certain wheedling. How ready that Madame Berriot was to rush and open or shut the door for her whenever she came into the room. And that Madame Lescaux who seemed right behind her whenever she dropped her handkerchief, or forgot her spectacles, even Mademoiselle Gilliat would hurry to open or shut the window. Madame Marius was graceful with her thanks, these things appeared quite natural to her.

She missed her daughter. Sometimes in the evening she would go along to the tiny room shared by her daughter with a Madame Straumer, whom Madame Marius thought the largest human creature she had ever seen. Taller than she by three inches, great of girth, the old woman was appalled by such weight of flesh, and the horse-like strength.

The huge woman would make a stiff bow whenever the old woman came into the room. And promptly enough she would go out and leave them.

" How are you getting on, Madeleine, child. Do you find the work hard ? I miss having you near me, especially in the night, sometimes I reach out a hand to touch your hair and I'm only touching that bony Mademoiselle Gilliat. Tell me what you are thinking ? "

" I am all right " Madeleine said.

" Is that all you have to say to me ? "

" Sometimes I think of Eugene. We should never have left him like that."

" You suppose he is thinking of us ? What rubbish. But for myself, I am beginning to like this place and I am glad I have come. I never want to journey any more. It makes me realize what a lot of journies are un-necessary. Do you still go to the early mass."

" I always go to the early mass."

" What kind of woman is that who shares this room with you?" she asked, and Madeleine said, "she is good, companionable, helpful. . . ."

" Does she ask questions ? " asked the old woman.

Madeleine shook her head.

" Nothing."

" You mind this laundering, perhaps you would like the cookhouse ? "

" I am so used to both, why should I mind ? "

" Put your arms round me, child, sometimes I am so terribly alone, I cannot explain it—I . . ."

" Here, one accepts everything, one does not think."

" We do not even sit in the window any more " said Madame Marius.

" I cannot always manage to come, mother."

" Well—no matter."

And, walking back to her room, she said to herself, " It is hard to know *what* she is thinking, sometimes I feel her mind is like a canyon, her thoughts drop to the bottom of it like stones, and lie there, hidden and undisturbed, locked away—no, I never know what she thinks. It is always a distance between us. She is like an ox that one has struck with a hammer. I shall not forget that terrible night when he returned, I saw her clearly then. One batters in vain against a shutter she seems to drawn down upon her feelings."

One morning, as she sat alone in the room, her chair facing the window, enjoying her ceremonial glass of wine, they brought her the letter.

" Thank-you, Sister " she said, taking this, laying it on her knee, " I had begun to think I had finished with this sort of thing," and not until she heard the door close did she pick up the envelope, reach for her spectacles.

" From Father Gerard again, I have no doubt. I know it could not be that Father Nollet, we never agreed upon a matter, but I will not think about that."

" Marseilles " she exclaimed, " then it is not from him. And since we paid our rent to the last minute it cannot be from that Monsieur Hamburger. Who then ? "

She tore open the envelope and drew out the sheet of paper. This was thick and crackled and she opened it. The heading caught her eye.

" Office of the Administration, Institute of the Good
Shepherd."

" Office of the administration . . . what on earth is this ? "
She put on her spectacles and started to read.

" Dear Madame,
            I wish to inform you that a week to-day there
was brought into this Institution a man by the name of Eugene
Marius, late Captain of the Marine. I had better say at once, that,
but for the help of a member of the Saint Vincent de Paul Society,
you might not yet have received such communication, for he
carried no identification and no papers of any kind. But it was
seen at once by certain tattoo marks upon the arms, the chest, and
the left forearm that he was or had been a sailor. This person was
in a condition of great distress, and from Monsieur Aristide
Labiche I have the following information.

Your son was removed from the pulpit of the bombed church of
St. Dominic, where it is understood he was under the impression
that he was on shipboard, for it was his shouts that first drew attention to his presence. He is now under observation. I regret to inform you that his is a condition that will deteriorate. His replies to
plain questions are garbled and quite incoherent. Asked where he
was going at the moment of his apprehension he replied only,
' Rumania, in ballast.'

He seems to us to be the victim of some aberration. Only studied
and careful observation can yield us anything. It is possible that in
the near future he will be removed from here to another institution
where his condition will be more carefully studied. It is essential
that both your daughter and yourself should come here at your
earliest, as it is important that we should know whether at this
juncture any recognition is possible. Your presence is highly
necessary and we shall be glad if you will make arrangements so as
to arrive here before half ten o'clock to-morrow morning, Tuesday,
and you will ask the receptionist for a Doctor Parette. It is also
necessary that you send or bring any of his clothes. Yours faithfully,
Anton Duschene, Secretary to the Administration."

The letter dropped from the old woman's hands. It swished
away on the highly polished floor, she watched it go. A light

breeze coming in through the open window sent it still further away, but her eyes never left it. Finally, it came to rest near a leg of Mademoiselle Gilliat's bed. She continued to stare at it. Then, almost involuntarily she shook herself.

She dropped to her knees. She could feel hardness of wood biting into her old knees, but she remained thus, looking out of the window, her eyes followed the gentle stir in the belt of poplar, their branches waved silently in the warmth of the sun.

" I must go, I must tell her . . ." who could not go, who could not move ; something seemed to be pressing her more and more to the floor, this wood had a sudden vise-like grip. She was knelt thus when the door opened and Sister Veronica came in, carrying a great poesy of fresh flowers in one hand, a big water jug in the other. And at first she did not notice the old woman upon her knees. Then, seeing her, she put down her flowers and jug on the table and went to her.

Falling on one knee, she said, " you are not ill, Madame ? "

Madame Marius did not turn her head, but continued to stare out at the trees.

" Madame. . . ."

This nun was of medium height, dark-eyed, pale of feature, her hands were gentle, her voice so soft as to be almost caressing. The old woman had liked her from the very first.

Feeling the hand on her shoulder she then moved.

" I am not ill, Sister Veronica, thank-you," but the nun immediately saw a change in her, and how the words seemed to drag themselves from the throat.

" You are certain you are not ill, Madame Marius ? "

The old woman tried to smile, but could not, she rose slowly to her feet,

" I am not ill, and I may rise of my own accord, thank you, Sister " she said, and walked away, the Sister watching her go, out through the still open door.

And when it had closed, Sister Veronica began to replace the dead flowers in the vases. As she came by Mademoiselle Gilliat's bed, she noticed the letter, picked it up, but did not read it, and placed it on the locker.

Madame Marius stood in the corridor. This was deserted. At the far end, through the great oaken door she could hear voices. This was the laundry. Madeleine was there, she would have to tell her.

As she stood there, her head a little inclined to her breast she seemed to be thinking, to be making a decision, then suddenly she started off up the corridor. Reaching the door to the laundry she did not hesitate, and she did not knock, but walked straight in and saw her, right across this large room, whose air gave off the hard, clean smell of soaps and soda, and somewhere there was a tap running, and the sound of steam.

Her daughter was alone in this room, was actually crossing its floor, bearing in her outstretched arms a great pile of snowy linen freshly drawn from the press. She had not seen her mother enter, who now went quickly to her, and catching her hand, exclaimed, " Madeleine, Madeleine," and something in her voice so frightening that this whole towering pile of linen fell about them, and Madeleine felt her hand grasped, and as her mother knelt she was pulled down with her. So they both knelt, their hands clutching, the daughter's free arm around her mother's shoulder. It would not matter if Madame Traumer came in, if anybody came in, they would not see, who together saw this single vision before their eyes, for Madeleine knew before the old woman had spoken.

" Overthrown " Madame Marius said.

Making a slow sign of the cross, the old woman said, " In the name of Jesus Christ and of his Holy Mother, and of his angels—it is not gone, it was never gone, not lost, I knew it, there is justice."

" What has happened to him ? " asked Madeleine.

" I have said he is overthrown."

And after a long pause, " come Madeleine you had better see the letter," and Madame Marius rose to her feet, and still holding her daughter's hand, pulled her after her, and the door opened and closed after them. Madame Traumer had suddenly appeared, thrown it wide, had whispered to Madeleine as she went out, " your mother, dear. Is she ill ? " and received only a shake of the head in reply. In silence they went down the corridor, and in the room the air was filled with many scents of newly-cut-flowers.

" Wait there " her mother said, who crossed to the locker and picked up the letter. " Outside " she said, " and somewhere away from those other women, they will soon be returning."

They walked down the drive, turned to the right, and coming behind a greenhouse suddenly stopped. Behind this there stood a rough wooden bench.

" Sit here " Madame Marius said.

They sat down.

" At first I thought you had lied to me, but it is true enough " said the old woman, and fixed a steady, searching eye upon her daughter's.

" Sometimes, child, I am angry with God, and I mean that. After all if one is not angry, the love one has for him is shallow and false. But I am not angry now. You will read the letter I have received. Do you remember one day I opened my door to a curious dwarf-like creature, whose name I could not catch, and whom I really thought was something from the circus down the road ? Well he was no dwarf and he was no clown as you may see."

From time to time she waved off the flies, and she tried to remember. Madeleine handed her back the letter. She did not speak.

" You will come with me. You see it is necessary that we go . . ."

" I will not come with you " Madeleine said.

" You will not come ? "

" I said I will not come " replied Madeleine.

" You mean that, truly ? "

" I mean that."

" Then I must go myself. I must drag myself out of here, I, who thought she had finished travelling, and I will only say that I do not understand——"

" You have never understood."

Madame Marius got up. She stood there looking down at her daughter.

" You are angry with me ? "

" I am not angry with anybody. I only wish to be left alone."

" Then as God is my judge, you will be left alone."

And the old woman turned away and walked slowly back to the house.

Already she could hear the chatter of that returning quartette, she had a sudden horror of meeting them in the drive, now, in this very moment when something was tugging at her, when she was empty, and could not speak, the word she would have spoken to her daughter frozen upon the tongue.

At the window of the little office, she stood, patiently waiting until the Mother Superior had finished something she was writing, then, she asked quietly, out of the turmoil within her, for the key to the luggage room, there were one or two things she would like to get from her black trunk. And the key had been taken off its hook and handed to her.

" Thank-you, Mother Superior " Madame Marius said, and she went off to the luggage house.

" Cruel is the word I had not the right to use. It was no use. I could not speak to her again. It shall be as she says. She will be left alone."

She opened the door of the luggage room and entered.

She could see packed in with other luggage her large black trunk. It was heavy, it would be awkward to get down, but she would ask no help. After a little struggle she was able to pull it clear from between two other trunks, and let it slide easily to the floor. She knelt down and inserting her key in the lock, threw back the heavy lid.

There was everything as tidily as she had laid them out in the Rue des Fleurs. She began to remove the top layer. What she required lay at its very bottom. She removed dress after dress, an overall, scarves, a silk shawl, a woollen pullover, shoes wrapped carefully in tissue paper, a writing compendium, a small brown brief-case, that, against the crush of letters, papers and photographs would not close. She leaned away from the trunk, looked round suddenly as though she thought somebody was watching her, then bent to her task again.

" There is nothing else but that " she thought, removing more and more of the things from the trunk. Coming upon a long parcel tied with string she rose to her feet and carried it across to the window. She did not know why, but something made her open it.

" The years I have treasured that " she exclaimed, as, unwrapping the parcel she removed from it a small wooden model of a cruiser, exquisitely carved in mahogany. Holding it up she beheld the name shining on her bow. CROILUS.

" Holding this little boat in my hand, it makes everything seem like a dream. It was the first model he ever carved for his little son," and the day was back, the hours, full and fresh and happy; she could see her son being presented with this boat by his father.

" It's still as beautiful as ever. Poor Alois " she said under her breath, "poor Alois. Drowned like a man this thirty years."

For a long time she held this model up against the light, staring at the bold bright name upon its bow. Carefully she re-wrapped it, and went back to her trunk. Around her were piled the things she had taken from it. She laid the model carefully on the floor, and resumed the emptying. Carefully re-wrapping the model she put it back in the trunk.

" Here they are."

And she withdrew the shirts, the socks, the suit that Madeleine had taken to the cleaners in the city.

She put everything back in its right order, fastened and locked the trunk, then, again struggling with its weight, she managed to get it back to its place on the shelf. She picked up the things and went out.

She again stopped at the office, asking for a large sheet of brown paper and some string. She thanked the sister and returned to her room.

It was near to lunch hour, and as usual she saw them sitting on their beds, awaiting the ring of the bell, the door to open. She passed them by and did not look at them. Then she folded up the things from the trunk, tied the parcel, and taking pen and ink from the window shelf she sat down on her bed and began to address it.

Captain E. Marius, c/o Dr. Parette,
Hospital of the Good Shepherd, . . .

The watching women sat on, all were looking at her, surprised, not by her silence, but by their own, as though the very air above them were charged with some forewarning, as though this tense and stooped woman, sat tight at the foot of her bed, scratching laboriously with her pen was holding with all her will some charged secret, and when, having finished writing she dropped the pen, Mademoiselle Gilliat cried, " Oh ! " as though she had been struck.

The pen rolled towards her, she bent and picked it up.

" Your pen, Madame Marius " she said, who did not answer, but took the pen pressed into her hand.

Madame Marius got up and walked straight to the door, opened it and left them.

" Perhaps she is ill " said Madame Bazin.

" Perhaps bad news," cried Madame Berriot, " these days there is always bad news."

" It is probably the daughter who is not so well " remarked Madame Lescaux.

The bell rang, the nun came in with the tray, lunch was served, one after another the women took their places, and as the nun looked round the table, she asked? " Where is Madame Marius ? "

" She has just gone out, she had a parcel for the post " Madame Bazin said.

" It is two hours yet to the collection " replied the novice, " no matter, if she is hungry she will soon return," and she left them.

" I often wonder what she carries in that black bag " Madame Berriot said.

" I never see her take it out, perhaps it is full of precious stones——"

" The soup's too thick for this weather."

" Father Aloysius is going to preach on Sunday morning after the nine mass."

" Is he ? "

And on and on throughout the meal, as they drank noisily of their soup, and tore at their bread, and filled their glasses with water.

" I've seen her drinking. She tipples in secret " said Madame Lescaux.

The novice, searching in the garden for the old woman found her seated alone on the bench behind the greenhouse.

" You are not having your lunch, Madame Marius ? "

" I am not very hungry. I felt I must come out and sit in the air for a while."

" You look somewhat exhausted, perhaps you have walked too far this morning."

" I have not walked this morning."

" Come now " the novice said, pressing, she helped Madame Marius rise from the bench.

" Maybe you felt a little faint " she said.

" Maybe " the old woman said, a thousand miles away.

" Francois will drive you to the station, Madame Marius " the Mother Superior said, " you will be away for the day ? "

" Yes, I shall be away for the day," the old woman replied.

The two women were standing in the small, red-tiled hall and they were waiting for Francois.

" It is not very far to the station " the Mother Superior said, studying Madame Marius who looked straight out through the door, feeling morning air upon her face.

It had rained in the night, and here and there a puddle

reflected the morning light, and there came to her nostrils the deep, heavy earth smells, and she saw the untidiness of flower-beds.

" Heavy rain during the night, Mother " she said.

" A storm. But it will be better towards mid-day."

" The station is not far " she added, " it won't rain again, I'm sure."

" The station " thought Madame Marius, already it was growing in her mind, the noise, the people, the jog of the train, the grind of wheels—into the world again.

" It's like stepping into the sea."

" What was that ? " asked the Mother Superior.

" Nothing. I hope this man won't be long."

" Your daughter is not accompanying you ? "

" No, she is not coming."

" I would have Sister Veronica or Sister Angela travel with you, Madame Marius, if you wish. Would you like that ? "

" There is a change in her " she thought, " this morning she looks fragile, it is so unlike her."

" There is nothing worrying you ? "

The old woman shook her head.

" Not now " she said.

She felt the nun's hand on her arm. " Nobody ill, I hope ? "

" Nobody ill " Madame Marius said.

" You are happy here, Madame ? "

" I am well content."

" Your daughter ? "

" I think she is happy, too."

" It is a long journey by yourself " said the Mother Superior.

The old woman drew herself erect, she turned and smiled at the nun. " It is all right, Mother. Thank you. You are very kind."

And she longed and hoped for the sound of the car, wanting to be off, away, on the noisy train, towards that place from which she had been glad to fly to sit in the corner of the carriage and hold to her silence and to her dread.

" Here is Francois."

The Mother Superior stepped out into the path.

" Lovely and fresh " she said, and as the car came to the door, she smiled at its old driver.

" Good morning, Francois. You will drive this lady to the station."

She stood waiting for the old woman to come out, she opened the door of the car, and as Madame Marius bent down to enter she clutched her arm, saying, " Francois would like to know the train on which you're returning. He will drive you back from the station."

The old woman sat down. But now she was unable to speak. She could only look out at the nun, whose large gracious smile seemed to be filling the car. The old woman gripped the handle,

" I don't know, Mother, it is all right. I will return safely," and she closed the door.

" In any case " said the Mother Superior, above the sudden roar of the engine, " in any case there is always a taxi at the station."

She watched the car go slowly down the drive. ·

" A very independent old woman indeed " thought the Mother Superior as she went inside.

Francois helped Madame Marius from the car, he bought her ticket, he picked up her tiny bag, he led her to the train, found her a seat, asked if she were comfortable, and when she said " yes," he still stood there, talking about the weather, the state of the country, the new wing for the house, all the time leaning in over the window. He had closed the door, and from time to time looked towards the engine.

" A good journey to you, Madame " he said, as the train began to move, and he stood waving to her, his face wreathed in a smile, the apple-red face with its quivering grey beard. She waved him back.

" Not a thought in his head " said the old woman to herself, " perhaps a happy man."

She sat alone in the carriage. She huddled in the corner, the train gathered speed, flashed through the tunnel.

" I shall never understand why she would not come."

" There was his way and there was mine. Nowhere did we meet. There will be no questions, and there will be no answers. I will see him, and then it is finished. He is overthrown and that is just."

Sometimes she would glance out of the window, watch the flashing fields, the flying telegraph poles, and sometimes she lay back and closed her eyes.

" He died on me long ago " she thought, and felt again this rising dread. " But I suppose I must."

At the station she was confused, helpless. She stood alone on the platform, the world rushed by. Then a porter came up and enquired where she wanted to go. She gave him the address. He put her into a taxi, she gave him ten francs, and he thanked her and the taxi drove off.

" This is the most dreadful place I've ever been in. Now I can see why he came here."

At the hospital entrance she paid off the taxi, it rolled away, and for a moment or two she stood on the pavement edge, a little nervous, hesitant. Then she walked slowly to the entrance. In answer to the porter she gave her name and her business.

" You will sit there, Madame " he said, and pointed to the long wooden bench set against the wall.

On this many people were already seated. Seeing the old woman come forward the crowd moved up a little, but not too much, one waited so long, one fought for one's comfort. Madame Marius sat down.

She felt assailed by smells, by the enormity of this waiting-room, by the pressure of the people on the bench, it was like fighting to hold one's tiny place in the swarming, onrushing world, and with one hand she gripped fiercely to the end of the bench.

Above her head hung the great clock, but she did not look at this, its tick was enough. Nurses passed up and down the corridor, a draught was blowing in through the half open door, it had not occurred to anybody to close it. Her feet began to feel cold upon the stone floor. A nurse came in, passed by.

The old woman saw only the flash of feet, the black shoes and grey stockings. She began wondering when her name would be called. Once she looked round, far down the bench, the row of faces immediately turned in her direction, and she lowered her eyes.

" Is it that I am lucky and others are not ? " she thought.

A telephone bell rang, a burly porter put his head through the door, surveyed the assembly, then called over his shoulder, " No " in a loud, nerve-shattering voice.

Looking up at the porter Madame Marius imagined herself to be listening to the harsh voice of this city.

Huddled at the end of the bench she listened now to the steady monotonous tick of the clock, and this ticking suddenly fell beneath the wheels of the rushing train, and the sounds were clear and distinct in her ears. For a moment she saw Madeleine buried under a cloud of linen, her son flat upon his back in the rotting room.

" Madame Marius ? "

She looked up.

" You are Madame Marius ? "

" I am Madame Marius."

Heads turned, bodies moved, the bench creaked, faces lighted up with natural curiosity. She saw a young, white-coated man standing over her, looking at her from behind a pair of horn-rimmed spectacles. She stood up.

" Please come this way " he said, and she followed him out. He fell into line with her as they walked up the corridor, at the end of which he stopped, and the old woman saw the glass fronted door, and read the name upon it in large black letters. DR. PARETTE.

The young man knocked.

" Dr. Parette. Madame Marius from Cassis."

" From Lyons " Madame Marius corrected.

Dr. Parette came out, a small round, bright-looking man, whose manner was quick and nervous, whose greenish eyes blinked at her, and he too, wore horn rimmed spectacles. For a second he looked at the woman.

" You are the mother of the man Marius ? "

" I am."

" Please come inside, Madame Marius."

The door closed. " Please sit down " he said, placing a chair for her on the other side of his desk.

" Thank you."

They both seated themselves. Again he was looking at her.

" Brought here nine to ten days ago " he said.

" That is it."

He relaxed in his chair. " I see."

" Where is he ? "

" Upstairs " Dr. Parette said.

Noticing her tenseness, he said very quietly as he arranged some notes on his desk, " relax, Madame. Nothing will be difficult."

" Thank you."

" There is little we can do " he said. " Perhaps he may recognise you. Certain people have been here, a Madame Lustigne, a man by the name of Varinet, a Lucy Briffaux. . . ."

He saw her hands crumble, tremble on her knees.

"Did the parcel arrive here, doctor. Posted yesterday. They were all the things I had."

" He is wearing them " Dr. Parette said.

" Where are you staying ? " he asked. " Your daughter, you have a daughter I understand. She did not come ? "

" She could not come " replied the old woman. " We are now at Lyons, and will remain there."

" We shall want your help " he said.

" Help ? What help ? "

" His present condition has not simply fallen upon him from the air."

" When may I see him ? "

" In a moment or two " replied Doctor Parette. He sat up suddenly in the chair, " d'you mind if I smoke, Madame ? "

" Not at all " she replied, and was amazed at the size of the pipe that he took from the drawer of his desk. He lit this, and slowly puffed.

" I shall not keep you very long " he said. " You are not of these parts ? "

" I am an utter stranger here."

" There are many others " the doctor replied. " Would it be true to say that your son has been looking for a ship for some time and has been un-successful, has been shipless many months."

" That is perfectly true. I have a feeling he came here to see one particular person who would not see him " replied the old woman.

She lowered her eyes, studied the prominent veins on the back of her hands.

" All these questions. Asking me what he already knows, I have no doubt," she thought.

" In the shipping world things are not always assured, Dr. Parette. If one is a sailor, things are not always cosy. One may have bad luck, and ships are as fragile as men, anyway I have seen the proof of it . . ."

" You are of a seafaring family, Madame Marius ? "

" Yes. *All* my people, what there were " she replied.

He detected a certain hostility, a grudge. He got up and coming from behind his desk he stood by her. Then he patted her shoulder and said, " you are not very helpful, Madame. Perhaps you do not realize the seriousness of the matter . . ."

" My son has been suffering an illusion for some time, he has persuaded himself that he is a ship's captain, and is angry when nobody will recognise that. What is the use of my answering what you already know, Doctor. Please take me to see my son. I have come some distance, and I am not young, and I have a train to catch which I cannot miss, since it is the last of the day."

" There was great difficulty in reaching you, Madame, and it was necessary that you should come, since, owing to his condition it would be necessary for you to assent to his being removed from here to another place. I do not wish to distress you. . . ."

" I could not be distressed further " Madame Marius said, and she moved back a little to allow him to pass through the door. She followed him. They walked very slowly down the corridor.

" When first I saw your son I said to myself, ' what a fine man this is, such splendid physique, such a fine presence, here is an intelligent man ', but when I talked to him it was very different. He was like a gentle clown. I could not imagine that such a man had ever met the blows of the sea. I thought perhaps he might have violent tendencies but such are markedly absent. He does not know who he is. But what he does know is that he is under way, is in fact aboard ship, and she is in ballast, she is moving towards the Greek islands. He keeps on telling us that.

" There is in the grounds at the back of this hospital, a lake, and he sits at the window and stares out at this for long periods, and yet though the sight of water should find some response in a seaman, he is yet inert, not a muscle of his face moves, he might be looking out at a solid brick wall. He talks to himself a lot. Once I distinctly heard the name, Manos. Does that have any connection in your mind, Madame ? "

" None at all."

" Or the name Madeau ? "

She shook her head. They had reached the end of the corridor. At the foot of the stairs she waited for a few moments whilst the doctor spoke to a passing nurse. They then began to mount towards the first floor.

" There is no lift here, unfortunately, Madame, though we are soon to have one."

" Is this place full of madmen ? " she asked.

The question, seeming to leap out at him, he stopped dead on the stairs.

" Are you afraid ? "

He placed a hand on her arm.

" I am not afraid."

" We will rest for a moment at the top of the stairs " Dr.

Parette said. " He is on the second floor. It is a small room, and he is quite alone, since he is harmless, and very quiet. Nobody will bother him and he will bother nobody. When you go in you will see a man seated in a chair. There is nothing to fear. I will go in and speak to him, you will wait a moment at the door. When I come out you may go in. We are hoping he will recognise you, since he recognises nobody else."

They climbed again.

" To what blackness am I walking ? " the old woman asked herself, " to see the ruin of a life, the end of my name. I pray to God he does not recognise me."

She hesitated a moment on the stair, and he waited for her. She saw him suddenly as child, puling, cradle snug.

" After that nothing is safe."

She went on.

" God has drawn down the blind. That is only just. If there is nothing inside that head but the tallest ship and the roar of the sea then I am thankful, for thus the horror is shut out, and my day's end will be hidden and secret in me. Even now it is hard to believe."

They had reached the door.

" A moment " Dr. Parette said.

She heard him speak through the door.

" Captain Marius, a visitor has come to see you."

A moment's silence and then the louder voice. " Your mother is here."

She wanted to hear this voice, she dreaded to hear it. She leaned against the door. The doctor went in. She waited. When he came out again he drew the door after him but did not close it.

" It is as I said. He has been like that this past hour. Something out there attracts him, what we do not know. There is a chair behind the door. Sit there, but do not speak for a minute or two. He will hear you, and when he turns round you will tell him who you are."

Madame Marius looked at the doctor.

" If I were not to see him, perhaps it would be for the best " she said.

" Madame Marius. It would be humble for you to go in." Gently he pushed her through the door.

He closed it so quietly that she would never have heard it.

He sensed her fear, he even saw her hand trembling on the back of the chair. He listened.

" They've even dressed him in his Captain's suit " she said.

Marius, seated in the chair was slumped in such a way as to give the body an appearance of being boneless. Looking at him she saw her husband and her son.

" Look at the arm that struck, hanging at his side like the dead branch of a tree. Look at the length of him, fallen. How early he seemed to smell the gutter, Look at his life. Look at the Captain."

Mumbling, she lowered her head, and when she raised it again he was looking at her, he had turned round in his chair. Madame Marius buried her face in her hands.

" And he sat high, and imperious and alone in his high tower," the words came suddenly into her mind, moved across it, weighted as stones.

" I will go to him " she thought, " I will go to him " she said, willing herself to rise, to drag clear of the chair, and slowly she went towards her son.

He looked at her as she approached, but seeing his eyes, she realized that he would not know who this person was. She stood still, looking down at him.

" It is another person " she thought, " I do not know this man."

She spoke. " Who are you ? "

His smile frightened her and she drew back a little.

237

" Lucy " Marius said, making to rise, not rising, falling back again.

" Who am I ? "

" Lucy " Marius said.

She put out a hand to touch him, drew it back, she retreated slowly back to her chair and sat down.

Her head sunk forward, she clasped her hands, her finger twined and untwined.

" That fine forehead " she said. " I can yet see my husband there, and yet it is crushed. How horrible life can be. It is only by some visitation of grace that one endures it."

Gradually, and almost shyly she looked up, looked about this room. He was standing now, leaning against the window, his head touching the pane, his raised hands pressed against the sash. She might never have entered this room, she might never have existed.

" A bare room " she thought, " just like the rooms at the Home."

Against her very will she found herself staring at him again.

" I am looking at a wreck. He doesn't even know himself."

From where she sat, she could see, by craning her head forward, a patch of water. That would be the lake, she thought.

" The distance between us is greater than any sea. I shall go back. She will be there, who paid the most and never once opened her mouth to complain."

A whisper behind her made her start, and she exclaimed, " oh ! " Dr. Parette was behind her, bending over her chair. She turned and looked at him.

" He thinks my name is Lucy. I have not denied it. Let it be."

She got up, said impatiently, yet with a curious, broken voice, " I want to go, doctor."

" He has not recognised you at all ? You did speak to him ? " She nodded her head.

" I once knew him when he was a man " she said.

" You agree then, that he should be removed to another place ? "

She nodded her head, said slowly, " it is so hopeless. Will he recover ? "

" I am unable to answer that " Dr. Parette said.

He saw that she was looking at her son. And then she said, almost under her breath.

" My husband, too, was a sailor. He drowned."

Then suddenly the doctor was not there. He was standing beside Marius. He was speaking to him.

" Are you ready ? " he asked. " We will cast off."

The old woman moved forward. She could see the lake more clearly, how its waters suddenly darkened as it reached towards the heavy presence of tall trees, their branches laden.

Dr. Parette had taken her son's arm. He walked him slowly down to where Madame Marius was standing.

" Your mother " he said.

" Lucy " Marius said.

" You had better go, Madame. We will write to you again."

" Indeed I had better go."

And she stood looking at these two men, and at the taller of them who at this moment smiled so blandly at nothing but a great sheet of deadened water, moving now towards some invisible sea, and she tried to say " good morning " and did not, and turned and walked out of the room.

" We must be under way " Dr. Parette said, leading him out.